LEGACY OF FEAR

A.J. McCarthy

Black Rose Writing | Texas

This is a work of fiction. Names, characters, businesses, places, events, and incidents are either the products of the author's imagination or used in a fictitious manner. Any resemblance to actual persons, living or dead, or actual events is purely coincidental.

ISBN: 978-1-68433-383-7
PUBLISHED BY BLACK ROSE WRITING
www.blackrosewriting.com

Printed in the United States of America
Suggested Retail Price (SRP) $18.95

Legacy of Fear is printed in Calluna

*The final word count for this book may not match your standard expectation versus the final page count. In an effort to reduce paper usage and energy costs, Black Rose Writing, as a planet-friendly publisher, does its best to eliminate unnecessary waste without lessening your reading experience.

This novel is dedicated to my late mother, whose strength of character and sense of humor inspired myself and many others to forge onwards, despite life's hardships.

ACKNOWLEDGEMENT

The town of Clear Point, the setting for this novel, is fictional, but its physical characteristics are based on the exceptionally lovely towns of Tofino and Ucluelet on the western coast of Vancouver Island, British Columbia.

LEGACY OF FEAR

Chapter 1

The whirr of the wheel and the crash of the waves were her musical accompaniments. Through the open window, a breeze carried the scent of salt air, a breeze with no hint of evil or ill-intent to warn her.

At this late hour, Emily Burton was at her peak, loving to work with a view of the night sky in front of her, knowing the Pacific Ocean rippled, mere steps away.

Her face tight with concentration, the clay changed shape under her long, slim fingers. A noise startled her, sending the vase-to-be into a crazy, twisting shape. She flicked a glance at Max. He slept like a log at her feet. At ten years old, the black lab's hearing was not as good as it used to be, certainly not good enough to be relied upon. She flipped the switch on the wheel. As it wound down, she moved to the window and squinted into the darkness.

Had she seen a human shape beside the tall red cedar tree? Did something move, or was the moonlight teasing her with shifting shadows through the clouds? The noise had sounded like a crack, followed by a loud thump. Had a branch broken and fallen to the ground?

It was common for wildlife to wander at night. It could be anything as small as a raccoon or as large as a bear. However, Emily knew it was unusual for them to come close to the house. Max's scent generally kept them away.

She removed the screen and leaned out the window.

"Is anyone there?" she yelled. Max roused from his pillow and padded over to stand beside her, like an old soldier who understood his duty.

There was no response.

Emily straightened and glanced at her watch. It was close to midnight and breathing life back into the vase was not an option that appealed to her. She cleaned her wheel and supplies before turning off the light. After casting a last quick glance out the window, she headed to the bathroom to prepare for bed.

Her bare feet were soundless on the dark hardwood floor. She paused by her bed, her hand on the edge of her quilt, as second thoughts assailed her.

Max tilted his head when she removed a flashlight from her night table drawer.

"I'll be right back. I want to check it out, just in case."

The spare bedroom was at the back of the house. Through the window, she shone the light across her backyard and was relieved to see eyes staring back at her. They were all present and accounted for. Nothing else seemed to be disturbed.

"Everybody's okay, Max. I think we can sleep easy tonight," she said, returning to her bedroom. She boosted Max onto the bed before sliding in beside him.

When she woke the next morning, Emily remembered the noise. A scrap of worry nibbled at her brain. She threw off the covers, tugged on her sweatpants and t-shirt, and encouraged Max to climb off the bed. Behind her, he treaded to the front of the house, but a low growl rumbled from deep inside him as she pulled open the door. Emily's throat constricted.

The wooden railing of her steps lay on the ground, twisted and broken. Her porch had seen better days, but she had been certain it was solid. Something larger than a raccoon had damaged it. If it was a bear, she might have more than a railing to worry about.

She hurried to the north side of her house and slid to a stop in front of the chicken coop. The fence and the building were intact, and the chickens went about their business as usual. It was the same view she had seen the night before.

"I'll be back to feed you. Give me a minute."

Emily sped past her vegetable garden and, seconds later, reached the goat pen. Molly and Millie bleated a greeting, happy to know they were about to be fed. Their fence stood straight and solid, and they hadn't been harmed.

Emily smiled in relief. Whatever crushed her railing the previous night had not disturbed the animals. The cracking of the wood had undoubtedly scared it away.

The goats nudged her as she poured some oats into their trough and tossed some hay beside it. She filled their water containers and promised to return to milk them as soon as she had time. First, the chickens needed their feed, and then she would have her own breakfast and coffee.

With her second mug of caffeine in hand, Emily stood on her porch and gazed toward the woods where she had seen movement the previous night. A gust of piercing wind lifted her shoulder-length brown hair and made her cross her arms over her chest. Her brown-eyed gaze shifted downward, and she surveyed the damage to her steps. She could handle a hammer and saw, she thought, but she would need to pick up some wood. And maybe some bear deterrent. He must be hungry if he had ventured so close to the house.

An hour later, ready for her day, Emily slammed shut the hatch of her seven-year-old Toyota SUV, helped Max onto the front seat, and headed for Clear Point, a town three kilometers from her house. The route was as familiar to her as her own face, following the shape of the coast, lined on both sides with towering western red cedar trees. Mary's Point, the store that sold local crafts and delicacies, occupied a place on Main Street between the coffee shop and the bait and tackle store. Emily supplied the shop with a variety of pottery products.

The tourist season had picked up as April brought the warmer weather. The western side of Vancouver Island in British Columbia drew people who enjoyed the beaches, along with surfing, fishing, and whale-watching. The university students would converge on the town in a couple of weeks, take on jobs in the tourist industry, and use every spare moment to ride the waves. Clear Point would be busy until the fall when it would cater to the retirees who enjoyed the crisp weather and the changing leaves.

Emily completed her delivery and pulled into her driveway just before noon, parking as close to the porch as possible. She may have been optimistic, but she had stocked up on enough lumber to replace not only the railing but the entire set of steps. It was an ambitious undertaking, but the internet was a wondrous thing. She would find instructions.

Emily set aside all thoughts of bears and stairs as she returned to her wheel and kiln. The physical labor of manipulating the pieces and of her weekly deep-clean of the workshop relaxed her. This room and its equipment had been the source of her livelihood for six years, ever since she had left the big city and its big-city jobs behind.

Early evening, she prepared for her nightly run on the beach, which would give her the energy and focus for her creative endeavors. Emily slipped out of her clay-encrusted overalls and replaced them with black, tight-fitting, spandex pants. She donned a light zippered jacket over her t-shirt as a concession to the spring-like temperatures and the bracing wind that rolled off the waves.

In the old days, Max would have accompanied her when she ran, but he had developed a bad hip. Morning strolls were fine for him, but she had to leave him behind if she wanted to have a good workout, and she needed one after a day spent hunched over a pottery wheel.

Emily jogged along the well-worn path through the trees down to the beach. Her sneakers thumped against the hard-packed sand, which never quite dried out between tides this time of year. Logs were scattered on the beach as if giants had played a game of 'Pick up Sticks.' Emily either weaved around them or jumped over them.

She filled her lungs with the fresh, clean air, a gift from the rain earlier in the day, and relished the coolness of it against her skin. The sunset showed its colors, fighting off the overcast sky. With spring inching closer to summer, the days grew longer, but Emily knew it would be almost dark by the time she returned home.

Up ahead, a large cluster of rocks populated with hardy trees jutted onto the sand, as if it strained to reach the huge 20-foot-high boulder that dominated its own spot on the beach, partially immersed in the ocean. At certain times of day, depending on the tide, the small, four-foot wide section of sand between the boulder and the rocks filled with ocean water, but Emily normally made it through and back before it became submerged. If not, she would climb over the lower rocks to avoid having to remove her shoes and slosh through the water.

Running through the opening, something moved in her peripheral vision. It came from the trees, tackled her hard, and slammed her to the ground. Pain rang through her head. The full force of a body came down on top of her. Strong fingers closed around her throat and choked her screams. Panicked, Emily clawed at the unknown attacker. She tried desperately to dislodge him, but her attempts were futile. The weight of a stranger pressed against her and pinned her against the soft sand. The dampness was cold upon her back.

Her strength waned.

Her vision faded into blackness.

Chapter 2

The female doctor's hands gently poked and prodded her. From the gurney, Emily stared at the sterile instruments and medical supplies on the counter beside her and wondered how she had ended up here. It was mere minutes since she had regained consciousness, and the doctor had revealed little of what had happened. All Emily knew was she had survived death by strangulation, which was more than enough to make her heartrate spike and her gut clench.

"I'm going to send you for a CT scan," Dr. Gordon said. "I don't think you have any serious injuries to your throat, but I want to be certain. At the same time, we'll check for a concussion."

"I want to know more…" Emily's voice was just above a whisper, the pain in her throat intense.

"I know," the doctor interrupted. "You'll talk to the police in a little while. First, we have to make sure your injuries are taken care of."

An orderly appeared and steered Emily's stretcher down the hallway to the radiology department. The small hospital served a few communities along the western coast of the island. It didn't take long to get from one end of the building to the other, but Emily was still surprised at the speed with which she was handled. Everyone was brisk and attentive. She supposed it wasn't every day they treated someone who had been attacked in such a violent way, not in this peaceful area of the world.

When the tests were complete, Emily was rolled back to the ER. She looked around and took in her surroundings. A man stood next to the nurses' station, and her gaze locked onto his face. He was tall, in his fifties, with a pristine appearance, despite the paunch that threatened the buttons of his uniform shirt. He straightened as his gaze connected with hers.

"Hey, how are you doing?" His smile was sympathetic, and he moved to stand beside the stretcher as the orderly left the room. The bright overhead lights reflected off his balding head.

"I'm glad to see you," she said. "I need to know what's going on. This guy came out of nowhere and attacked me."

Emily had known Ted Bowen, head of the Clear Point division of the Royal Canadian Mounted Police, ever since she had moved to the town. He was a respected and familiar sight in the area. His hand closed around hers, and she grasped it like a lifeline.

"I know," he said, his expression dismayed. "Everybody's feeling the shock of it. I'm sorry to bother you with this, but I'm going to have to ask you some questions."

"I have a lot of ..."

"Oh my God, Em, I got here as fast as I could!" The blonde-haired woman ignored the police chief as she rushed to Emily's side and grabbed her free hand.

"What the hell happened? Someone attacked you? And that poor man. I couldn't believe it when Doug told me. What's going on?" Her blue-eyed gaze swiveled to Ted. "Who did this?"

"We don't know yet. This is my first opportunity to speak to Emily." Ted glared at the woman with a raised eyebrow.

"What do you mean by 'that poor man'?" Emily's head pivoted toward Ted. "What does she mean?"

"You didn't tell her?" the woman said.

"I just got here. I told you that." Ted's face was creased in a deep frown.

"Oh, Emily. It's horrible. There..."

"Francie, this is official police business. I'll deal with it," Ted said, his voice firm.

Emily saw her friend bristle, and impatience surged up inside of her.

"Will someone please tell me what's going on? I don't care which one of you it is," Emily croaked.

Ted darted a quick glance at the other woman before he focused on Emily.

"From what we can piece together, a man walking on the beach witnessed the attack on you, and he intervened."

Emily's heartbeat quickened. She hoped this other man could answer her questions, but when she saw the expressions on Ted and Francie's faces, she doubted she would be happy with the rest of the story.

"Unfortunately," Ted said, "he didn't succeed."

"The guy got away," Emily said, disheartened.

"Yes." Ted cast a glance at Francie. "And the man who tried to help you didn't survive."

Emily's eyes widened. "He died?"

"Yes, seemingly from a broken neck."

Her mouth opened, but no sound came out. She looked at Francie in disbelief. Her friend's downcast expression confirmed Ted's story.

"Oh my God," Emily managed to say. "That poor man. He died because of me."

Tears filled her eyes before they slid down her cheeks. Francie's arm came around her shoulder.

"Don't think that way." Her friend's voice was gentle. "It wasn't your fault. It was the man that attacked you. He's the one to blame."

"We suspect he died instantly," Ted said. "We're doing everything we can. I called in IHIT. They're on their way from Vancouver."

"IHIT?" Emily said.

"Integrated Homicide Investigation Team. They're made up of RCMP and police officers from other departments on the mainland. They'll lead the investigation."

Emily's mind whirled. What had started as a normal run on the beach had turned into a nightmare, and an innocent person had lost his life.

"Who was he? The man who was killed?"

"A tourist," Ted said. "He and his wife were visiting Clear Point. He decided to take a walk on the beach after dinner."

"Oh God." Images filled Emily's mind of a wife pacing the floor, worrying about her husband, crying when she received a visit from a grim-faced police officer. She would be devastated.

"Why? I don't understand why someone would attack me and kill someone else. There's no reason."

"It's probably some crazy person. He didn't even know you," Francie said. "No one around here would do something like that."

Emily silently agreed. Violence didn't exist in Clear Point. The sole explanation that made sense was that a mentally-unbalanced tourist, or a vagrant passing through the town, had gone berserk.

"Do you remember anything? Can you tell me what happened?" Ted broke into her thoughts.

"I...it's all so blurry in my mind. I ran through the passageway, and I saw a movement. Nothing clear, just something from the corner of my eye." The fingers of her right hand fluttered across her throat. "Then someone tackled me from the side."

Emily looked at the concerned faces of Ted and Francie.

"I have a vague recollection of pain...and then...nothing. Did I lose consciousness right away? Why can't I remember more?"

"You took a blow to the head. You may have passed out almost immediately," Ted agreed.

Emily could see the disappointment in his eyes. She wanted to give him more, but she had nothing else to offer.

"Was there anyone else around who saw what happened?" she said.

"Shortly after, someone found the two of you, but it was too late to save your rescuer, and the perpetrator had escaped," Ted said.

"How will you find him? The man who did this?"

"We'll do everything we can, I promise."

A wave of dizziness washed over Emily. She laid her head back against the pillow and stared at the ceiling. Francie squeezed her hand.

"Do you think you have a chance of catching him?" she said, grasping for a kernel of hope.

"I don't know," the police chief said. "I don't want to make you any promises, but we're going to do our best, and IHIT is made up of professionals. They see this kind of thing every day."

A movement came from the direction of the nurses' station and drew their attention. A few seconds later, a tall, strongly-built man appeared at the door. His blue eyes were frantic, and his cap sat askew on top of a mop of light brown hair.

"Em, I got here as fast as I could. I was out on the boat. Are you all right?"

"Oh, Trevor," she said, as his arms closed around her in a strong hug. A single sob escaped her lips as she clung to him.

Through her own distress, Emily felt Trevor's body tremble, and she sensed his rage. Her friend was the quintessential hippie, Zen to the max. She had never seen him so upset, and the sight increased her own anguish.

"We'll find this guy," he said, as he pulled back to look at her, his hands clutching her upper arms. Emily gave him a watery nod and took a few deep breaths.

Ted cleared his throat. "It's a police matter, Trevor. We'll take care of finding him."

"We can help," Trevor's fists were clenched by his side. "There's got to be something we can do."

"The more information that can be found and given to the police, the better, but I don't want any vigilante hijinks going on." He shook his finger at Emily's friend, like a schoolmaster admonishing his students.

"I'm not going to organize a posse, Ted, but you can be sure we won't sit back and let someone get away with this," Trevor said.

"I understand that, and I understand all of you are worried about Emily. So am I, but please let us do our jobs."

"It had to be a random act of violence," Emily said. "The guy is most likely long gone."

"You were almost killed, for God's sake!" Trevor turned to her, his eyes wide.

"I know. I don't understand it," Emily said. "And...and that man...I hate to imagine what he went through." She lifted shaking fingers to her face and pressed on her eyes. Sobs shook her body.

"I'm afraid you're going to have to leave," the nurse said, wedging herself in front of Trevor. "She can't be upset like this. She needs to rest."

The woman snapped up the side-rail of the stretcher as Emily watched her grim-faced friends sidle out of the room. Ted appeared at her side, his face resembling a basset hound as he bent over her.

"Emily, I'm going to step out. I've got some calls to make, but there are going to be more questions, from me and IHIT. You can count on that."

"I don't know what else I can tell you. I don't remember anything," she said.

"I know, but they're still going to investigate, and you're going to be called upon."

The nurse cleared her throat and shot Ted a pointed look. He nodded and gave Emily's shoulder a squeeze before he left to join the others.

While the nurse attached the blood pressure band to her arm, Emily heard loud whispers from the other side of the doorway.

"She can't be left alone. What if he comes back?" Trevor said.

Emily's hand jerked involuntarily. She hadn't thought of that. She had focused on the idea that it was a random act of violence, but the thought of going home to an empty house didn't appeal to her.

"Don't worry. She won't be left alone," Francie said. "Doug and I will see to that."

CHAPTER 3

Emily learned through an excited orderly that the IHIT team had arrived by helicopter. According to the gossip among the staff, the forensic experts scoured the beach area, while the lead investigators questioned the sole witness to date, the man who had come upon Emily and the dead body.

Emily knew she would be next on their list of interviewees.

Ten minutes later, a harried-looking Dr. Gordon entered the hospital room where Emily had been moved and confirmed her suspicions.

"There are two police officers from Vancouver here, along with Ted," she said. "They insist on asking you some questions. I'll give them a limited amount of time. You've suffered a trauma, and you have a concussion. I have no choice except to let them talk to you. But don't worry; I'll intervene when I see fit and let you get some rest."

"I appreciate it. Besides, there isn't much for me to tell them. I remember very little of what happened."

A brisk knock at the door interrupted them. The doctor rolled her eyes before she went to open the door.

Two strangers entered the room and nodded at the doctor before they focused on Emily. Behind them, Ted shuffled in and sent a quick smile her way. He leaned back against the windowsill and crossed his arms.

"Hello, Ms. Burton," the first man said, his expression solemn. He was tall and thin, with sparse medium-brown hair, brown eyes, and coffee-yellowed teeth. Despite the late hour and the fact they had flown to Clear Point by helicopter to face an emergency, his suit was crisp and unrumpled, his tie perfectly adjusted. "My name is Dave Humble. I'm the chief investigator in this case. This is my partner, Rick Wallace." He gestured to the man beside him. He was also tall and thin, but his smile held a flash of sincerity, and his clothing looked like it had been picked up off the floor and thrown on in a hurry.

"As I'm sure you're aware, we have to ask you some questions about the events tonight. The doctor has kindly allowed us some time with you."

Inspector Humble didn't make any attempt to hide the sarcasm in his last remark. Emily's heart sank as she realized he didn't intend to make this easier for anyone.

"If you don't mind, my partner will record this interview. We don't want to miss anything."

Before she had a chance to offer her opinion on whether she minded or not, a small rectangular device was set on the bed beside her.

Inspector Humble identified all the people in the room and recited the date and hour. Emily felt like she had morphed into another world, far from the reality of her own. Her brain was fuzzy, and the tiny red blinking light of the recorder mesmerized her.

"Ms. Burton?" The inspector's raised voice caught her attention. "I need you to confirm that you live at 67 South Beach Road."

"Yes, I do."

"Do you live alone?"

"Yes."

"I want you to start at the beginning and tell me exactly what happened tonight."

Emily cleared her throat and tried to focus. "I went for a run on the beach..."

"Do you often do that?" Humble said.

"Yes, every day, unless the weather is bad."

"Alone?"

"Usually. Sometimes, my friend Francie comes with me."

"Full name, please."

"Francie Miller." Emily watched the other detective scribble notes in a small pad, despite the recording of the interview.

"Continue," Inspector Humble said.

"I always run along the same route, and as I ran through the pass, from the corner of my eye, I saw something move. The next thing I knew, someone pounced on me from the side, and I hit the ground."

"Did you struggle? Try to fight the person off?"

"I remember twisting around...I remember pain...in my head. I was terrified." She glanced toward Ted. He gave her an encouraging smile.

"Did you see the attacker's face?" Humble said.

"I don't think so. I can't remember it."

"Hair color? Was he wearing a hat?"

"I don't know."

"Do you remember anything about his clothing?

"No, I don't."

"Was he tall, short, fat, skinny?"

"I'm sorry. I have no idea. It happened so fast, and for some reason, I can't remember any details," Emily said. His questions made her realize how little she knew about the incident. *How could she not know?*

"Did he speak or shout?"

"I don't think so. I don't remember anything like that."

Inspector Humble shot a glance at his partner before he returned his gaze to Emily.

"Was there anyone else around when you were attacked?"

"I didn't see anyone." Emily was almost certain she had been alone on that stretch of beach.

"Is the beach normally deserted at that hour?"

"Often, but not always."

"But tonight, it was?"

"I think so. I don't remember seeing anyone else." The pounding between her eyes intensified.

"Can you think of anyone who may want to harm you?" he said.

"No, not at all." Of this, Emily was convinced.

"You have no enemies?"

His stare reflected his skepticism. *Did she look like the type of person who would have enemies?*

"Not that I know of."

"Not that you know of," he repeated. "Lucky you."

Emily narrowed her eyes. This man did not live up to his name. His sarcasm and arrogance were palpable. She glanced at Ted again, who stared at the IHIT inspector with a heavy frown.

Dr. Gordon's voice came from behind Emily's left shoulder.

"I think that's enough questions for now. Emily has been through a terrible trauma, and she needs her rest. I also should add that it's quite normal for victims, and particularly concussed victims, to have trouble with their memory immediately after the incident. She needs time."

The doctor's intervention consoled Emily, but her relief was short-lived.

"I'm almost done," the inspector said, with the air of someone accustomed to having his way. He turned back to Emily. "Did you know the man who was killed tonight?"

Emily's heart sank at the reminder. "I don't think so. What was his name?"

"Mario Hart. You didn't know him?"

"No. We'd never met," she said softly. Having a name associated with the tragedy seemed to make it worse.

"You're in good physical condition, wouldn't you say, Ms. Burton? I mean, you exercise. I'm sure you eat well."

The sudden change in questioning confused her. "Yes. I'd say so."

"Perhaps, you were acquainted with this man? Perhaps, you'd met on the beach at some other time, and you were interested in him. Romantically, I mean. Maybe, he rejected you. Is that possible?"

Emily's eyes widened as the implication of what he said sank in. Ted straightened from the windowsill and dropped his arms to his sides.

"That's not true. How could you say something so awful?" Emily said. She glanced at the other IHIT inspector, hoping he would admonish his partner. His expression remained bland.

"As an investigator, it's something I have to look at. What if you weren't attacked? What if you were the attacker, and you killed Mr. Hart, and you just happened to get hurt in the process?"

"That's enough, Detective," Dr. Gordon said, her voice hard and brisk. "You're upsetting the patient, and I insist you leave, all of you."

Emily had a vague awareness of the men gathering their things. Ted crossed to the bed, gave her a sympathetic smile, squeezed her shoulder, and followed the other law enforcement officers from the room.

"What a terrible man. How could he think I'd kill someone?" Emily said, her voice breaking.

"Not that I'm defending his methods, but I think he's simply doing his job." Dr. Gordon wrapped a blood pressure band around Emily's arm. "They have to study everything, especially in the case of a homicide. Just to let you know, your hands were swabbed for evidence while you were unconscious. Those tests, along with the rest of their investigations, will narrow down the possibilities. You don't have to worry. But you do have to get some rest. I'm going to adjust the lights in here and leave you alone for a bit. Then, we'll make arrangements for you to get home."

The doctor covered her with another blanket, dimmed the lights, and left the room. Emily closed her eyes. She hoped to shut out the disturbing thoughts that raced through her mind.

She wondered about the man who had lost his life trying to help her. *What was he like? Did he have a large family? Children? What did he do for a living? His loved ones would be crushed. His co-workers would be baffled by the fact that he had left for a vacation and never returned. Would they blame her? It was conceivable. Everyone wanted someone to blame for the bad things that happened to them. The killer was an unknown. She was real.*

An hour later, Francie held Emily's arm as she guided her out of the hospital and to the waiting car. Dr. Gordon had told Emily to get plenty of rest and to expect dizzy spells and headaches. She received instructions to return to the hospital if her symptoms couldn't be alleviated with over-the-counter medication.

"You're a lucky woman," the doctor said. "But you have to take care of yourself. You've suffered a trauma, and your body needs time to heal."

Emily smiled faintly at the woman. It seemed like such a tiny price to pay compared to her savior, who had sacrificed his life.

Several hours after Emily's fateful run, Francie pulled her car up to Emily's home. Darkness cloaked the house, and a concerned bark came from inside as Emily climbed the steps, holding onto Francie's arm. Trevor had come by earlier to let Max outside, but the dog would be worried about his mistress. They were seldom separated.

"Doug is on his way over," Francie said as Emily comforted her old dog.

"I hate to bother you guys like this. I'm sure, by tomorrow night, I'll be able to stay alone. It's just that..."

"Don't even think about it. You know we don't mind. We'll stay with you for as long as you like. Or you can stay with us."

"I know how Winnie would feel about Max invading her space," Emily said, referring to Francie's less-than-friendly cat.

"Winnie needs a wake-up call. Anyway, we'll worry about that another day. For now, you need to get your rest."

Emily sank onto the couch, and Max curled up beside her, resting his chin on her lap, his gaze fixed on her face. She flinched when she heard heavy footsteps on the porch and released a sigh of relief when Doug's familiar face appeared in the doorway. He threw a glance at Francie before focusing on Emily. He crossed over to her, knelt on the floor at her feet, and took her two hands between his much larger ones.

"I couldn't believe it when I heard."

"I still can't believe it," Emily said, her voice choked. With his dark, crew-cut hair and deep brown eyes, Doug had the appearance of a harmless teddy bear. Of medium height, he had a powerful build, rendering the teddy bear-look deceptive. Emily knew he could be fiercely protective of those he loved.

"Can I make you something, Em?" Francie said. "Are you hungry?"

"No, thanks. I have no appetite at all."

"What did the police say?" Doug asked.

Emily filled him in on the little she knew. Her throat closed when she thought of the man who had lost his life. Doug's hand closed over hers.

"I wish there was something I could say that'd make you feel better." Doug's voice rang with sincerity.

"Just having you guys around is appreciated more than you know. I don't like to impose on you like this."

"You're not imposing," he said. "We're happy to be here with you. I just wish the circumstances were better."

"Emily, it's time for you to get some sleep," Francie said.

"I'll try, but no matter how tired my body is, I'm not sure my mind will rest." She pushed herself to her feet. Her battered and bruised muscles ached.

"I'll take care of making sure all the windows and doors are locked. You'll be safe," Doug said.

Emily's heart sank. She had never locked her doors until now. Clear Point had always been a haven of security for her, and she never experienced the slightest fear living here.

"C'mon, Max. It's time for bed," she said. She couldn't decide which ached more, her body or her spirit.

The dog's claws clicked on the hardwood floor as he followed her to her bedroom, the brightness of a full moon shining on the floorboards, lighting the way.

CHAPTER 4

Emily resisted the urge to grimace. The coffee was strong and bitter on her tongue. In front of her sat a plate of fried eggs too undercooked for her taste, tofu sausages dangerously close to being burnt, and slices of avocado not quite ripened. Francie was a dear friend, but cooking was not her strong point. Nevertheless, Emily appreciated the effort and remained determined to see it through.

"How's your head?" Doug asked with a concerned look from his seat on the opposite side of the table.

"I have a bit of a headache, but I'm sure it'll pass."

Her head throbbed like a jackhammer in slow motion, but she didn't want to worry anyone or create another spate of fussing on Francie's part. Her friend had already objected to Emily getting out of bed and had insisted she eat a breakfast large enough to feed a lumberjack. She had also forced her to take two painkillers while Emily would have preferred to take one.

The jarring ring of the telephone set off a larger series of throbs inside Emily's head.

She was thankful when Francie grabbed it on the second ring and left the room to talk to the caller. She returned to the kitchen with a look of apprehension.

"That was from the IHIT detectives. They want to come by and ask some more questions," she said.

"What more can I tell them? I remember so little. They know that." Emily didn't know if she could handle another question period with Dave Humble.

"We should call them back and tell them not to come," Doug said. "It's going to upset you for nothing."

Emily waved her hand dismissively. "No, it's okay. I'll get it over with. It shouldn't take long."

Within a half hour, the two officers, along with the ever-present Ted, were at her door. Inspector Humble, as expected, was dressed fastidiously, while his partner looked like he could use another cup of coffee or two.

Francie, despite her reluctance to have the authorities in Emily's home, was her usual hospitable self and served hot coffee to everyone. She received a grateful smile from Inspector Wallace in return.

The two officers sat on the worn, red plaid couch while Emily faced them in an equally-worn and mismatched blue striped armchair. Ted dragged a wooden chair from the kitchen. Inspector Humble's gaze swept the room, taking in her second-hand furnishings and handcrafted decorations, but his expression remained unchanged.

Doug and Francie, once the coffee was served, were asked to leave. Through the front window, Emily watched the two of them pace back and forth on the porch. She knew Doug would have his hands full trying to keep Francie from forcing her way back into the house.

On the coffee table in the center of the living room, the recorder was set, and the second interview began.

"Tell me why you were on the beach at that hour," Inspector Humble said.

"Again?" Emily glanced at Ted, hoping he would intervene and tell her she didn't have to reply to the same questions she had answered the previous night. He shrugged his apology.

"Yes," Humble said.

She gave in to the inevitable. "I always run at that hour. It suits my schedule."

"And you always run alone?"

"Most of the time. Sometimes Francie comes with me, maybe once a week." Emily gestured toward the woman who peered at them through the front window.

"Why wasn't she with you last night?"

"She knows my routine, and if she wants to come along, she'll show up. It's as simple as that."

"And you don't meet up with anyone while you're running?"

"Nothing planned if that's what you mean. Sometimes, I'll see people I know along the way. I just say hello and keep running."

"Do you often see the same people? Any regulars?"

His tone was casual, but it didn't dispel Emily's suspicions after the implications he had made the previous night. *Did he hope to trap her into admitting to a clandestine affair? A preplanned meeting that had gone terribly wrong?*

"No, I wouldn't say so," she said. "Sometimes, I won't see anyone. Other nights, I may see a dozen people. It depends on the weather. It depends on the time of year. It's never the same."

"You always run in the same direction and take the same path?"

"Yes. I already told you that." She ran a hand through her hair.

"Never had any incidents?"

"Never."

He stared at her, his expression intense. Perhaps she was paranoid, but it seemed like Inspector Humble didn't like her. He may not believe she was the perpetrator of the crime, but he might think the fault, in the end, lay at her door. On the other hand, maybe he had hit upon a nerve already burdened with guilt.

Finally, he spoke. "There's not a lot of crime in Clear Point. It's a pretty quiet place. From what I hear, everyone's nice and friendly. Who would do something like this?"

"You're asking me? I have no idea."

"There's nobody you know who's threatened you?"

"No, there's no one," she said, shaking her head.

"Do you have a boyfriend?"

"No."

"Any exes?"

"I have an ex-husband."

"What's his name?" Inspector Wallace poised his pen over his pad.

"You can't think Alan had anything to do with this," Emily said with a frown.

"Did you part on good terms?" Humble countered.

Emily remembered the pain and anger she had felt when Alan told her he was leaving. She remembered exploding at him, telling him what a terrible person he was, wanting to know how he could leave her after all the promises he had made. And he had retaliated, making her feel small and worthless. The divorce was quickly arranged, both of them eager to be rid of the other, but for different reasons. Alan wanted to start a new life. Emily wanted to escape the pain of being considered less than a real woman. They hadn't spoken since the last papers were signed.

"I guess not." She stared at her hands in her lap.

"What's his full name?"

"Alan Tanner."

"Burton is your maiden name?"

"Yes, I took it back," she said, lifting her head.

She knew Alan had stopped loving her, but she had a difficult time imagining he would want her dead. It was incomprehensible to her that he would make a special trip to Clear Point, watch her habits, and set up a trap to intercept and kill her. The thought was painful, like a knife stab to the heart.

"Is there anyone else you can think of who'd want to harm you?" The detective's voice shook her from her thoughts.

"No, of course not. It isn't even possible Alan would want to kill me." Emily felt the need to express her opinion once again.

"Nevertheless, we have to check it out. It's routine to look at and eliminate the spouses and ex-spouses first."

The strength drained from Emily's body. Instead of having the impression the police were there to help her, she felt intimidated.

"You still don't remember anything about your attacker?"

She shook her head. "I would've told you if I'd remembered anything. I wish I did. I really do."

"And you can't think of anything unusual that may have happened over the last few days or weeks?"

"No, nothing." Her gaze swept the room until her focus fell upon her two friends. They stood on the porch and stared at her broken railing.

"Oh," Emily said, her hand at her throat. "I...there may be something...but I doubt it."

"What is it? Anything may help." Ted's voice was shaded with desperation.

"The night before last, there was a noise, a loud bang. At first, I thought it was a raccoon or a bear, maybe."

"What time was this at?" Inspector Wallace asked.

"Around midnight. I was working at the wheel when I heard it."

"The wheel? What're you talking about?" Humble said.

"My pottery wheel. I often work at night. And it was an unusually loud noise."

"Did you go outside to investigate?"

"No, I looked out, but saw nothing...no, that's not true. I thought I caught sight of a shape in the trees." Her voice became louder and more animated as the memory returned. "At first, I thought it was human, but when I saw the damage, I decided it had to be a bear."

"Damage?" Ted said. "Are you talking about the railing out there?"

"Yes." She turned toward him. "A raccoon couldn't do that. The animals were fine. They hadn't been disturbed. I assured myself of that before going to bed, but I didn't notice the railing until the next morning. Do you think...?"

"We won't think anything until we have a chance to look into it further," the lead detective said. The other man strolled to a corner of the room to talk on his cell phone. He ended the call and returned to the group.

"They're on their way." He addressed Inspector Humble.

"Who?" Emily said.

"The crime scene investigators," Humble responded. "We'll try to determine if an animal or a human broke your railing. In the meantime, make sure those other two don't touch anything out there," he added, sending his partner to the door.

* * *

Emily lay down for a few minutes to rest. Her headache had not abated, and she had been slammed by a wave of fatigue. She knew her concussion caused a large part of the pain, but the investigators were also tireless with their questions.

Inspector Humble insisted she walk them through her activities the night of the noise, and he made her sit at the wheel while it spun dizzily. She described each step of that night, guiding them around the house as she did so. From the porch, she pointed out the area of trees where she had seen the shape that had been either human or bear.

When Humble said he wanted Emily to help them reconstruct the scene on the beach, Francie put her foot down. "That's impossible. Can't you see she's exhausted? You can't expect her to go traipsing around the beach, especially not so soon after it happened."

Humble had the grace to look sheepish, an expression that didn't sit well on him.

"I suppose we don't have to do it today, but I'm afraid I'll need you to walk us through it as soon as possible."

Emily nodded her assent and shot a grateful glance at her friend. She told them she wanted to rest for a few minutes while the forensics team worked on her porch and in her yard. Without waiting for a response, she went to her bedroom, crawled under the quilt, and curled into a ball on her side.

Sleep wasn't possible, not with the back-and-forth shouting between the law enforcement officers, and not with the heavy footsteps on the porch and in her house. But she closed her eyes against the harsh sunlight and the constant strain, and she relished what little time she had alone.

Emily had lived on her own in this house for close to six years, ever since the breakup with Alan. She never considered herself a loner, but she had come to enjoy and cherish her life as it was, with the freedom to live the existence of her choosing. At this moment, she longed for the peace and quiet she had grown accustomed to, and she wanted nothing more than to see everyone leave her home.

Those feelings were shared by someone else. Max nudged the bedroom door open and climbed onto the bed beside her, resting his chin on her hip. Emily stroked his head and drew comfort from the old dog.

Half an hour later, a light knock on the door signaled the end of her respite.

"Em, I hate to bother you, but it seems they're done. They'd like to talk to you before they leave," Francie said.

Emily rolled over and smiled at her friend. "If it'll get them out of here faster, I'll be right out."

"I thought you'd say that. I'll let them know."

As she joined the policemen, Emily gazed around the living room, not sure what she expected to find, but the interior of the house seemed to be the same as usual. She presumed the exterior would not be in the same condition.

"We've searched for evidence on the railing and on much of the outside area," Inspector Humble said. "We didn't find anything to confirm a human being had been present the night before last. But we can pretty much conclude it wasn't a bear."

"How can you say that?"

"Any animal that applied that much force to the railing would've left some fur behind, and there was none. There were no large tracks either. As for human tracks, there are plenty in the driveway, way too many to decipher. And there's too much foliage among the trees to find anything conclusive. Not to mention the fact it rained hard since that night, which would've washed away anything worthwhile."

"So, in other words, you've eliminated the possibility it was an animal, so it has to have been human," Emily said.

"Correct."

She shivered. *Who had been prowling around her home? Could it have been the killer? What had scared him off?*

Humble glanced at his partner and nodded.

"We'll be in touch if there's anything," he said.

Emily's eyes widened. "That's it? You're just going to leave? What can you tell me about the investigation? Did you find any other evidence? Over there, I mean," she said, waving her hand toward the beach. She hated to even think of the spot where an innocent man had been murdered.

"I'm not able to share details with you," Humble said. "But we're working on the premise it was a random attack."

"You said it could be my ex-husband."

"I said we had to eliminate him as a suspect. It's standard procedure to follow. My gut, on the other hand, tells me it was probably a random attack."

"But what do I do? I could've been killed. Now, you're saying he may have been right outside my door the night before. I need to know you're going to catch him."

The police detective huffed out a breath.

"I know you believe Vancouver Island is the epitome of clean living, and you think it's crime-free. But, like any other place on the planet, this area has a criminal element. So, the possibility you ran into someone's path must be explored, just as we have to consider your ex-husband or any other people of interest."

"What criminal element? You know something or someone?" She looked at Ted with raised brows. She had never heard of any criminal activities in the area.

"There isn't any one person we can point our finger at, but we have avenues to explore. That's all I can tell you."

"You're telling me this guy is a criminal? I ran by him, and he decided to kill me?"

"No, I'm saying that's one possibility we'll investigate. Let us do our job, and we'll let you know what we find."

Emily pinned him with her gaze. "Do you still think I did it?"

"We're not ruling anything out," he said with a stare to match hers.

Emily turned to look out the window. She thought about the man who had lost his life, and grief stabbed her in the chest. She had never met him, but she imagined the pain his family was going through.

"How are they?" she said, turning toward the cop. "Mr. Hart's family. Have you spoken to them?"

For the first time, a flash of empathy flitted across the detective's face.

"They're about as well as you could expect under the circumstances."

"Can I see them? Talk to them?" she said.

"Emily, they've left the island," Ted said, stepping forward. "And, besides, it wouldn't be a good idea. Why put yourself through that?"

"I want to tell them how sorry I am for what happened. I feel responsible."

"You shouldn't. They're not blaming you. I spoke to them, and they expressed concern for you. They wanted to know how you were doing."

For Emily, this was worse than hearing they hated her. That they were willing to show kindness to someone who was connected to the murder of their loved one was too much to bear. Emily knew she would break down. She hurried from the room.

Chapter 5

Over the next few days, Emily received a lot of support from her friends, with an almost steady stream of sympathetic visitors who dropped by during the day and early evening. Many offered to stay over or invited her to stay at their home. Emily thanked them, but she knew if she became dependent on others it would be more difficult to get back on her feet. In her opinion, jumping into the icy water and letting her body adjust was the best option.

One of the most difficult tasks over the week had been discussing the case with her family. Her seventy-year-old father lived in Abbotsford, a suburb south of Vancouver, and he had seen the news coverage of the murder in Clear Point. Thankfully, the identities of the victims involved had been withheld, but Emily didn't know how long it would be before her name became public. The next day, minutes after the last police officer left, he phoned Emily, seeking an update and reassurance.

"Everyone's shook up around here, Dad. It's not something we're used to," she said, struggling to maintain an indifferent tone.

"Do you know the person that was murdered? Was it someone local?"

"No, it was a tourist. I thought they'd said that on the news."

"Oh, maybe they did. Wasn't someone else attacked and hurt?"

"Yes, a local woman. She's going to be okay. Don't worry." It was a white lie, Emily told herself.

"Well, of course, I'm going to worry if something like that happens so close to you."

Emily heard the concern in his voice and knew her decision to keep the truth from her father had been the best one to make. She didn't want to upset him. After a few more words of comfort, their conversation ended with Emily assuring him she would be extra careful.

Emily took a fortifying breath after disconnecting. She needed to call her sister. Lisa was two years her senior and took her role as big sister seriously. She lived in Kelowna, almost seven hundred kilometers inland, which meant the two women didn't see each other often, but they maintained a strong long-distance contact.

"Nice to hear from you," her sister said, slightly breathless. Lisa always sounded like she had rushed to pick up the phone.

Emily caught up on Lisa's news, which consisted of numerous events in her children's lives. She had a girl and a boy, respectively aged seven and five. From the way she described it, she never had a moment to herself.

"Enough about me. What's new in your life?" Lisa said.

"Well…"

"Oh no, what is it?"

"I'm fine," she hastened to say before her sister went into panic mode. Lisa was always able to read Emily's tone of voice. Unfortunately, what she had to say would not put her sister at ease. "It's just that an incident occurred here."

Emily went on to tell her sister about the attack on the beach and the murder of a tourist.

"You didn't tell me about this? I heard about it on the news, but I didn't know it was you. I'm only finding out now?"

"It happened yesterday. I didn't have time to call you until now. And, I knew you'd be upset…"

"Upset?" Lisa said, her voice rising. "My baby sister was almost murdered, and you think I'm not going to be upset?"

"This is precisely why I hate to tell you. You overreact."

"How can you say that? What the hell. I don't believe this."

Emily could picture her sibling in her mind. Her brown eyes would be wide, and her face would be reddened with emotion. Emily had witnessed it several times over the course of her lifetime.

"Lisa, take a deep breath. I'm fine."

"Did they get the guy? Do they think it's Alan?"

"What? Why would you say that?" It was bad enough to hear it from the cops, but for her sister to think her ex-husband hated her enough to kill her was too much.

"He's the obvious first choice," Lisa said.

"He is not. Do you actually think Alan is capable of something like that?" Silence filled the air for a moment.

"No, I guess not. He's too much of a wuss," her sister said.

"Lisa!"

"It's true. If he wasn't, he would've stuck around in the first place. For better or for worse, remember?"

Emily closed her eyes. Leave it to her sister to bring that up. She already regretted telling Lisa the news.

"Do they have any suspects?" the other woman said.

"Not yet. The theory is that he's long gone. Obviously, it's not a local."

"How can you be sure?"

"Because I know all the locals," Emily said. "There's no one here who'd do something like that."

"I'll drive out tomorrow."

Emily rolled her eyes. It was just like her sister to make an impetuous decision like that. It would take her at least twelve hours to get to Clear Point, and she would have to organize her family before she would be comfortable leaving them.

"Don't be silly. There's nothing for you to do here. I'm fine," Emily said.

"You must be traumatized. You can't stay alone."

"I admit I'm shook up, but it's nothing I can't handle. And I'm not alone. Francie and Doug are staying with me."

It was a small lie. Doug and Francie would not stay indefinitely, and she didn't want to tear her sister away from her family when it wasn't necessary. Besides, as much as she loved Lisa, Emily didn't think she could handle the constant fretting.

"You need me with you." Lisa's voice grew less insistent, and Emily knew her sister had rethought her hasty offer.

"You need to be with your family. I'll be all right. I'll call you often just so you know everything's okay."

"I'm not sure about this, Em."

"I am. And, another thing, please don't mention this to Dad. He knows about the murder, but not my involvement. There's no need to upset him."

Lisa agreed on that point. Emily hung up with a promise to keep her sister updated, either by e-mail or by phone, the instant she had any news. Disconnecting, she closed her eyes and dragged in several deep breaths. She decided to do some yoga to clear her mind of negative vibes.

Chapter 6

Emily sat upright in her bed, a scream forming in her throat. She had been dreaming. It began harmlessly enough with a daytime walk on the beach, a sprightly Max by her side. She spotted a surfer on the waves. To get a better look, she lifted her hand to shield her eyes from the glaring sun, wanting to see if it was someone she knew. She heard gunshots coming from behind her. The man on the water waved his arms and yelled at her, telling her to duck. She dived onto the sand and prayed she wouldn't be struck by a bullet.

That was when she woke, but the gunshots didn't stop. They were not imaginary, and it wasn't a single popping sound. It was more like the rat-a-tat-tat of a machine gun.

Max was also on full alert, but whether it was because of the noise or Emily's reaction to it was unknown.

A week had passed since the incident on the beach. It haunted her and took little to bring it to the forefront of her mind. Any sharp, unusual noise made her heart beat triple-time. Several moments later, she realized it wasn't the sound of a machine gun that reached her ears.

"What the hell? It's six o'clock on a Saturday morning."

Emily threw off the covers, slid out of bed, and stalked to the window.

The cool morning air caressed her face as she peered out, trying to make out the direction from which the noise came. She thought it sounded like hammering, but from many hammers at the same time. She frowned and wondered who would make such a racket at this hour on a weekend morning.

Emily shrugged on an oversized sweater and headed to the kitchen. She punched the button on the coffeemaker and slid her feet into her boots before she opened the door. Max nudged past her and plodded into the trees beside the house.

Francie and Doug had stayed with Emily for two nights after the attack, and that was plenty of time for her to yearn for her time alone. She loved her friends, but they were set on smothering her with concern. Since then, she had stayed alone and hugged Max close to her at night for comfort.

While she waited for her pet to return, Emily eyed the still-broken railing and the pile of fresh lumber waiting to be transformed. Pushing aside thoughts of the chore, she breathed in the fresh ocean air, never failing to appreciate how lucky she was to live in this little portion of paradise.

She had been born and raised in the large, bustling city of Vancouver on the mainland, and although her present home carried the same name as that city, Vancouver Island was as different from its namesake as chalk and cheese.

As a child and teenager, Emily spent all her summers in Clear Point and grew to love the small-town life, the beautiful scenery, and the smell of the trees and the ocean. Her maternal grandmother had grown up here as an only child but left to marry and live in the city of Kamloops, in the interior of British Columbia. The family home was handed down to Emily's mother, who kept it as a summer getaway, much to the delight of her two daughters. It had remained in the family, and when Emily had scraped together the means, she became the proud owner of the property.

Emily knew the sound of banging noises in downtown Vancouver wouldn't have disturbed her sleep, but she had grown accustomed to sleeping to the soft melody of the ocean.

Max trudged back to her, and she went inside to make coffee and breakfast. Once that task was completed, she would see to the chickens and the goats before she investigated the noise nearby.

As the coffeemaker gurgled, she thought about her telephone conversation with Dave Humble the previous day. The latest news was that a similar attack had occurred on the waterfront in the city of Vancouver. The woman managed to escape unharmed, and no one else was involved or hurt. They now leaned toward the theory the perpetrator had moved to the mainland and he may be targeting women. In that case, the attack on Emily would have been random, and Mario Hart had been murdered because of his intervention and for no other reason.

All the same, to reassure Emily and the rest of the population of Clear Point, the RCMP had assigned a patrol officer to the beach area, and the police presence in the town increased. According to the authorities, Emily could return to her previous way of life.

Needless to say, they forgot to consider the fact walking on a deserted beach filled her with fear, and she had trouble sleeping at night.

Dressed in her everyday wear of worn jeans, a plaid shirt over a t-shirt, and a pair of waterproof boots, Emily and Max set off toward the house where her neighbor used to live. She suspected they would find the source of the early-morning noise in that direction.

Emily hadn't regained enough physical strength to resume her nightly run. She didn't know if she would overcome the psychological barrier to ever run again. For now, she limited her exercise to sedate strolls on the beach, in broad daylight, with Max by her side and a heavy walking stick in her hand. If she had the misfortune of being approached by a dangerous-looking stranger, she would have something with which to defend herself.

Luckily, that was never the case. The beach in daytime remained a popular place for surfers and the hardier sun worshippers. As the spring advanced and the weather warmed, it would teem with people.

The wind off the water whipped at Emily's hair and tugged on her shirt. Her boots slapped against the hard, damp sand under her feet. The hum of a seaplane could be heard over her right shoulder. She wondered if Doug made a flight to a nearby town or took some tourists on a sightseeing trip. He was one of the seaplane pilots that serviced the area, and he ran a brisk business.

As Emily drew closer to her neighbor's house, the noises grew louder. There was no doubt there were hammers and saws at work. She rounded the corner, and her eyes widened at the sight. At least three men worked on the roof, stripping off the old roofing tiles. A few more changed windows, and two others built something off to the side.

Curious, Emily stopped and gazed at the house. It held a lot of memories for her. It had been deserted for over six months, ever since Mr. Felch had passed away. She had enjoyed her neighbor's company, and she knew the feeling had been mutual.

A tall, imposing man advanced toward her. Emily assumed he oversaw the construction job and therefore should be harmless, but her stomach clenched, nevertheless. Her gaze flickered to the other men who worked several feet away, and a few of them glanced in her direction. She was safe, she reminded herself. After all, it was daylight, and there were people nearby. She straightened her shoulders.

"Hi, I'm Emily. I live next door," she said, making an effort to respond to him as she would have before the attack.

"Dustin Reeves," he said, one hand in the pocket of his worn jeans. The other scratched Max behind the ears. His ball cap covered most of his sandy brown hair and shadowed his eyes. The lower part of his face was expressionless, his jaw taut.

"I didn't know the Felch place had been sold," Emily said. "I'm surprised. News usually travels fast around here."

"Yeah, it was a pretty quick turnaround," the man said with a shrug. "I've got a construction job going on here. It's not safe to hang around."

"I don't want to be a bother. I just thought it'd be a good idea to meet my new neighbors. Are they here?"

"No," he said, his voice abrupt. "You live next door, you said?"

Emily rethought the wisdom of giving too much information to a stranger.

"Not quite next door, no. Farther down...with my boyfriend...he's a cop," she said, her face growing warm.

The man's lips twitched.

"I'm glad to know that. If there's any trouble, I'll know where to go. I bet he's a big burly guy, right?"

"Yeah," Emily said, her voice low, her eyes averted. "I think I'll get going. I'll drop by some other time when the owners are here."

"I'll let them know you dropped by to extend a welcome. Emily, was it? And your boyfriend's name is...?"

"Bob."

"Bob, of course. I'll be sure to remember that."

Emily realized the man saw through her ruse and would have a good laugh at her expense when she walked away. With his co-workers, he would share the joke about the woman who was so afraid of him she had invented a cop boyfriend.

She turned and headed home without another word.

"God, I'm a fool, Max," she said when she had put enough distance between herself and the man named Dustin. "He's sure to tell the owners, and they're going to think I'm an idiot. I've turned into a crazy lady. People will start talking behind their hands as I walk by, saying I used to be normal until you-know-what happened. I'll have a weird look in my eyes, and my socks won't match. Everybody'll shake their heads, and tsk-tsk, and say it's a shame."

Max, ambling beside her, grumbled agreeably.

Emily's house came into view, and she stopped for a moment to stare at it with objectivity. It wasn't big or fancy. It was a bungalow with three bedrooms, one of which served as her workshop. It had everything she needed in her life as a single woman.

She also had the chickens and the goats, and in the garden, she grew enough vegetables to sustain her year-round, with a little extra to give to friends. She didn't want for anything. All she yearned for was to get through this period of fear, guilt, and doubts. With any luck, she would come out on the other side, if not whole, at least able to function as she had before.

Chapter 7

Emily and Max strolled by the house, which seemed to be deserted. On the return trip, she stopped and stood with her hands on her hips, her head cocked to the side, and stared at the former Felch home. She couldn't see a car in the driveway; no one hung around outside.

"C'mon, Max, we'll just go a little closer. I'm curious to see what's been done."

She had often been a guest in the house. It had needed an overhaul, having deteriorated since the death of Mrs. Felch at least ten years earlier.

As she drew closer, Emily admired the new windows on the beach side of the house and the white wood siding. Since her encounter with the foreman, the construction mess had been cleared away and a few shrubs added to give it a more natural appearance. His team worked fast, she thought.

Unable to stop herself, she moved to the back of the house. She had spent many hours on the porch with Mr. Felch, sipping lemonade while listening to his stories. Shaded with large cedar trees and unchanged by the recent construction, the porch ran the length of the bungalow. It was wide enough to accommodate a swing, along with a table and several chairs.

It happened the instant her foot settled on the second step.

"Curious, are you?"

Emily whirled around to face the source of the voice, her heart hammering in her throat. A few feet away, a man sat in a white rattan chair. A tree cast a dark shadow over his face, but most of his body was visible. He wore blue jeans and a black t-shirt. His bare arms were tanned and muscled.

"I...I'm sorry. I didn't know you were there," Emily said, her hand over her heart. She moved her right foot back and searched for the step without taking her eyes off the stranger.

"I can see that. Do you always prowl around people's houses when you think they're not home?"

Emily wasn't sure if she had angered the man or not. His tone was smooth and seemed to hold a touch of amusement. Perhaps he wanted to catch her off-guard. The urge to turn and run pulsed through her body. She took another step backward, missed the step, and lost her balance.

A squawk of distress escaped her lips, replaced by a gasp of fear when a strong hand gripped her arm and pulled her upright.

"You?" she said. "I thought you said you were the foreman?"

"I didn't say anything of the sort. You made an assumption," Dustin Reeves said. He released her arm and leaned against the door of the house, his arms crossed over his chest.

"You own this house? Why didn't you tell me that from the start?" Confusion replaced her fear.

"You referred to the owners as 'they', and since I'm not plural, I said 'they' weren't at home."

Emily wasn't brave enough to challenge him, not today. The encounter had shaken her more than she wanted to admit. Mumbling another apology, she turned and hurried toward the beach and home.

•   •   •

"It was very strange. I don't think I like him."

"I don't understand what he did that was so wrong."

Emily fidgeted, the rough bark of the log digging into the back of her legs. She tore her gaze from the sight of the advancing tide to look at her friend. Francie had joined her for a brisk walk on the beach. Emily still couldn't jog without risking a wave of dizziness. As they walked, the conversation turned to the subject of her new neighbor. Tired, Emily suggested they take a break.

"He lied to me," she said.

"I'm sure he thought he was being funny. And don't forget you lied to him first," Francie said with a grin.

Emily groaned. She had shared the story about her idiotic claim of having a cop boyfriend living with her. She ran her hands through her hair before she slumped forward, her elbows on her knees and her chin in her palms.

"I don't know myself anymore, Francie. I used to be friendly and trusting. I wasn't afraid of strangers. I didn't feel I had to lie to them to protect myself. I didn't see fault in people where there may be none."

Francie laid her hand on Emily's knee and leaned ahead to get into her line of vision.

"It's normal for you to feel this way. You had a horrible experience. You'll come out of it. You've done it before."

"It's not the same thing," Emily said, as she picked up a branch and drew shapes in the sand.

"You're right. This time you were physically hurt and terrified. With Alan, you were emotionally destroyed. What I'm getting at is that you're strong and resilient. You overcame a terrible experience in your past, and you'll do it again. The first step is to put this whole thing behind you."

Emily snorted. "That's easier said than done. It's impossible to erase from my mind."

"I'm not telling you to erase it. I'm telling you to stop focusing on it so much. Think about other things."

Emily knew Francie meant well, but she didn't have a clue about what went on inside Emily's mind or how the attack had affected her.

It had taken Emily a long time to learn how to put bad experiences behind her and to live in the present. It had involved radically changing her lifestyle and her life choices. But she didn't think she could have done it without the help of her friends, and she was grateful for them.

Emily and Francie had known each other since they were small children. Francie had lived her entire life in Clear Point, and the two girls had spent their summers together. They would part with tears at the end of August every year and reunite with joy in the spring.

They were as different as two people could be, both in physique and in character. Francie, with her natural sun-bleached blond hair, stood a few inches taller than Emily and was more muscular. An avid surfer, she taught the sport to both tourists and locals. She was also an extrovert, someone who always needed to be surrounded by people. Emily, on the other hand, enjoyed her friends, but she enjoyed her solitude just as much.

"Thanks. That's why I like hanging out with you," Emily said with a wink.

"However," Francie said, raising her index finger. "I have to add, you have a few strides to take in starting up another relationship."

"Oh no, you don't. We're not getting into that."

"Why not? It's time. You're thirty-two."

"I didn't know I had an expiry date."

"Doug and I have been married eight years."

"That's wonderful, but it's not for me," Emily said with conviction.

"Alan was a bad apple. There are a lot of good ones out there. They're lined up, waiting for their chance," Francie said with a knowing nod.

Emily laughed for what seemed like the first time in many days. "You don't give up. I'll give you that."

"C'mon, let's get back. We've got plans tonight."

They turned their backs to the ocean and made their way through the trees toward Emily's house.

•   •   •

The two women, accompanied by Doug, went to Bob's Brew, their favorite pub on the main street in Clear Point, to meet up with friends.

On weekends, the bars and restaurants were jammed with tourists or Vancouverites searching for good times and adventure. Emily and her friends preferred to go out during the week to share a drink, catch up on the news, and have a game of pool or two.

The owner of the bar had tried to imitate an Irish drinking establishment with the dark mahogany woodwork and the Guinness poster art, but the roots of the area had naturally sprung up. A fishing net was cast over a framed photo of the cliffs of Moher, and lobster traps stacked beside the bar were used to store surplus bottles of Jameson Irish Whiskey.

Despite its identity crisis, it fulfilled all the needs of a friendly neighborhood bar. It was dimly-lit with comfortable benches and stools, and it had a spot in the back with a pool table and heavy wooden armchairs. The constant clang and thump of pool balls mingled with the rumble of voices.

This evening, the usual group held court. Will McCade arrived first and reserved a table for them. When he spotted the three friends, his teeth flashed white against his dark beard, and his blue eyes sparkled with good humor. He was casually, but neatly, dressed in jeans and a light jacket over a t-shirt.

Will became a permanent resident of Clear Point three years ago, when he took over a multi-generational family fishing business. He had spent his summers working the boats with his grandfather and had learned to love the life and the habitat as much as his predecessors. After spending several years traveling, he returned to Clear Point to settle down.

Will slid into the booth beside Emily. He gave her a wink and a smile before he nudged her over a little to make room. The consensus among her friends was that Will had his eye on Emily, and he had for a long time. She tended to agree with them, but she had resolved to keep him at arms-length, despite his good looks and charm. She wasn't interested in romantic involvement.

Emily, Francie, Trevor, and Will had been inseparable friends during those beautiful summer months every year. Francie was like a sister to her, and both Trevor and Will were like treasured brothers. She couldn't imagine having a romantic relationship with either of them.

Despite her resolution, she wasn't immune to Will's smiles and good nature. He had everyone wrapped around his little finger. Why should she be different?

A few minutes later, Trevor sauntered over to join them. As usual, his hair was ruffled, his shirt was oversized, and his pants slouched low on his hips. The sandals on his feet were well-worn and tattered. Trevor had lived in Clear Point all his life, grown up on the fishing boats, did a stint as a tour boat crew member, and now managed his own surf shop. He had a deep love of everything about Clear Point, having come from a long line of Daltons who had called this side of Vancouver Island home. For Emily, he epitomized the spirit of Clear Point: cheerful, laid-back, friendly, and always willing to help a friend.

Unbidden, the image of her new neighbor popped into her mind. She shook her head to clear it. Although she didn't know him well enough, he was clearly a mainlander, new to this area. He was the polar opposite of someone like Trevor, and he would never fit in with this crowd.

Gratitude welled up inside her. A choice she made years ago had brought her to Clear Point and this group of people. Although the town had been a significant part of her childhood and teenage years, she had never dreamed it would become her permanent home. It had taken a series of unfortunate events to get her to this point, and she was thankful for the result, despite the latest misfortune.

"Thanks, Mel," Emily said to the waitress as she set a craft beer in front of her. Her friends reached for the BBQ chicken wings and nachos on the platters in the center of the table, while Emily helped herself to the veggies and dip, having long ago become a vegetarian.

"How're you doing, Em?" Will asked, his expression serious. The others stopped their conversation and focused their attention on Emily.

"I'm doing okay. I'd be lying if I said I was a hundred percent, but each day it gets a little easier. I think that's normal."

"Of course it is," Francie said.

"You know you just have to say the word and any of us will be over there in the blink of an eye," Trevor added.

"I know that. You guys are great. I appreciate it, but I'm settling back into my routine. I'm getting my rest, and the headaches aren't as bad, so there's nothing to worry about."

"Emily met the guy who bought Alfred Felch's house." Francie changed the subject and set off a round of questions about the new resident. Emily had little to contribute other than the fact he had renovated the house and she had the impression he liked his privacy.

The group made their way to the pool tables to join a few other acquaintances and take up the challenges that were tossed around. As Emily watched Francie and Doug compete with a loving fierceness, Will sidled up and bumped into her gently.

"I must say you're looking lovely tonight, Miss Emily."

Emily laughed. She wore her oldest pair of jeans and a t-shirt inscribed with 'I must be psychic because my underwear says Medium.' On her feet, she wore mud-splattered sneakers.

"You're so full of it, Will."

"Not at all. I'm into the whole beach bum chic look."

"I'm far from being a beach bum."

"Just because you're not into surfing, doesn't mean you can't be a beach bum."

"I'm just not a water baby, that's all." She shrugged off the arm that snuck across her shoulders.

"I bet you I could make you love the water."

"I doubt it."

"I bet you I could make you love other things." His breath was hot in her ear as he leaned closer.

"You're relentless, you know that?" Emily laughed. "Why don't you turn your charm on Charlotte? She'd be perfect for you."

Both of their gazes turned to the petite, blond woman who watched the pool game from the other side of the room.

"I'm crushed. How could you pawn me off on another woman? You're supposed to jealously keep me for yourself."

His voice was playful, but Emily detected an undercurrent of wistfulness in his tone.

"I believe in sharing," she said, with a smile and a desire to keep the atmosphere light.

"Oh, that sounds kinky." Will raised an eyebrow and winked.

They both turned at the sound of a cheer. Doug's fist was raised in victory.

"Bring on the next loser. Who is it?" Doug shouted.

"Prepare to be beaten," Will said. He stepped over to claim the pool stick from Francie.

"You should give him a chance," her friend said as she arrived at Emily's side.

"And you should know better than to even suggest it."

"Alan was an asshole."

"I know, but I loved that asshole before I realized he was an asshole."

"Not all of them are," Francie said, gesturing toward Doug and Will. "And you won't know if you don't take a chance. Look at him. He's perfect. He's gorgeous, athletic, funny, charming, and I could go on and on. Christ, I'd go for him if I wasn't already in love and happily married to Doug."

"I know, I know. I'm being stupid, it's just..."

"It's just time. Look at that butt."

Emily moved her gaze to Will as he leaned over the pool table.

"Yeah, he has a nice butt. I'll give him that."

CHAPTER 8

Emily gazed with pride at the fruits of her labor from the morning. All the pieces she had removed from the kiln had been packed in crates and boxes with the care a mother would bestow upon a newborn baby. Another collection was ready to be baked later in the day when she returned from her delivery to Mary's Point.

She backed the SUV up to the still-unrepaired porch steps and left the hatch open. With a crate of pottery in her arms, she took her time going down the steps, her head twisted at an odd angle, watching her feet.

"Let me help you with that."

Emily squealed and teetered on the steps. The crate slipped from her grasp, and she knew she would see her hard work crash to the ground. Two large hands reached out and rescued the box.

"You scared the hell out of me." Emily had one hand to her forehead, the other over her heart. "Why did you sneak up on me like that?"

"Sorry about that. I didn't mean to scare you, but I wasn't sneaking up on you," Dustin Reeves said.

Emily sat on the top step and took several deep breaths. It was unusual for her to be so jumpy, but the last thing she had expected was to hear a strange voice. She watched as her neighbor placed the crate in the back of the vehicle.

"I should've spoken up," he said. "Especially after what happened to you."

"How do you know about that?" She lifted her head, and her gaze pierced his.

"Everybody knows about it. It's the talk of the town."

Emily's shoulders slumped. Of course, the murder would be discussed everywhere from the gas station to the hardware store. The people of the town talked of little else. Many of them had given up solitary walks and now locked their doors, even in the middle of the day. Emily knew, with time, the fear would fade, and people would go back to their regular way of life, but it was still too fresh in everyone's thoughts.

"Do you have any more boxes to bring out?"

"It's okay. I can do it," she said, straightening.

"I can help. It's the least I can do after I scared the life out of you."

Emily hesitated. *This man was a stranger. Was it wise to let him into her home?*

Dustin stepped back and raised his hands to each side.

"I get it. You're not sure about me. I don't blame you."

Emily shifted her gaze to the trees that separated her home from the ocean. She had loved this town for so long. It had brought her peace and happiness, even through the darkest days of her life. It nourished her friendly and trusting spirit. She hated that someone had chipped away at that spirit.

She turned back to her neighbor, her shoulders straight. "Follow me." She led the way to her workshop.

"Wow, this is quite the setup you have." He stood with his hands on his hips and contemplated the room. Emily followed his gaze. She took it for granted, but she had to admit she had a workshop of which she could be proud. Everything was neat and in its place. It was organized in a way not to waste space. The kiln resided in an insulated corner, and her wheel was stationed near the window, with shelves lining the walls filled with works-in-progress and the tools of her trade.

Dustin grabbed the largest of the two remaining boxes while she took the other, and Emily's finished stock was soon secure in the SUV.

"You aren't nervous about staying here alone?" Dustin turned back toward her.

"No. I'm fine." She twisted the tips of her hair around a finger.

"From what I hear, they haven't caught the killer." His brows were lowered, and his hands were on his hips again.

"That's true, but he's moved onto Vancouver now. It won't be long before they catch him."

Emily heard the doubt in her own voice. She didn't like the way he stared at her, as if he could read her mind. And she didn't like the way he stirred up old fears.

"I'm fine here. I lock my doors, and I'm being extra careful," she said. "I'm not the slightest bit worried."

He gazed at her for a moment before he shrugged his shoulders.

"I can fix that for you if you want." He nodded toward the broken railing.

"Thanks, but I can take care of it. I just haven't had time yet."

"I'm pretty handy with a hammer," he said. "I worked on the renovations at my house."

"I appreciate the offer, but I'll be able to do it." She stared at him for a moment, her head tilted to one side. "Why are you being so nice, all of a sudden?"

His lips twisted. "I may have been a little...unneighborly the other day and I thought I'd try to make up for it."

"Uh-huh. Well, I appreciate your neighborly help this morning. Clear Point has a small-town, helpful character. You'll catch on."

She gave him a smile and a wave as she urged Max into the vehicle and pulled out of the driveway. In her rear-view mirror, she glimpsed him as he stood and watched her progress.

●　　　　●　　　　●

Emily didn't sleep well that night. Her neighbor had stirred up unpleasant memories. She had lied to him. *Of course, she was worried. How could she not be?* You don't come that close to losing your life and not worry about the fact the person responsible remained out there somewhere and was perhaps willing to murder again. She locked her doors whenever she was in the house, day or night, and she double-checked them before going to bed. Her sense of security had vanished the day of the attack, along with her capacity to trust people.

After staring at the ceiling for longer than she cared to, she crawled out of bed and went to her workshop. She flipped the switch of her pottery wheel. As it spun, Emily relaxed. The hum of the wheel combined with the incessant crashing of the waves on the beach created a symphony of calming music.

She pulled the container of clay toward her, reached in, and grabbed a clump. Plopping it in the middle of the wheel, she wet her hands with water from the bowl that sat ready and waiting for her.

Emily wrapped her hands around the clay and relished its coolness as it changed shape according to the demands of her fingers. She could mold and shape the clay in any way she wished. If she wanted to destroy it, she could. If she wanted to turn it into something beautiful, she would. If it was destined to be something plain and practical, then so be it. But she would decide. She would determine the result.

Emily had no particular purpose in mind for this mass of clay. Not this time. She needed it to calm her, and she let her emotions guide her toward the finished product. In the end, the creation was smooth and undulating, mimicking the waves of her emotions. It would be a vase, and she would paint a dancing woman on it, she decided, a woman who didn't care who watched her and simply wanted to feel the music and live in the moment.

She closed her eyes and pictured herself dancing on a beach as the waves provided a rolling crescendo. The sand caressed her feet, her muscles pulled as she stretched and twisted. She absorbed the smell of the salt air, and the coolness of the ocean breeze.

The last of the tension fled her body. Emily set the piece aside to dry, cleaned her tools, scrubbed the clay from her hands, and climbed into bed. She fell asleep as soon as her head hit the pillow.

She awoke to the sound of soft morning rain, enough to keep the tourists off the beach and send them flocking to the shops and restaurants. Layla, Mary's assistant from the shop, called to place an order for more bowls and vases. Emily needed both the money and the distraction, so she headed back to the wheel and threw herself into the task.

Mid-afternoon, she stood and stretched, working the kinks out of her back. The rain had stopped, and she needed fresh air and exercise. Max lifted his head when he heard the scrape of the drawer where she kept his leash. They embarked on their thirty-minute walk to Clear Point.

In the town, Emily greeted the storeowners and residents she met, sometimes stopping to chat for a few minutes. She gave directions to some tourists who were looking for a restaurant, and she helped the elderly Mrs. Walsh take her groceries into her house. She declined the offer of coffee and cookies, hoping to get to her destination before the end of the day.

She headed in the direction of the water, passing restaurants, stores selling beachwear, whale-watching guides, ice cream vendors, and fish taco stands. Emily attached Max's leash to a pole. He settled beside the steps of Trevor's surf shop and prepared for a nap on the sun-warmed grass.

The shop was crowded. Emily bumped elbows and shoulders with strangers eager to purchase top-quality surf gear. It occurred to her this might not be a good time to visit her friend. She turned toward the door, but a familiar voice brought her up short.

"Where're you going?"

Trevor's scruffy head appeared above the crowd of shoppers.

"You're busy," she said. "I just stopped by to say hi."

"I'm not too busy for you. Let's go for a coffee."

"You don't have time."

"The guys can handle it. It's mostly browsers anyway."

They each bought a coffee at the shop next door and took it outside to drink at one of the picnic tables.

"You don't look like you've been sleeping well." Trevor's expression was concerned.

"Is it that bad?" Emily said, twisting her hair around her finger.

"No, but I can tell. Everybody thinks I'm clueless, but I know what's going on," he said. "You're still worried about the guy being out there."

"Can I ask you a question?" she said, tilting her head to the side.

"Since when do you have to ask permission?"

"Do you think he's still here?"

Trevor's brow creased. "I doubt it," he said. "I agree with Ted. I think it was a transient, high on something, and he's moved on. Why would anyone want to hurt you?"

"I don't know. I can't think of anyone who'd hate me enough to want to kill me."

"I can guarantee you there's no one."

"I guess. I spend a lot of time thinking about it and wondering how something like that could happen."

"Have you remembered anything?" Trevor said. He twirled his coffee cup between his hands.

"Nothing specific, no. I mean, there's not much to remember, is there? He was dressed in black from head to toe..."

Emily froze, and her mind raced.

"What is it?" Trevor said, his eyes wide.

"Why didn't I realize this?"

"Christ, what is it? You're scaring me." His hand reached out to wrap around her fingers.

"I think he wore a wet suit."

"Really?"

"Yeah, the kind you sell them in your shop. What do you call that? What's that material?" she said, snapping her fingers.

"Neoprene?"

"Yes, neoprene, that's it. That's what it felt like."

"It's strange you didn't remember it before."

"Maybe it was the knock on my head. Maybe I forgot, and it's just now come back to me." The words rushed past her lips.

"That's great news."

"Why are you staring at me like that? You don't seem to think it's good news."

"I'm worried about you, that's all. I didn't realize you had serious memory problems."

"I didn't realize it either, until now. I should go see Ted," she said, rubbing her temples.

"You look pale. Do you have a headache? Why don't I drive you home, and you can rest a bit? There'll be lots of time to talk to the police."

"I'll be okay. The walk will do me good, but I think you're right. I'll go home, relax, and do some yoga before I talk to the cops. Maybe I'll remember something else."

As she started to rise from her seat, she heard a voice behind her.

"What are you guys up to?"

Will settled on the bench beside her, nodding at Trevor.

"I was just about to leave," Emily said.

"You look upset. What's wrong?" He shifted his gaze between her and Trevor.

"Emily remembered some things from the night of the attack," Trevor said.

"Like what?" Will's gaze pierced hers.

"The guy wore a wet suit," she said.

"That could be important. It means the guy's a surfer." Will glanced at Trevor as if for confirmation.

"Yeah, along with ninety percent of the people in this town," she said. "I don't know how much it's worth, but I'll tell the police and see what they think."

"Is there anything I can do? Do you want me to give you a lift home?" Will said.

"I'm good. Thanks for the offer. Max and I will be on our way. The walk will do us good," she repeated.

Emily went home with mixed feelings. On the one hand, she was happy she remembered something that might be useful to the investigation, but, on the other hand, she was concerned about her memory and how many other things she may have forgotten.

They took the beach route back from town. Max was unleashed, and he bounded in front of her, acting uncharacteristically young. Several people took advantage of the break in the weather, some of them hitting the waves.

She shook her head at the sight of the wetsuits. *Why hadn't she thought of it before?* The memory of the material under her fingers was vivid and intense.

As Emily approached her house, an unexpected but familiar sound reached her ears. She frowned and hurried through the trees to her front lawn, coming to an abrupt stop.

"What are you doing?" she said.

Dustin glanced over his shoulder before he pushed himself off his knees to turn and face her.

"I was just getting this done."

Sturdy new steps replaced her old ones, and a new railing leaned against the porch, waiting to be installed.

"I told you I'd take care of it," she said. She folded her arms across her chest, her lips pressed together.

"I know, but I had a few spare minutes today, and I thought I'd give you a hand. I heard people around here are like that. They help each other out," he said with raised brows.

Emily's anger deflated. He was right. He wanted to fit in, and she fought him for no reason. Another indication she wasn't herself these days.

"I'm sorry." Her voice softened. "I guess I overreacted. I appreciate the help."

Between the two of them, they erected the railing, and Emily was pleased with the final product.

"So, is that what you do for a living, carpentry?" she asked Dustin, as they sat on the porch, a tall glass of lemonade in each of their hands.

"No. It's just a hobby." He stared toward the trees, his expression set.

"What do you do then?"

"I'm a writer."

"That's interesting. What have you written?"

"Nothing you would've read."

"Try me," she said with a smile.

He hesitated for a moment. "The Concept and the Symbiosis of the Holobiont," he said. He leaned back in his chair and stared at her with a slight smile on his lips.

"Well, you've got me there. What is that, a textbook or something?"

"Or something."

"So, you're some sort of expert on...holobionts?"

"I try."

"You know I'll google it, don't you?"

"Go right ahead. I'll quiz you some time."

"You don't strike me as a writer," she said.

"What do I strike you as?"

"I don't know, but you don't seem like the writer type. And you don't look like a holobiontist."

He laughed as he got to his feet.

"Maybe you're not as good a judge as you thought you were."

CHAPTER 9

Emily searched her brain for hours that night and tried to remember something besides the feel of neoprene beneath her fingers. The fact the murderer was a surfer hit a worrisome note for her. Most of the locals surfed. It was one of the many attractions of Clear Point. Of course, out-of-towners came here to take advantage of the waves, but on a Thursday night in the spring, it was less common. She hated to think the killer could be someone she knew.

Clear Point was her home. She loved it here. She loved the small-town atmosphere. She loved that she was acquainted with all the residents personally. She loved the ocean and the fishing boats and the sights and smells that surrounded her. She couldn't imagine all of that tarnished by a criminal element.

On the other hand, if this was the same person who had attacked someone in Vancouver, why did he wear a wetsuit? Was it a disguise that made him blend in with the locals while also serving the purpose of covering him up? It was a strong possibility, but it would mean he had planned the attack ahead of time. It hadn't been a spur-of-the-moment decision. Had he stalked her? Or had he waited for the first person to come by that spot, specifically a woman, knowing she would be easier to overpower?

Unable to sleep, yet too distracted to work at the wheel, Emily paced. She sat down long enough to ingest a chamomile tea and paced some more until she felt tired enough to go to bed.

After a few hours of sleep, Emily packed up her truck earlier than usual and headed into town. Instead of stopping at Mary's shop, she continued down Main Street and parked in front of a building that had been a small school in a previous life. It now housed the local police force.

Force might have been an ambitious word. Apart from Ted, the department consisted of two men and another part-timer to help with the evening and weekend patrols. Of course, they were part of the national RCMP force, but since the town was so small and crime almost non-existent, there wasn't a need for a large local staff. As a result of the murder, two other officers from Vancouver had been sent to Clear Point on a temporary basis to reassure the population, but Emily was certain their residency would be short-lived.

Born and raised in Clear Point, Ted would give his life to protect the town he had called home for all of his fifty-three years. He was backed by his deputy, Ralph David, a twenty-year resident, and Rob Abbott, a young twenty-something who had family in the area.

"Nice of you to drop by," the chief said.

Emily smiled. She appreciated the way Ted made it sound as if she was here for a friendly visit. She was certain his thoughts strayed to the murder every time he laid eyes upon her.

"What can I do for you?" He gestured toward a chair in front of his desk.

"I remembered something. I don't know if it's important."

Ted sat straight in his chair and reached for his pen, the smile disappearing from his face. "Everything's important. What is it?"

"I remember what he wore. It was completely black. It covered his arms and legs, maybe even his hair. It was like a wet suit, in neoprene."

Ted nodded his head but had yet to write a word on his pad. "That'd explain the lack of hair," he said.

"What?"

"We didn't find any hair, blood, or skin on your hands. You would've fought him, tried to pull his hair. I know you don't remember it, but instinctively everyone would do it. The head covering would explain the lack of evidence."

Emily absorbed that information. She didn't remember pulling his hair.

"Do you think it could be someone local, Ted?" she said, her forehead creased.

"I hope not, really I do. I'll pass this information along to IHIT, and they may be in touch with you again with a few more questions."

Emily returned home, her mind in a fog. She had intended to run other errands while in town but had lost all desire to do anything except shelter herself in the security of her home. If it was secure, she thought wryly.

Emily shook two aspirins out of a bottle, tossed them into her mouth, and washed them down with a large glass of water. Her head had throbbed since she had left the police station. Under normal circumstances, she would have used aromatherapy to relieve the pain, but today she fell back on pharmaceuticals. She was tired and cranky and frustrated with herself for not remembering more of what had happened that disastrous day. The fact the man had worn a full-body wetsuit was significant. The more she remembered, the more she would be able to help the investigation, but her memories were blocked.

"Let's go for a walk, Max. I need to stretch my legs."

White clouds filled the sky, and a cool breeze came off the ocean. Emily zipped up her sweater and thrust her hands inside her pockets. The diehard surfers were in the water, challenging the waves. Others stood by and observed.

On a normal day, she would have shouted a few words of encouragement, or stopped to chat with the bystanders, but today she wasn't in the mood. Her thoughts were too muddled.

She rounded the bend and saw the shape of a man sitting in a chair on the end of the dock. She groaned aloud. She didn't need to have a conversation with anyone right now. But she knew she had been spotted, and to turn around and leave at this point would have been too obvious. Besides, he had made an effort to fit into the island spirit. The least she could do was be friendly, she thought.

Max trotted ahead to greet the man and seemed content to sit on his haunches beside the chair, getting his ears scratched. As she got closer, Emily noticed her neighbor stared at her with a furrowed forehead.

"Why are you looking at me like that?" she said.

"You don't look like your usual perky self."

"I'm fine. Just a little tired." She kicked at a stone in the sand with the toe of her sneaker.

"Did your palm reader give you bad news?"

The tone of his voice made Emily lift her head. She leaned closer until she was a few inches from his face. He didn't move or react except for a raising of his brows. She took a deep breath through her nostrils and straightened.

"I'm disappointed," he said. "I thought you were going to kiss me."

"Have you been drinking?"

"Are you my mother now? Was it going to be a motherly kiss? Now, I'm truly disappointed." His words were slurred. "By the way, where's good old Bob these days? I haven't had the pleasure of meeting him yet." Dustin's raucous laugh grated on Emily's nerves.

"You shouldn't be out on the dock if you're drunk," She crossed her arms over her chest and ignored his attempt to embarrass her.

He shook his head and took a long sip from a tall glass that was half-filled with a clear liquid.

"You're really something," he said. "You should learn to mind your own business."

"I'm concerned for your safety. What's wrong with that?"

"You should be concerned about your own safety."

Emily looked him in the eye and tried to determine if what he said was a threat, a warning, or an expression of concern.

"Any news about the case?" he said with a lifted eyebrow.

"Not much. I remembered something, and I told the police about it. That was it."

He took another sip and stared at the waves as they worked their way toward the dock.

"You should stop remembering. It won't do you any good."

"What do you mean?"

"I mean memory is overrated. Just forget about everything, and you'll be better off."

"You're very cynical today."

Another shrug and another sip.

"Why? Why are you here, living by yourself?" she said, overcome with curiosity about this man and his out-of-character behavior. "Why are you so unhappy?"

"First, might I remind you that you also live by yourself, and second, what makes you think I'm unhappy?"

Emily let out a short, humorless laugh. "You can ask that? It looks like you may have a drinking problem. And that's usually a sign someone is unhappy."

"Thank you, Miss AA, for those words of wisdom. But I can tell you I don't have a drinking problem. Actually, what I have is a drinking solution. Besides, it's a special day, so I'm allowed."

"What's so special about today?"

"It's an anniversary of sorts, and I like to celebrate it with a little drink."

Emily got the picture. She also had some unhappy anniversaries in her repertoire. They were never easy, but she didn't turn to alcohol to help ease the pain. She found other means to reduce stress and eliminate bad memories. But, somehow, she didn't picture Dustin as a yoga and meditation kind of guy.

"But enough about me; let's get back to your problem," he said.

Emily groaned. She had enjoyed a brief respite from her problem while she thought about his.

"What do you suggest I do?" She placed her hands on her hips.

"If I were you, I'd lock my doors and keep my mouth shut."

"I have been locking my doors, and I disagree about not remembering and keeping my mouth shut. We're talking about a murderer. I can't let him get away with it. Maybe he'll do it again."

"Maybe he'll come back for you again."

"They think he's gone to Vancouver."

He snorted. "Yeah, right. As if they know."

Emily shook her head. It was no use arguing with him. He was too drunk and much too cynical.

"Anyway, you don't have to listen to me," he continued. "I just don't think you should go blabbing about the case with everyone you meet. You don't know who you can trust."

"I'm not talking about it with everyone I meet. I've discussed it with my closest friends, people I do trust. And I have to tell the police as much as I can. Besides, it's my decision."

He lifted his glass in a toast.

"Here's to bad decisions."

Chapter 10

The chair creaked as Emily sat and hit the switch on the pottery wheel. She stared at the mound of clay in the center and watched it turn and turn, not knowing what she wanted to create. She felt powerless, even in her own studio.

The memory of her disturbing conversation with Dustin the previous day hung over her head like the dark clouds that released their fury this afternoon. The rain and wind lashed at the house and forced her to close the window except for a tiny slit to allow a smidgeon of fresh air into the overly-warm room.

The kiln was full and baking at its maximum temperature. Emily compensated for the heat by wearing shorts and a camisole. She adjusted the volume on her phone and put her earbuds in place. The smooth voice of Diane Krall filled her ears.

Her hand reached toward the switch, about to shut off the wheel and give up before she even started. The tips of her fingers were an inch away from their target when she stopped.

"Since when do I give up," she said. Max's ears twitched, but he didn't move. "I've been through some tough times, and I've never given up. Yes, I've been forced to make difficult decisions, and I changed directions, but I've never given up. This is my life now, and I love it. That won't change."

Emily wet her fingers and wrapped them around the mound of clay. The shape formed under her guidance until she created a bowl. It would be strong and beautiful.

She leaned back to admire her work and stretch the kinks out of her back. Her head throbbed, and a strange queasiness rippled through her stomach.

"When am I going to get over these headaches, Max?"

The dog didn't move except for the slightest tweak of his tail.

"I feel awful," she said, one hand to her stomach, the other to her forehead. "It's too warm in here. Let's get out of here for a bit."

She stood and was struck by a wave of dizziness. Her hand grabbed the shelf beside her. But her dog and his complete motionlessness drew her attention.

"Max?"

Emily stumbled over to kneel beside her pet.

"Max?" she said, her voice rising. The animal's eyes opened and tried to focus on her before they closed again. Panic set in and she leaned down to wrap her arms around the dog and try to lift him. Another wave of dizziness hit her. She couldn't draw enough air into her lungs.

Emily didn't trust herself to stand without falling. She crawled to the window and pressed the heels of her hands against the bottom of the frame. She used what little strength she had left to shove until the window opened with a screech and a groan. Emily let herself fall forward, her head and shoulders hanging out the window. Her lungs sucked in cold, fresh air, and her head cleared.

"I'm coming," she said, her voice as unsteady as her body. Hoping she had the strength to help her pet, Emily started the journey back to Max, but a voice made her turn to the window.

"What's wrong?"

"I...I don't know." She squinted at the man who peered through the window at her. "I don't feel well. But I need help with Max. Please, help me."

Dustin climbed through the opening and hurried over to the dog. He kneeled over Max seconds before Emily's stomach gave up the fight and emptied its contents into the wastepaper basket.

"Is he all right?" she said, once she caught her breath.

"He's alive," Dustin said. He left the dog and came over to her, his face etched with concern.

"I'm okay. Take care of Max." She shoved to no avail on his chest as he held his arms out toward her.

"I've got to get you out of here," he said.

"I can do it."

She struggled to get to her feet but lost her balance as dizziness, once again, assaulted her. One arm slid around her back and another under her knees. His chest was solid under her cheek as Dustin hurried from the room.

"No, please," she said. "Get Max out. He needs help."

"I'm going to get you into the fresh air first. Then I'll get him."

Emily realized there was no point in arguing. The quicker he fulfilled his mission, the sooner he would get back to her dog.

The air was cool and damp, and the roof of the veranda protected her from the rain that had slowed to a drizzle. Dustin deposited her in a wicker chair and returned inside. Emily closed her eyes and took deep breaths of the blessedly fresh air. She didn't know what had caused the nausea or Max's collapse, but she realized there was something in the room that needed to be cleared from her lungs.

"What are you doing?" she said when Dustin came back with a throw blanket to tuck around her. "You have to get Max."

"I'm going. My priority right now is to make sure you're all right."

"I'm fine," she said, her voice croaking. "Please hurry."

She wanted to throw off the blanket and run back into the house, but she knew her legs wouldn't hold her. She depended on Dustin, even though she didn't agree with his priorities.

A few moments later, he returned to the porch with the limp dog draped over his arms. Emily suppressed a whimper when she saw him. She slid onto the floor beside the animal as Dustin laid him at her feet.

"We have to get him to the vet," she said, tears of concern in her voice.

"We have to get you to the hospital," her neighbor said with the firmness of a drill sergeant. "You have all the symptoms of carbon monoxide poisoning."

"No, it must be something I ate. I have a detector."

"Then how do you explain Max?"

Her gaze lifted from the dog to the man as the wail of a siren reached her ears.

"I called 9-1-1," he said. "The ambulance will take you to the hospital. I'll take Max to the vet."

She released a breath of gratitude. The vehicle pulled into the driveway before she could express the words.

Emily realized there was a good chance these were the same medics who had attended to her on the night of the murder, but they were professional enough not to remind her of the fact. They asked the necessary questions, took her vital signs, and bundled her onto a stretcher. One of them took the time to examine Max but could only recommend the dog be taken to a vet as soon as possible.

CHAPTER 11

It was déjà vu.

Once again, Emily stared at the interior of a sterile examining room at the hospital. Francie flew into the room, her eyes wide with concern.

"Are you okay? I came as soon as I got the call."

Emily believed her. Her friend wore old sweatpants, and a t-shirt spotted with tomato sauce stains. A crooked ponytail held back her hair and emphasized her reddened face.

"Who called you?" Emily said, her voice weak.

"Someone from here called and told me you'd been brought in by ambulance for carbon monoxide poisoning. What the hell happened?"

"I don't know. I have a detector. It should've sounded an alarm." Tears formed in Emily's eyes. "I'm so worried about Max. He was unconscious."

"Where is he?" Francie glanced around the room as if expecting to see Max lying on a stretcher.

"Dustin took him to the vet. Once the ambulance came for me, I was okay on my own." She grabbed Francie's hand. "Could you call the vet for me please? Can you find out if he's okay?"

"Of course, I will," Francie said, patting her hand.

The curtain was shoved aside, and a nurse came in, an assortment of tubes, vials, and syringes in a box in his hands.

"Not in here, you're not." He gestured toward the phone in Francie's hand. "Go to the waiting room if you have to make a call."

With a grimace, Francie scooted from the room.

"Doesn't it drive you crazy when someone shouts into a cell phone in a public place? Sometimes I wish they'd never invented the stupid things," the nurse said, as he secured an elastic strap around her arm and proceeded to fill vials with her blood.

"When will I be able to leave?"

"Not for a few hours yet. We have to make sure all the gas has left your bloodstream."

"Is there some way to speed it up?"

The man chuckled. "You don't like our accommodations? You've got somewhere you have to be?"

"Yes," she said, ignoring his first question. "I have to go to the vet to make sure my dog is okay."

His expression turned sympathetic. "I understand, but we can't let you go anywhere until we're sure you're okay. The doctor will pass by in a little while and let you know more."

With quick efficiency, he packed up his box of supplies and left the room. Emily shifted on the stretcher. She wanted to get up and sneak out of the hospital. She felt fine lying down, but the memory of the faintness she had experienced in her house lingered, and she knew she would not get far on her own.

She was torn between physical weakness, extreme nausea, and concern for Max. Emily was in the unenviable position of being trapped in a hospital emergency room, not knowing what was going on or what had happened to bring her here.

• • •

"The vet said he'll be okay. He'll be tired and sluggish for a bit, but he'll come around."

"Why couldn't he come home?" Emily said.

"For the same reason you're still in here. The poison has to be cleared from his lungs."

Dustin stood by her stretcher, disheveled, with a rip in his t-shirt and his jeans splashed with mud. Running through the rain and dragging himself through her window had left tell-tale signs. Francie returned and stood on the other side of the stretcher. She eyed Dustin with interest, having just met him for the first time.

"I don't understand how it happened." Emily shook her head.

"You're operating a propane-fueled oven in that room. That's your answer," Francie said. "I always told you it was dangerous."

"But the window was open a bit, and the detector..."

"Could've been faulty," Dustin said.

Emily closed her eyes. The worry over Max and the subsequent relief had sapped what little strength she had left. She wanted to be home in her bed, with Max beside her, and she wanted to sleep for twelve hours. Her eyes opened when the doctor swung into the room, and Emily wondered if she would soon have at least part of her wish come true.

Dr. Wilson smiled at the three of them before he focused his attention on Emily.

"Good news. The last blood test revealed the toxicity has left your system. You're very lucky. Things would've been much worse if you hadn't gotten out when you did."

"I realize that." She threw a glance at Dustin. "Can I go home now?"

"Yes, but you may be woozy for a while. It wouldn't be a good idea to stay alone."

"I'll stay with her," Francie said. She gave Emily a look that dared her to say otherwise.

Too tired to argue, Emily didn't care if a herd of hyenas moved in with her. She wanted to go home. She focused on the doctor's hand as he filled out a form until she sensed a movement by the door. She turned her head to meet Ted's gaze, his lips turned slightly upward.

"Are they going to spring you from this joint, or will we have to sneak you out?"

Emily smiled. "It looks like I can walk out free and clear."

"Good," he said. "You had a close call there. Thankfully, Reeves was nearby. You wouldn't have been so lucky."

"So I've been told," Emily said.

Dustin shrugged a shoulder and shifted from foot to foot. He looked like he wanted to be anywhere but in the overcrowded room.

"How's Max?" the cop said. His gaze shifted between Emily and Dustin.

The older man nodded and smiled as Dustin filled him in on the vet's diagnosis.

"The firefighters have been through your place, Emily, and I have to say the cause of the CO poisoning is a bit of a mystery. There doesn't seem to be anything suspicious."

"They couldn't find the cause?" Emily said, her brows furrowed.

"Well, the fumes must have come from the oven. For some reason, the circuit breaker for the vent tripped."

"Tripped?" Francie said. "What would cause it to trip?"

"They couldn't find a reason. It could be it was overworked. At any rate, it's something you should have checked out by an electrician, just to make sure you don't have a serious problem. You don't want to go through this again."

"She said she had a detector," Dustin said.

"Yep, I was getting to that. I'm afraid that was a case of human error,"

Ted said with a frown in Emily's direction. "The last time you changed the batteries, you put them in wrong."

"That can't be. I always test it," Emily said. She searched her memory for the last time she had taken care of that chore. She always made it coincide with the adjustment of the hour to or from daylight savings time. It hadn't been long ago, and she was sure she had tested it after replacing the batteries.

"You may have been distracted last time," Ted said. "It happens. You don't have to beat yourself up over it."

"If Max hadn't survived and it was my fault, I'd definitely beat myself up over it." Her eyes were filled with heat.

Francie's hand closed over hers. "The main thing is everyone's going to be okay, and you'll get everything looked at. Let's get you home."

CHAPTER 12

Despite all she had been through, Emily spent a restless night in her bed. Part of the problem was not having Max beside her. She was accustomed to the presence of his warm solid body. Another part was the memory of how she had felt when she had been under the effects of gas poisoning. It was a horrible sensation of helplessness.

The final part was bewilderment over how it had all come about. It was strange to have two seemingly unrelated problems collide to create a near-tragedy, like an aircraft's landing gear failing at the same time as their communication system.

The concern of the authorities reached as far as encouraging her to have her electrical system checked. Foul play didn't enter into their picture. Emily tried to force it out of her mind.

"I'm getting paranoid," she said to herself. "This whole thing has made me see evil behind every door. I hate it."

Her frustration made sleep impossible until she finally dozed off an hour before dawn.

By eight o'clock, she was in her truck and headed in the direction of the veterinary clinic. Francie insisted on driving, claiming her friend might have some residual effects from the CO poisoning. Emily didn't argue. She wanted to see her dog, and she didn't care how she got there. If she had to put up with Francie's worrying for a couple more hours, she would do it.

"There's my boy," she said, tears in her voice when the old dog ambled out of the back room accompanied by one of the clinic's assistants. His step quickened when he spotted his mistress, and he moved into her arms for a hug.

"Max, I'm so sorry you went through this. It's all my fault."

"It is not," Francie said from behind her. "Whatever happened, it was an accident. Let it go."

Emily didn't argue. She settled the bill and helped Max into the truck, climbing into the back seat beside him and letting Francie take them home.

Two hours later, Emily settled on the couch beside Max as Francie's car pulled out of the driveway, glad to be on her own again. Any lingering effects from the previous day had diminished to almost nothing, and she reassured her friend she would take it easy for the rest of the day. Whether she did so or not remained to be seen, but she relished her time alone.

The goats and chickens received some attention that afternoon. She made minor headway in her vegetable garden, fighting the constant onslaught of weeds but gave up when her strength flagged.

Emily returned to the house and stood in the doorway that led to her workshop. Her gaze swept over her pottery wheel, her shelves of supplies, and half-finished creations before it moved to the oven. Her heart lay heavy in her chest. Pottery was her passion, and this workshop had always been an oasis for her. Now, it had turned against her. The equipment she had installed with hope and pride had almost killed her and Max.

She wanted to vent all the anger and frustration and pain she had reined in since the night of the attack.

Over the course of the six years since Alan had left her, she had built a new lifestyle. She had made the decision to throw off her past, look inside of herself, and live the type of life that felt right for her. Gone was the stress-filled nine-to-five job. Gone was the big city life. She concentrated on her health. She used yoga and meditation to keep her on an even keel and keep at bay all her anger and disappointment.

Emily didn't know if that would work for her now. The bricks in her carefully-built wall were being smashed one by one. At some point, the wall would not be strong enough to stand on its own, and her vulnerability would be exposed.

Deflated, Emily went to the kitchen and found some ingredients for her supper. She would bolster her mind and her spirit by taking care of her body. Spinach, tofu, beets, and asparagus arrayed her kitchen counter when she heard a pounding on the door. Max's bark echoed through the house as he lumbered over, tail wagging, to greet the unknown visitor.

None of Emily's friends would have knocked, and never with such vehemence. They would have simply walked in.

Drying her hands on a towel, Emily hurried to the door. Her neighbor could be seen on the other side of the screen.

"Can I come in?"

"Of course," she said, stepping aside. "I was just getting something together for supper. Would you like to join me?"

"No, thanks. But let me guess. Tofu?" Dustin said, his face creased in fake pain.

Emily rolled her eyes. "What's wrong with tofu?"

"I bet you're vegan, right?"

"Wrong. Vegetarian. I have my own chickens to give me my eggs and goats for the milk."

"Hmm." A forced smile twisted his lips.

"What do you have against vegetarians?"

"Nothing. I just don't see the point of it." He held up his hands in a defensive gesture. "But I don't want to start what I'm sure will be a heated discussion, so let's just change the subject."

Emily bit her tongue and reminded herself this man had saved her life.

"To what do I owe the honor of your visit?" she said with her own fake smile.

"I just wanted to check up on you to see if you're safe."

"Why wouldn't I be?"

He circled the living room and craned his neck to peer into the kitchen. "How many doors do you have?" he said.

"What?"

"Doors. Entrances. How many?" Dustin turned back to her.

"Two...three, I guess, if you include the patio doors in the back."

"I do." He headed for the back of the house.

"What are you doing?" She hurried after him.

He didn't respond. Emily caught up to him at the patio doors that led out onto her rear deck.

"Watch it. You'll break it," she said, as he yanked on the handle and tested the lock.

"A five-year-old could break through this." He shot her a glare.

"Up until now, I've never even locked my doors. I'm not going to go overboard. Besides, why are you concerned about this now? Is it because of the gas leak? They said it was accidental."

"Yeah, that's what they said."

There it was again, she thought, that cynical tone. "You don't believe them?"

"I might, but there's something weird about it. You tested your detector. What changed?"

Instead of being alarmed, relief pulsed through Emily. Someone believed her when she said she had tested the carbon monoxide detector. That went a long way to making her feel sane again.

"You think it could be deliberate," she stated.

"It could've been accidental, or it could've been deliberate. Let's say I'm suspicious by nature."

To give herself a chance to think, Emily turned and walked into the kitchen. She removed a jug of ice water from the fridge, filled two glasses, and handed one to Dustin. As she returned the jug to the fridge, a chair scraped against the floor behind her.

"So, how do you want to handle this?"

"Handle what?" she said, turning.

He leaned back in the chair and rested an ankle over the opposite knee. "Your safety."

"My safety is my concern." She bristled against his interference, without understanding her reluctance to accept it. "And I won't do anything besides what I'm already doing, which is locking the doors and being extra careful. Besides, I have Max to protect me."

Both of their gazes moved to the old dog, his greying fur made more visible by the fact he lay on the floor on his side.

"Max, come here," Dustin said.

The lab opened his eyes, laboriously pulled himself to his feet, and limped over to the man, his joints stiff. He earned a vigorous ear scratch for his efforts while Emily received a 'Yeah, right' look.

"He hears okay, and has a good loud bark," she said, not sure who she tried to convince.

"You have a spare room?"

"No."

"This place looks big enough to have a spare room." He surveyed his surroundings as if a sign pointing to the spare room would appear out of nowhere.

"I do have a spare room, but no, you can't sleep in it."

"Then you can sleep in mine."

"Again, no."

He glared at her for a moment.

"Fine, have it your way," he said, as he stood and headed for the door. He stopped as he walked by the kitchen counter, grabbed a pen, and scribbled on a pad.

The door slammed behind him as Emily stared at his phone number.

CHAPTER 13

Francie called and invited Emily to join her and Doug, along with Trevor and Will, at the pub for dinner that evening. At first, Emily refused. She wasn't in the mood for being sociable and had the urge to cocoon on the couch with Max, maybe watch a sad movie or two. But Francie was nothing if not persistent, and she badgered Emily into joining them. Once there, she was glad to have given in. Her friends always made her feel better, no matter how rough the seas.

It was standing room only in the bar that night. Emily and her group had arrived early enough to get a table, but moving around involved a lot of nudging, bumping, and elbow-rubbing. Shouts and cheers resonated from the back where the pool table resided. The crowd was, by and large, made up of strangers, primarily tourists from the mainland. More than a few of them had too much to drink, and the noise level rose in direct proportion to the alcohol consumption. On a couple of occasions, Emily had to remove an unwanted hand from her waist or other areas. She was always polite but firm when she told them she wasn't interested.

The evening broke up a little after midnight for the group of friends. Everyone said their goodbyes in the parking lot. It was a warm night, and a lot of people milled around. Francie put her hand on Emily's arm.

"Are you okay to get home? We could follow you or give you a lift. You can get your truck tomorrow."

"Of course, I'm okay. I only drank two beers all night."

"I know that. But if you're afraid to go home alone, we can go with you."

"I'll be fine, but thanks for the offer."

Trevor appeared at her side. "I'll take you home."

Emily laughed. "It's okay, guys. I'm perfectly safe. I'll drive straight home. Max is there. There's no problem."

Emily gave her friends a wave as she pulled out of the parking lot with her truck. She admitted she put on a better show than she felt. She was apprehensive about walking into a dark, almost empty house. *But she couldn't live in fear, could she?* Besides, the consensus was the attack had been random, and the perpetrator was long gone. She reminded herself of that fact.

The section of the road between the pub and her home was dimly-lit, curving, and sparsely populated. Emily drove as if on auto-pilot. She was tired, and she had driven this route so many times she knew every bump and crevice in her path.

Startled out of her half-daze, Emily glanced at the bright headlights in her rear-view mirror. A truck or large SUV had appeared out of nowhere. *Where had he come from? Had she passed it and not noticed? Had he pulled out of a driveway?* The reflection of the lights blinded her and made the color and make of the vehicle indistinguishable. The truck gained on her, coming closer to her back bumper. Emily's gaze shifted with unease from the road in front of her to the brightness in the mirror.

She didn't want to brake for fear the driver would run into her, but she didn't want to speed up for fear of losing control. All she wanted was for the driver to get off her bumper and pass her. Yet, when they came upon a straight stretch of road, he didn't make a move to pass. Instead, he moved closer.

To Emily, it resembled an overused scene from a movie, and she half-expected the truck to pull up alongside her and try to drive her off the road. She would be trapped in her car in the ditch, a sitting duck.

Emily pictured this section of the road in her mind. She had traveled it by car and on foot many times. She considered her options. Leading him to her home was not one of them, and the next town was twenty kilometers away. She wouldn't be able to keep this up for that distance.

Emily's fingers gripped the steering wheel until her knuckles turned white. Her heart raced. She focused on the shoulder of the road and searched for the opening she needed. Without touching the brakes and hoping her tires would hold their grip, she swung the steering wheel sharply to the right and accelerated.

Her truck fishtailed as it hit the gravel. Branches bounced off her windshield and scratched the side of the vehicle as it plunged through the trees. Tires screeched behind her. She hit the switch to shut off her headlights. There was nothing to do about the brake lights except to avoid touching the brake pedal.

The path, too narrow and overgrown for anything other than walking, connected the road to the beach. Traveling it by truck would be challenging, if not impossible, especially in the pitch dark.

A glance in her rear-view mirror told Emily her follower hadn't given up. He had nudged his truck into the pathway, which meant he wasn't some random nutcase that liked to tailgate people on the road. He had a purpose in mind, and she didn't like to think about what that purpose might be.

Emily urged her truck over shrubs and small trees while she kept an eye on her tracker in her rear-view mirror. When he stopped, turned off the headlights, and climbed out of the truck, she knew she had a decision to make. He would move much faster by foot than she would by truck in these conditions. Abandoning her vehicle would be her best hope. Emily had an excellent knowledge of the terrain. She prayed it was better than his.

She tumbled out of the truck and ran as soon as she got her footing. The branches grasped at her clothing like tiny, little fingers. She heard and smelled the ocean and knew it lay just past the tree line, but she didn't know what she would do when she reached the end of the bushes and emerged onto the sand. *How could she hide from her pursuer if she was in plain sight?*

The half-moon shed enough light for her to make out the ground in front of her, but she knew it gave him the same advantage. Branches snapped behind her. She didn't look back. It would slow her down and increase her chances of tripping. Besides, she already sensed he had gained on her.

Emily glanced up at the sky and realized she would have a second chance in a moment. *Would she be able to pull the same trick again? Would it be more successful this time?*

The moon disappeared behind a large cloud, and Emily dived to the left. She narrowly missed hitting her head on the boulder as she slid behind it and down into the small cavity below. The foxes who often camped here were off somewhere else, she thought. Otherwise, she would have had another problem on her hands.

Her heart pounded in her ears, and her breath rasped. She tried to calm both. She needed to hear the footsteps of the man. And she needed to make sure he did not hear her. A branch broke on the opposite side of the boulder. Emily held her breath. She wanted to hear more noise, preferably his footsteps heading back toward his truck.

The night stilled as if nature also held its breath and waited to see what would happen. Another branch cracked, but Emily couldn't distinguish from which direction the sound came. It was followed by a noise that sounded like the thrashing of bushes. He searched where she had last been spotted.

Emily was confident she was well-hidden, but if he had a flashlight application on his cell phone, which most people did, it would be game over. As if she had willed it, a bright light flashed across the trees in front of her. Emily knew he stood to the right of the boulder. She curled her body inward as much as possible, thankful for her dark clothing. She pulled her sleeves over her hands, covered her face, and wished she'd had the time to cover the opening with branches.

Leaves rustled, and branches popped. Emily caught a glimpse of a light in her peripheral vision as it flashed across the boulder and over the crevice. She held her breath and anticipated the moment when a hand would close over her wrist and pull her out of her hiding place.

Time seemed to crawl until she heard him move away. She let herself breathe, but she didn't dare move a muscle, not until she was sure he had left. Her legs were cramped, and she longed to stretch them out, but it wasn't worth the risk.

In the distance, a motor roared to life. The man was now in his vehicle. This presented two possibilities: either she was safe, and he had left, or he tried to trick her into thinking so. She waited until the distinct sound of a truck battling with the overgrowth reached her ears before she unfurled her body and crawled out of the hole.

She was lucky. She had no idea what the man's intention had been, who he was, or if he was the killer who had come back to finish her off. But she was certain she had escaped something that would have been, at the very least, unpleasant. Her body twitched with shivers.

Emily stayed in the shelter of the trees as much as possible and made her way back to her own truck, standing outside the vehicle for a few minutes. She debated whether she should fight to back it out of the woods in the dark and risk finding him waiting for her on the road somewhere, or to go home by foot.

She chose the second option, even though the thought of going home alone didn't appeal to her. If this person, whoever he might be, knew where she lived, he might wait for her there. On the other hand, she had to get to Max.

With her decision made, Emily headed toward the ocean, letting the familiar sounds and smells guide her. Emerging onto the sand, she had misgivings. The reflection of the night sky on the water had always calmed and soothed her in the past. Now, it made her feel exposed. Walking on the sand would be faster and easier to manage than the coarse brush in the woods, but she would be more visible. The memory of the last time she was on the beach in the dark lingered. It hadn't gone well then. She prayed history wouldn't repeat itself.

Emily gazed at the length of beach that lay between her and her house. *She could reach it within ten minutes, but what would she find there?*

She crept alongside the tree line, her gaze constantly swiveling around her. She remembered what had pounced out of the bushes at her a few short weeks ago. This time, Emily carried a large branch with a sharp point at the end, and her gaze remained on the trees. If someone jumped out at her, she would at least be prepared and could perhaps put up a better fight.

Within eyeshot of her house, she crouched in the shrubs and observed her surroundings. Nothing looked out of place, but the man could have hidden his vehicle along the road and arrived on foot. He could be hiding inside the house at this moment. Emily knew there was no way she would be able to stay at her home tonight, but she couldn't abandon Max either. She took a fortifying breath and approached the house, the stick held in front of her like a jousting lance.

The porch creaked when she set foot on it, and she was relieved to hear a bark from within. Opening the door, she found Max wagging his tail on the other side.

"C'mon boy, we have to get out of here," she said in a low voice.

There wasn't anything she couldn't live without for a few hours. All she wanted was her dog, who didn't hesitate to follow her down the steps. She led him to the beach and, once again, headed south.

Chapter 14

The light guided her. She didn't know if he always left a light on in the house, or if he was still awake, but she was thankful for the beacon. It was after one o'clock in the morning. She would have expected him to be asleep.

She rapped twice, waited half a minute, and took a startled step back when the door was flung open. Dustin's hair was ruffled, and his clothing was disheveled, but he was wide awake.

"What are you doing here?" he said, his eyebrows lowered.

"I..."

She wasn't sure where to start. She hadn't thought any further than getting herself and Max out of harm's way.

"Why aren't you asleep?" Emily said. It was a stupid thing to ask, but she needed time to organize her thoughts.

"I'm working. I hadn't planned on entertaining anyone at this hour." His voice was gruff.

"I'm sorry. I should've called someone else, but this place was the closest, and all I could think of was getting away."

"Did something happen?" His expression transformed into one of concern. He grasped her elbow and tugged her into the house. Max ambled past her.

Shock set in. She had run on adrenaline since the headlights had appeared in her rear-view mirror. Dustin must have noticed the trembling of her limbs. His grip held firm on her elbow as he led her to the couch. Emily didn't need any encouragement. She sank into the softness, dropped her head between her knees, and gulped for air.

"Here. Take this."

She lifted her head to see he held a cool glass of water. She nodded and took a big gulp. Her equilibrium returned. Dustin sat across from her in an armchair, his expression serious, and stared at her as if she was an explosive he didn't quite know how to defuse.

"Why don't you start from the beginning? Where were you tonight?"

Emily explained about the pub and her decision to go home on her own.

When she reached the part about watching the headlights of the truck advance upon her, her voice held a slight tremor.

"What kind of car was it?" he said.

"It wasn't a car. It was either a pickup truck or an SUV. It was the same height or a bit higher than mine. And I think he had his high beams on. They were very bright."

"About ninety percent of the vehicles around here are either pickup trucks or SUVs. Did you see the color?"

"I think it was dark-colored."

"Hmm."

"I know. I know. I'm not much help." She rubbed her hands over her face.

"What happened next?"

Emily told him about her decision to turn onto the pathway. This earned some raised eyebrows from Dustin, whether in admiration or disbelief, she wasn't sure. She described how she had hidden under the rock and waited for her pursuer to leave.

"When he got out of his truck, did the light come on inside the cab?"

Emily tried to retrieve the image of the man as he climbed out of his vehicle. She shrugged her shoulders. "I think it did, but he was so far away, I couldn't see him clearly," she said.

"You're sure it was a man?"

"I think so. I assumed so. I guess, now that I think about it, it could've been a woman, but this person seemed quite tall. That's about all I was able to make out."

"You didn't think to call 9-1-1?" His tone was like that of a disappointed father toward a teenager.

Emily grimaced. "When I was driving, it took all my concentration to keep the car on the road. Then I was in such a hurry to hide I left my phone behind. But in all fairness, I wouldn't have been able to use it while I was hiding. He would've heard me."

"So, you came to me. That's a bit surprising. Last night, you weren't open to my help."

"Well, I guess if there'd been anyone else who lived close by, I may have gone to them, but you're the lucky winner tonight."

"I certainly am."

Emily thought she detected sarcasm in his tone, but she had more important things to worry about. "I have to call the police and file a report."

"Definitely."

"You don't seem sure." She tilted her head as she gazed at him.

"I'm just thinking, that's all."

"Are you thinking it's the killer?" She cursed the tremor that returned to her voice. The idea the same man who murdered an innocent person could have been so close to her tonight terrified her.

"What's your theory?" he said.

Emily rubbed the back of her neck, stood, and walked to the window. "I don't know. I don't want to think I could've been within a few feet of a murderer. But I have no idea who else it could be unless it was one of the guys from the bar."

"Did some guy show an interest in you?" he said, his eyes narrowed.

"A couple of them did. It was crowded tonight." She returned to the couch and wrung her hands.

"Did one of these guys say anything suspicious or weird? Did they look like the guy who followed you?"

"I can't analyze every word or gesture I heard or saw." Emily ran her hands through her hair. "I don't know what to think."

"It's okay. Just relax for a few minutes. I'm going to call Ted."

He placed the call to the police, spoke for a few minutes, and set the phone on a side table before he turned back to Emily. "Do you want something hot to drink? A coffee?"

"No, thanks."

"Are you sure you're not hurt?"

"I'm fine. There's no need to fuss."

His lips were clamped together as he paced back and forth between the couch and the window, sneaking glances outside. Noticing a change in his posture, she knew the police had arrived.

The chief entered the house first, and his deputy followed close behind. The older man's gaze pinned Emily and never left her as he crossed the room.

"Are you okay? What happened?" He sat on the couch beside her.

Emily drew a shaky breath and repeated the events of the evening while Ralph took notes. Halfway through her recounting, Ted interrupted her to confer with his colleague. The younger man made a phone call to send someone to secure the pathway where she had sought refuge.

"What do you think?" she said when she finished her story.

"I think I'll report it to IHIT," Ted said without hesitation.

"You think it's the killer? You think he's back?" The expression on Ted's face made Emily's heartbeat accelerate.

"Or, he never left." Dustin drew her attention. His comment didn't help to relieve her tension.

Ted threw him a glare before he returned his gaze to Emily.

"I don't know," the police officer said. "But I won't take any chances. It'll be up to Inspector Humble to decide how to treat this."

Emily shivered. She had relied on the presumption the killer had gone to the mainland and was no longer a threat to her. All along, she could have been in danger. He may have been watching her, following her, perhaps even...

Her head snapped up.

"Do you think this guy could've had something to do with the gas leak?"

Ted raised a hand. "Let's not get carried away. There was no indication of foul play at your house. We can't look for bogeymen in every corner."

"I didn't see a bogeyman tonight."

"I know that. I didn't say you had, but we're not going to panic before we even have a chance to investigate. IHIT will be informed there's been another incident in which you're involved, and they'll be here first thing in the morning. In the meantime, you need to stay somewhere safe, as a precaution."

The last statement was said with a meaningful glance in Dustin's direction, who responded with a shrug Emily assumed was affirmative. She had no desire to return to her house by herself. She knew she could call on Francie to stay with her or take her in, but she was here now, and staying here would be the simplest choice.

Ted seemed satisfied he had covered as many bases as possible; he stood and nodded at Ralph.

"We'll be off. I'll call you first thing in the morning and let you know what to expect from IHIT."

"I'll wait for your call," Emily said. Ted gave her a smile and a pat on the shoulder.

"Don't worry, Em. We're on this. For now, you have to remember to not take any chances."

"I didn't take chances. I was just going about my life as usual."

"I know that, but let's just be extra attentive." His gaze swept the room as if danger hid behind the furniture. "I'll be in touch," he said, but his words were directed to Dustin.

When the door banged shut behind the two police officers, Emily turned to her perhaps-unwilling host. "I appreciate you letting me sleep on your couch tonight."

"I'll do even better than the couch," Dustin said. "I'll offer you the spare room. It's right next to mine, and you'll be safe."

Emily stared at him. She heard Lisa's voice in her head saying, 'You don't even know this guy, and you slept in the room next to him? Why didn't you call someone else?' But, for some reason, she felt safe with Dustin. After all, he had already come to her rescue before. If he wanted to harm her, he'd had plenty of opportunity.

The spare room was basic. There was a bed. That was all. At least he had clean linens, which Emily accepted so she could prepare the bed for the night. He lent her a pair of his pajamas that were so big on her she resembled a small child, but she was grateful to have something. Her own clothing was filthy with the dirt she had gathered while hiding under the rock.

After a hot shower, she emerged from the room, self-conscious in his pajamas. She wanted to get a glass of water and hoped she wouldn't run into her host. Of course, luck wasn't with her. She walked into the kitchen to find Dustin sitting at the table with a cup of coffee in front of him.

"You can drink coffee this late at night?" She kept her voice light as she filled her glass.

"Doesn't bother me." He didn't look at her. His index finger scrolled through an application on his tablet.

"I'd be awake all night. I drink chamomile tea in the evening to help me relax."

"Do you brew up some kind of potion too? Maybe chant a little?"

"Funny guy."

"Are you better now?" He pulled his gaze away from the device to study her.

"Yes. Much. Thanks for letting me stay here and use your shower and pajamas."

He shrugged. "No worries."

A sudden wave of despair overwhelmed Emily. She lowered herself onto the chair opposite him. "What am I going to do?"

"You'll start by talking to IHIT tomorrow. Don't leave anything out. Then, maybe they can offer you some sort of protection."

"You mean like a bodyguard?"

"Likely not to that extent, but maybe they'll assign someone to watch your house, or at the very least, do a drive-by every once in a while."

"You don't think they'll look at it as a serious threat?"

"I don't know what they'll think, but if they do, any kind of protection will depend on who they can spare to keep an eye on you."

"Around here, none. It'd have to be someone from another district."

"Exactly, and how many of them are available?"

Emily stared into her glass. She had a feeling she wouldn't get much help from the RCMP. She shoved her chair back. "I'm going to bed. I'm exhausted."

Before she reached the hallway, Dustin's voice made her pause for a moment.

"Don't worry. I won't let anything happen to you."

Chapter 15

Emily felt older than Max looked. Even carrying the boxes of finished pottery to the truck, something she did every day, was a huge effort. She could blame it on two things: lack of sleep and lack of exercise. The former was because she worried about being attacked in her sleep, and the latter was because she worried about being attacked while running on the beach.

Emily had shared coffee and toast with Dustin that morning before the expected visit from the IHIT detectives.

She rehashed the incident for the two policemen, and they reassured her they would investigate with all their available resources. Already, evidence had been gathered from the scene, and it was on its way to Vancouver for analysis.

"Do you think the killer is back?" She fixed Inspector Humble with her gaze and tried to evaluate his facial expression.

"We don't know for sure. It could've been someone else who watched you at the bar and followed you. You said there were a lot of drunks, and a few of them tried to make conversation with you. It could've been one of them. You need to remember the killer took a lot of precautions on the beach so he wouldn't leave any evidence behind. What are the chances of him chasing after you on a public road in his own vehicle with nothing to disguise himself? Of course, we'll study it from all angles, given what's already happened to you, but we're not ready to say it's the same person."

"No, of course not," she said under her breath. The lack of information and the not knowing was worse than being told there was a killer on the loose and she needed to protect herself.

The investigator looked at her with narrowed eyes.

"You know," he said. "You've always referred to your attacker as a 'he', and we've always gone along with that assumption, but have you ever considered the possibility it was a woman?"

Emily's head jerked back. "It couldn't be a woman. She'd have to be so strong. I was knocked to the ground and strangled."

Inspector Humble shrugged. "You may be physically fit, but you're not that heavy. A taller, stronger woman could do it, especially if she was enraged."

"Why would she be enraged? What have I done to make anyone angry?" Emily said, her brow wrinkled in confusion. "She'd also have to be strong enough to kill that man."

"The element of surprise is more powerful than you realize," Humble said. "I'm just throwing it out there. We shouldn't assume it's a man. From everything you've told me, you have no proof of that. You didn't hear a man's voice or see a man's face. A lot of women surf and a lot of women drive pickup trucks. Let's not write off the possibility."

Emily was stunned into silence. She couldn't wrap her mind around the thought a woman could have been the killer.

After the detectives left, Dustin escorted her back to her house. They strolled along the beach, neither speaking, both embroiled in their thoughts, with Max plodding beside them. Emily assumed Dustin's thoughts involved the logistics of her safety, while hers were made up of disbelief, fear, and anger.

As expected, Dustin insisted on checking the doors and windows and on walking through the house to make sure nothing was disturbed.

"I can stay here with you if you like," he said, his gaze sweeping the room.

"We've already discussed this. I have work to do, and so do you. It's broad daylight. Nothing's going to happen."

"And you'll call Doug for tonight?"

"Yep."

"Let me know if he can't make it."

When the door closed behind him, Emily doubled-checked to make sure it was locked. She gazed around her home, the safe haven that was no longer. In the kitchen, she stared at a protection kit she had made. It included a sharp carving knife and a hammer, along with a flashlight and her cell phone, all in a basket with a long, curved handle. It might not be much, but those were the only weapons she had at her disposal. She would make sure they were always beside her.

Dustin had looked at her collection but hadn't passed comment. His dubious expression said it all. She assumed he couldn't come up with anything better.

The phone rang as she stood by the window and watched her neighbor head toward the beach. The screen displayed her sister's number. Emily took a strengthening breath and dropped onto the couch.

"Hey," she said.

"Hey yourself. How are things going?"

"They're going."

"I don't like your tone of voice. You don't sound right," Lisa said.

"You can deduce that from a few words?"

"I'm your sister, remember? A few words are all it takes. Give. What's up?"

Emily started by telling her about the carbon monoxide incident but placed more emphasis on Max's near-miss than her own health issues.

"You never found the cause?"

"No, not yet. To tell you the truth, I haven't had a lot of time."

She wondered if she set herself up for misery but knew she had little choice. If Lisa found out later, there would be hell to pay. Emily told her about the events of the previous night.

"What the hell?" Lisa shouted. "You told me there was no chance of the killer being in Clear Point. What's going on?"

"There's nothing to worry about."

"Someone tried to kill you twice. And you're not even sure the gas leak wasn't deliberately set up."

"I don't know anyone tried to kill me last night." Emily ignored her last remark. "It was some guy that followed me, that's all."

Emily didn't know how she could convince her sister she wasn't in danger when she was far from convinced herself.

"Are you crazy? God, what am I going to do?" Lisa said.

"There's nothing you can do. I'm taking precautions, and I have a lot of friends who help me out."

"I could go and stay with you. I could help you deal with the police. I could help you catch the guy," she said. Emily heard her swear emphatically. "I'll have to see what I can do. Noah came home from kindergarten with chickenpox today, and it's a matter of time before Jess gets it."

"Oh no. Those poor kids. Don't worry about me. I have a lot of help. The police are doing their job. What can you do for me besides give me moral support? And you're already doing that. Take care of your family. That's what counts."

"I want to be with you."

Emily heard the disappointment in her sister's voice, and tears came to her eyes. Despite all her drama and bluster, Lisa's heart was in the right place. It was obvious she was torn between her family's immediate needs and the desire to help Emily.

"I know. I promise I'll keep you up-to-date."

"Okay, but if the kids aren't too sick, I'll come to spend some time with you."

"It's a deal." Emily realized it was the only way to appease her. "I love you loads. Give the kids a big hug for me, especially Noah. Tell him I think he's a real trooper."

Emily lay on the couch for several minutes after she hung up, depleted of emotions. Max padded over and laid his chin on her shoulder. His tongue snuck out for a quick lick on the cheek.

"Thanks, Bud. I needed that."

She allowed herself to wallow in self-pity. After a few minutes, determined to get over her funk, she closed her eyes and took a deep breath. She concentrated on each part of her body in turn, relaxing each one, until a blanket of calm settled over her.

Emily wanted to overcome her worries and fears while keeping said worries and fears hidden from those around her. Call it pride, call it independence, she hated to be fussed over.

As she lay there, her thoughts returned to the conversation with Inspector Humble and his remarks about the perpetrator being a woman. Emily attempted to be open-minded. She reviewed the events that had happened to date and tried to imagine a woman as the responsible party. It was not easy. She wasn't a big person, but she would like to think she was fit enough to take on another female. Besides, she didn't know any woman strong enough to break a man's neck, except for...Francie, she thought.

A choking sound came from deep inside of her. *What kind of poison ran through her brain? How could she even consider for a moment that the friend she had known since childhood, the woman who was always ready to help her, was a cold-blooded killer?*

Tears came to her eyes, and she let them flow. Her life had hit a low point.

• • •

The truck rattled into the parking lot of the shop. Dustin had helped her retrieve it that morning. Emily made a mental note to ask Doug to look it over. She suspected it may have sustained a bit of damage during its escapade in the woods the previous night, apart from the obvious scratches.

Emily worked her way around the other cars in the lot to back up to the door at the rear of the building. As she held the door open to let Max jump out, a shout came from behind her. She turned to see Trevor loping her way.

"Hey, how's it going?" She forced a bright smile.

"Good. I'm on my way to work," he said. "You're up and at it earlier than usual."

"Yeah, I wanted to get things done today."

"Everything okay?"

Emily judged by the nonchalant expression on Trevor's face news of the incident in the woods hadn't made it to the ears of the locals yet. Guilt flooded her for not confiding in her friend, but she didn't have the strength to go through the whole story again. Not yet.

"Of course," she said.

"You don't look okay."

Emily raised an eyebrow.

"It's true. You seem tired," Trevor said with a shrug.

"I guess I am, a little."

"Are you sick, or are you still worried about the...you know...the incident?"

Emily sighed. "I'm not sick, Trev. Maybe I'm a little concerned, but it's nothing for you to worry about."

"Of course, I'll worry. You're my friend."

"I appreciate it, but I'm fine," she said as she lifted the hatch.

"The cops any closer to finding who did it?"

"Not that I know of."

"You'll let me know, won't you?" He pinned her with his gaze, his eyes creased in a squint against the sun.

"Of course."

Trevor opened his arms, and Emily stepped into them for a hug. She smelled sea and salt when he pulled her close. Her vision went black for a split second, and a jolt of shock shot through her body.

"What's wrong?" He held her at arm's length. "You're trembling."

"Nothing," she said, avoiding his eyes. "I just got one of those shivers. I'm okay. But I have to get this stuff inside."

Trevor shrugged and grabbed a box out of the truck.

"I can do it. You have to get going," Emily said. She had never been good at hiding her emotions, and with her friends, it was much more difficult.

Trevor brushed aside her protests and headed for the door. All four boxes were tucked into the back room within minutes, and Emily watched Trevor amble across the parking lot to the main street. Her body and her mind had gone numb.

"Not Trevor," she whispered. He had a gentle soul. It was the smell. The smell of sea and salt had recalled a memory of a dark body pressing her into the sand, dressed in neoprene and smelling like the ocean. But most of the people in this town smelled of the ocean. They lived beside it; they worked on it; it was a huge part of their lives. She was certain the memory Trevor had triggered was a by-product of his closeness to the ocean, not his closeness to the crime.

CHAPTER 16

The house was as quiet as an empty church. Emily hadn't turned on the radio or the television and had done little since dinnertime except sit and stare at the trees through her ocean-facing window. The dark clouds and the increasing winds warned of a storm.

It wasn't the first time in her life Emily was alone, but it was one of the few times she was lonely. She had called Francie earlier in the day, hoping she would be available to hang out with her that evening. She needed to reaffirm their friendship. She needed to look in her eyes and see the friend who had always been there.

It turned out Francie had a date night planned with Doug. She must have detected something in Emily's tone because she offered to put off her date, but Emily wouldn't hear of it. They promised to get together another night.

Instead, Emily sat and stewed in her solitude and worry.

The way people asked Emily how she was and how she felt about the murder had grown old for her. She wanted to put it aside. It was nothing short of a miracle the news of the man who had followed her into the woods hadn't spread like wildfire throughout the town. Ted and his deputies must have decided to be close-mouthed about the incident.

Yes, she'd had another scare last night, but she had gone over it a thousand times in her mind. She was more and more convinced it had been a random incident with an overly amorous tourist. That was the most likely scenario.

As Inspector Humble had pointed out, the man hadn't taken any precautions to hide his identity. And quite a few men in that bar had been inebriated. The fact he had gotten behind the wheel of a vehicle was reprehensible. She imagined he would be capable of terrorizing a lone woman. And she refused to consider the possibility it was a woman.

The shrill ringing of the phone interrupted her thoughts. Certain Francie had decided to check on her, Emily didn't look at the call display. When she heard the deep voice on the other end of the line, she hesitated for a moment, until she recognized Will's warm baritone.

"How's it goin', Toots?"

Emily smiled. "It's going fine, thanks."

"I spoke to Trevor today. He said you don't look good."

"Gee, that's nice to hear. I'm so glad you called to boost my spirits. And I'm happy to know you guys talk about me behind my back."

"We're just concerned," he said. "I have a proposition for you."

"You always have a proposition for me."

His chuckle sounded good to her ears. "This time it's a serious, well-meaning proposition."

"What is it?" she said.

"Why don't I sleep in your spare room?"

"What's the big attraction with my spare room lately?"

"Why? Who else has been sleeping there?"

Emily detected a tinge of hurt in his voice, mixed with curiosity.

"No one. I'm just kidding. Thanks for the offer, Will, but I'm fine. I don't need a babysitter."

"I won't get in your way, and I promise I won't make any inappropriate advances. Unless you want me to, of course."

Emily laughed. "Don't worry about me. But, if I need you, I promise I'll call."

"I'll be there in a flash, girl."

"I know. Thanks."

Some of the loneliness left Emily after she hung up. She knew she could ask her friends for anything.

"Come on, Max. You can do your business, and then we'll head to bed."

The lab understood the routine. He padded over to the door and went outside for a few minutes as his mistress watched from the doorway. Rain pelted the windows, pushed by strong winds off the ocean. Max didn't stray too far from the house, which suited Emily. His dark fur blended into the night, making it difficult to keep track of his movements. He earned a few words of praise when he climbed onto the porch and brushed past her on his way into the house.

He shook the rain off his coat, followed her to her room, and settled on the bed as she prepared for the night. Soon, they were both curled up, one sound asleep on top of the covers, and the other wide awake under them. Emily listened to the wind howl through the trees and the crevices of the house. Occasionally, there would be a clicking of branches against the windows.

It sounded like she starred in her own horror movie, where the foolish heroine would venture outside in her nightgown, unarmed, to investigate a noise. She would yell at her to get back in the house and tell her to stop being so ridiculous.

But, since Emily owned this scene, she would not do anything stupid. Instead, she would cower in her bed and lie awake until morning.

Her head lifted off the pillow at the same moment Max lifted his head and perked his ears. They both heard the same banging noise. Emily wanted to ignore it, but Max had other ideas. He barked, jumped off the bed, and headed to the door.

"Max. No. Get back here."

The dog ignored her. The banging grew louder and heavier. She couldn't stay in her room while Max faced whatever lurked out there. She swung her legs out of bed and headed after him. *As every stupid horror movie heroine before her had done.*

"Max, get back here," she shouted from across the room.

Someone pounded on the door, and Emily had no intention of letting him or her in. Max barked with an unusual determination, and nothing she said would deter him. Her only choice was to go and drag him away from the door. The visitor was tall, broad, and dressed in dark clothing, but from this distance, he was unrecognizable. Her heart pounded in her chest.

Emily's basket sat on the coffee table. She grabbed the knife in one hand and her phone in the other, fumbling to find the numbers 9-1-1. She ran to stand beside Max and held her right arm high with the knife in it, so the person would know better than to break down the door.

"Open the damn door!"

She may not have recognized the face, but the voice was unmistakable.

"What the hell." She ended the call before punching in the last digit.

Emily unlocked the door and pulled it open. "What are you doing here?"

"I went for a nice walk and thought I'd drop in for a cup of tea," Dustin said as he shoved past her and dripped water onto the hardwood floor.

"Very funny. You scared the life out of me."

His contrite expression lasted a second. "It couldn't be helped."

"You're shaking water everywhere."

"You should be thanking me instead of growling at me."

"For what? Terrifying me? Dragging me and Max out of bed so I can skulk around with a knife?"

"I came here to make sure you're all right. Tonight's not a good night to be alone."

"I'm fine." She didn't sound as defiant as she had hoped. The backpack he slid off his shoulder drew her attention. "What's that for?"

"Just some personal things."

"Personal things?"

"Emily, are you having trouble keeping up?" he said as he faced her. "I'm going to stay the night."

"I don't need you."

"I don't care."

"You're practically a stranger."

"Again, I don't care. And I don't think you should say we're strangers. We've been through a lot together in a short amount of time. Unless you can pick me up and throw me out of here, I'm not leaving."

"I'll call the police."

"Go ahead. I already talked to Ted and told him I'd be here. He was happy to hear it."

"I don't believe this." She let her hands drop to her sides.

"I'll just help myself to some coffee. Thanks for the offer."

Chapter 17

Emily thought the worst would be having a man sleep in the room next to her. She thought it would be awkward and uncomfortable, and sleep would evade her.

She slept like a baby.

The worst part was getting up in the morning and finding a man installed at her kitchen table with a coffee in his hand and a tablet propped in front of him. She had run her fingers through her hair and thrown on a robe, but she felt strange fixing herself breakfast while Dustin made himself at home and appeared a lot more put-together than she did.

She saw by the dirty knife and the crumbs on the counter that he had made himself some toast with peanut butter. At least that absolved her of the obligation to offer something more substantial, like bacon and eggs. For one thing, she didn't keep any bacon or any other meat products in the house, and she would have to go out to visit the chickens to get some eggs. The wind and rain hadn't let up since the night before, and she didn't like disturbing her hens in their nice warm nest.

"So, what do you normally do on a Saturday?" He lifted his head and acknowledged her presence.

"The same as I do most days of the week. I work on my pottery, and I do my own thing around here," she said, enjoying the first taste of caffeine on her lips.

"You make a living year-round with pottery?"

"Yep. There's a nice demand for my stuff. Besides, I live simply. I don't need to make a huge pile of money."

A noise gurgled in his throat that could have been a laugh, a cough, or a sudden swallowing of a comment.

"What do you do for a living, Mr. Hotshot?" she said.

"I already told you. I'm writing a technical book."

"And you got a big advance payment, enough to allow you to buy and renovate a nice house here in Clear Point."

"Yeah, why not?"

"I don't believe you. I think you're hiding something." Her eyes narrowed over her coffee mug.

"Maybe I am, maybe I'm not. What matters is that it's my business and only my business. That being said, I've got to get home and get to work."

He pushed his chair back and scooped up the backpack that sat on the floor beside him.

"What the hell is that?" Emily said.

He swung around to face her, his backpack in his hand. Emily marched over to him and grabbed one of the straps.

"Let go of that." Dustin tugged on the other strap.

"You have a gun in there." She glared at the offending item. "What the hell are you doing with a gun?"

"It's registered. I have all the paperwork." He jerked the zippers closed and concealed the contents.

"That's a handgun. I may not be an expert, but I'm fairly sure you can't legally carry a handgun in a backpack."

"Then, forget you ever saw it."

"First of all, why do you own a gun, and second of all, why did you bring it into my home? I don't like guns."

"I repeat, forget you ever saw it."

"Dustin, answer my question," she said, her hands on her hips.

He rolled his eyes. "I've owned a gun for years, for target practice. It's safe. I know how to use it. And the reason for bringing it here is obvious."

"You were going to shoot an intruder? That's crazy."

"I wouldn't fire without thinking. Give me some credit. I wanted to have a margin of protection. At least, it could be used to scare someone away."

"Is it loaded?"

"You don't have to worry about this," he said with a sigh.

His mollifying tone raised Emily's suspicions. "It's loaded, isn't it? You don't want to tell me. You spent the night in here with a loaded gun. I don't believe it."

She stalked to the other side of the room and back, her arms crossed over her chest. Emily hated guns of all types. She abhorred violence toward humans or animals, and as far as she was concerned, guns bred violence.

"Take a pill..."

"Don't you dare tell me to take a pill," she said. Heat rose in her face. "I forbid you to come into my house with a gun, and certainly not a loaded one."

"Okay, I got the message. I'll take it home and put it away. You'll never see it again."

"I hope not." She hoped her tone let him know she was dead serious.

"I'll see you later."

"There's no need to see me later. I'm fine." Emily fumed. At this point, she didn't know if she ever wanted to see him again.

He turned as he pulled open the front door. "You know, I was going to tell you that you finally looked like you got a good night's sleep. I'll be back later."

The door slammed shut behind him before Emily could get out another word.

She took a deep breath and unclenched her fists. She decided this guy was not good for her well-being. She would do an hour of yoga and meditation before getting into her pottery, or else her creativity would be nil.

CHAPTER 18

Emily met her friends at Bob's Brew. At first, she'd had second thoughts about returning to the bar but decided she would ask someone to follow her home as a precaution. Paranoia couldn't cloud her life, she thought, and if she wanted to see her friends, she would.

The usual gang gathered around their table, along with a few others who came to Clear Point on weekends and had been welcomed into the group. They weren't the city dweller types, but rather the surfer dudes who held down regular jobs elsewhere and came to Clear Point for the waves and the atmosphere.

The heavy wooden door swung open every few minutes to let more people fill the pub, and the line-up for the pool tables increased in proportion. The friends stayed in their spot and passed the time with a few drinks and a lot of conversation.

Emily stood with her back to the door. Across from her, she saw Will's eyebrows lower, and she wondered at the cause. His gaze darted between her and something over her left shoulder. Her stomach clenched as she turned to see Dustin stroll in their direction, his gaze fixed on her.

She groaned and had a premonition things were about to become complicated. When she made eye contact with him, a smile took over his face that silenced everyone in its orbit. In her limited experience, she had never seen such a smile, and it left her stunned.

"Hey, sorry I'm late."

Emily's mouth dropped open. He made it sound like they had planned to meet. Her brows drew together. *What game was this?*

"What are you doing here?" she hissed at him.

He ignored her and blasted his killer smile at her friends.

"I'm Dustin Reeves. How are you guys tonight?" he said as he extended his hand to each person in turn.

The weekenders accepted him at face value and introduced themselves, but both Will and Trevor wore identical stone faces. Francie stared at Emily with open speculation, and Doug appeared confused.

Emily watched in amazement as her typically close-mouthed neighbor became a back-slapping, let-me-buy-you-a-beer, social butterfly. Her friends loosened up and seemed to cave into his charm until he dropped the bomb.

"That was some storm last night, wasn't it?" Dustin said. "I was worried the roof would blow off Emily's house, but she slept like a log through the whole thing."

The mouths of her four closest friends collectively dropped open.

"Dustin, maybe you should clarify that statement," Emily said through clenched teeth.

"Clarify, honey? Do you really want me to clarify things in front of everybody?" he said with a mischievous smile. His arm snaked around her waist and pulled her up against him. Emily shook her head.

"No, on second thought, you leave that to me," she said with a glare.

Emily had no intention of getting into long-winded, easy-to-misunderstand explanations in a crowded bar. She would talk to her friends tomorrow and straighten out the confusion.

"What the hell is your game?" she said, loud enough for only Dustin to hear.

"It's pretty obvious, isn't it? I want the word to get out that you're not alone."

He said this with another glowing smile that would lead any observer to believe he was madly in love with her.

Emily sipped her drink and let that remark sink in, torn between blurting out the truth to her friends or allowing Dustin the benefit of the doubt. She needed time to process his logic.

"I like the name of this place," he said, leaning closer to her. "Bob's Brew. That wouldn't be your boyfriend, Bob, would it? I wouldn't want to have any problems with a big, burly cop."

Emily turned wide eyes on him. "Will you stop with that? You know why I made up that story. I couldn't take any chances."

"My point exactly."

A firm hand grabbed her arm, and Francie's voice rasped in her ear. "Come with me."

Emily rolled her eyes, knowing she could expect to be grilled to within an inch of her life.

"I'm busy," she said, hoping for a reprieve.

"Don't worry. This won't take long." Emily was tugged down the hallway.

The bang of the bathroom door reverberated through the air as Francie fired questions at Emily.

"You slept with him without telling me? Why would you do that? I'm mean he's gorgeous and everything, but why didn't you tell me you guys had something going on?"

Under normal circumstances, Emily would have spilled her guts to Francie, but something held her back. *Was it the suggestion the killer could have been a woman, and Francie was the only one Emily knew who was strong enough to attack her? Was it a general feeling of distrust that had taken over her mind?*

Dustin was right about one thing. All the signs pointed to the fact she could be in danger. And if playing along with his game, even to the point of keeping secrets from her best friend, would make her safer, she would do it. She loved Francie, but her friend could not keep things to herself, especially when it involved juicy gossip. Emily would explain everything to Francie later, hoping she would understand despite the hurt feelings she was sure to have.

"It was a little too fresh to discuss with anyone," Emily said, her stomach sinking at the lameness of her excuse.

"Fresh? Since last night? Were you glued to him all day, without a minute to give me a call? You arrived here alone. You could've pulled me aside."

"I'm sorry. What can I say?"

"I'll forgive you if you give me details."

"Details?" Emily's eyebrows soared upward.

"Yes. What made you change your mind about him? Never mind. He's a real cutie, I can see that. But you didn't seem that interested in him. And you've told me you didn't want to become involved with anyone."

"I changed my mind," she said, shrugging her shoulders.

Emily hated this charade.

A group of three women came into the small room and saved her from further interrogation. Emily gestured to Francie that she intended to leave. They nudged and shoved their way back to their group of friends. Dustin seemed to get along well with most of the gang, with the possible exception of Will and Trevor, who appeared to reserve judgment.

As she approached, she felt awkward and unsure about what she should do, but Dustin smiled and reached out to grab her hand and pull her to his side. She fit snugly under his arm, and for a moment, she didn't know how to react. Many pairs of eyes scrutinized her, and she wondered what she needed to do to stay on script.

The warmth of his lips touched her forehead for a moment. She tried to act nonchalant but had no idea if she succeeded. The smug, satisfied look on Francie's face led Emily to assume she fooled her, and she was relieved a major test had been passed. If she could fool Francie, she could fool anyone.

Emily relaxed as the evening progressed. Whether it was the wine, the company, or the seeming easing of tension on the parts of Will and Trevor, she had a good time. A jolt of shock ran through her when Dustin put his arm around her shoulder, nuzzled her ear, and suggested they head home.

"So soon?" Emily tried to ignore the sensation in the pit of her stomach.

"It's one-thirty in the morning. How late do you usually stay out?"

"It's that late? You're right. I should get home." She had time to say a quick goodbye to her friends before Dustin steered her toward the exit.

Emily shivered as a breeze tickled her neck. The night had cooled by a few degrees over the past several hours.

"My truck's over here." Dustin pointed to the left.

"You don't have to drive me home. I have my own vehicle."

"We'll get your truck tomorrow," he said. He slipped his arm around her waist and steered her toward his truck. "I saw how many glasses of wine you had. It wouldn't be responsible of you to drive home."

"What about you? You drank too."

"I had two beers. I nursed them all night. There's no need to worry about me."

Emily accepted the lift with grace. She didn't see the point in doing otherwise. Besides, he didn't have to go out of his way to drop her off. But when they arrived at her house, he pulled the truck into the driveway and shut it off.

"Hey, what are you doing?" she said, her eyes wide.

"What do you mean, what am I doing? We're home."

"No, I'm home. You live next door."

He ignored her and reached behind him to retrieve his backpack.

"Until things work out, I live here," he said. "All your friends know it now. Nobody will bother us."

Distracted by the sight of the bag, Emily said, "Is your gun in there?"

"I promised you you'd never see it again, remember?"

She glared at him. "Are you trying to sidestep the question?"

"Are you always this suspicious?"

Emily's mouth twisted, and her shoulders slumped. "I never used to be suspicious of anyone. My sister always told me I trust too easily. Now, I think of everyone as an enemy."

"Let's go inside."

"I don't need a babysitter," Emily said, but her defiance had slipped away.

"You can call me whatever you like. I'm staying."

Gone was the amiable back-slapper. Back was the bossy neighbor - times two.

Chapter 19

She stared at the digital clock on her bedside table in wonder. Against all odds, Emily had slept well for the second night in a row. It was nine o'clock in the morning. She didn't sleep that late at the best of times. Turning her head, she saw Max gazing at her with a concerned expression in his brown eyes.

"I'm okay, Max. Just a little sleep-in, that's all." She grimaced as memory returned. "Maybe it's not so okay. I may have a man sitting in our kitchen."

She threw on her robe, left the bedroom, and girded herself for a morning confrontation. However, the kitchen was empty, and Emily commended herself for being the first to get out of bed. Her self-congratulations were cut short when she realized a fresh pot of hot coffee was in the coffee-maker, a plate of sliced fruit sat in the middle of the table, and a note was propped up against the salt and pepper shakers.

'Have a great day' was scrawled across the paper.

"He must be bipolar," Emily mumbled to herself.

The strangeness of both the situation and her roommate didn't stop her from enjoying the coffee and fruit while planning her day. She needed to make another delivery to the store, and she had some banking to do, followed by a bit of grocery shopping.

A knock on the door put a stop to her musing. She glanced outside the window to see Will's truck in the driveway. With a smile, she greeted her friend.

"This is a nice surprise," she said.

"I hoped to hear that."

"Why wouldn't you? You know I love it when you drop by."

"Yeah, well that was before your new friend came along," he said, his disapproval evident. He craned his neck to look over her shoulder toward the kitchen.

Emily chewed on her lip, uncertain how to respond. Will was her friend, and she hated keeping secrets from him. But, at the same time, having people think Dustin was her boyfriend gave her a certain degree of protection.

"I refuse to believe your relationship is as serious as he tried to make it seem," Will said. His gaze searched her face, seemingly looking for a sign of confirmation or denial. Emily shrugged.

"Can I get you something?" she said. "I have some coffee in the pot."

"Actually, I came by to see if you wanted a surf lesson today. I've been promising you one for a long time."

Emily groaned. "Will, you know I don't like surfing."

"Only because you don't know how. Let me show you. It'll give you a chance to get your mind off things."

"I don't know...I have work to do."

"Work can wait. Come on. It's a beautiful day. It can't be wasted."

"I wouldn't be wasting it if I worked in my garden."

"We'll be back in an hour, two tops. And I guarantee you'll enjoy yourself," he said with a grin.

That smile was hard to resist. Besides, she agreed with him about getting her mind off things. She needed to replace the negativity with something positive, and a new learning experience was the perfect opportunity.

"All right, but you have to keep in mind I'm not a strong swimmer, not compared to you, and I have no experience."

"Today's the day we're going to change that. Go get ready." He smiled and waved his hand in the direction of her bedroom.

Emily hurried to get changed. With the decision made, she looked forward to something different to do with her day. And Will's company always boosted her spirits.

She emerged a few minutes later in her jogging shorts and a t-shirt. A red band secured her hair in a ponytail, and the scent of sunscreen trailed behind her.

The back of Will's black pickup truck already had two boards propped in it, and she smiled at his confidence. They drove for a few minutes to reach the area Will considered a good spot for beginning surfers.

Emily had attempted the sport before. The first time had been many years ago when she had been a teenager in Clear Point. Trevor had tried to teach her the basics, but her lack of comfort with ocean water and her total inability to find balance on the board drove her to give up. Will had claimed he would succeed where Trevor had failed, and today she would give him the chance to back up his claim.

With infinite patience, Will explained the principles of surfing, along with some of the misconceptions, before he lifted the boards out of the truck. She wiggled into the extra wet suit he had brought with him, repressing a shiver when she first touched the material. She struggled to clear her mind of the memory of the last time she had touched neoprene. Around her ankle, she attached the strap that was connected to the board. When she fell off, the board would stay close to her. Emily didn't think it would be long before she would find herself flailing in the water.

Side by side, they straddled the boards and paddled out past the waves. Will explained she was graced with perfect ocean conditions for a beginner. The waves were high enough to give her some experience, but not so high as to be impossible. He seemed convinced this would be the beginning of her personal surfing craze. Emily remained skeptical.

She had never been a strong swimmer. Despite the summers Emily spent by the ocean, she had succeeded in mastering only the dog-paddle. Her sister, on the other hand, had a wall covered in blue ribbons from the swimming competitions she had won.

They turned their boards toward the beach and bobbed on the ocean as Will explained more about the dos and don'ts of surfing. He glanced over his shoulder, and his body tensed.

"Up on your knees," he said.

Emily complied, sneaking a peek to see what she would have to conquer. She saw a wave, but it didn't appear to be big enough to ride. A second later, she looked again, and it had more than doubled in size. She knew her goal at this point was to kneel on the board and ride the wave without falling off.

She glanced to her right to see Will standing on his board. He had told her what to do as the wave advanced on them, but even so, when it reached her, she was unprepared. She flipped into the water while the surfboard tugged on her ankle. A strong set of arms wrapped around her middle and pulled her up long before she ran out of breath.

"You did great," Will shouted into her ear.

"I fell off." She gasped and spit water out of her mouth.

"You lasted a second or two. Next time you'll do better."

He was right. The next time she held on a little longer, but after an hour, every muscle in her body screamed. Emily thought she was in good shape. She ran every day, and her job involved manual labor, but she wasn't prepared for the strength and stamina it took to handle a surfboard. If nothing else, she had developed more admiration for surfers and their physical endurance.

"Uncle!"

"You want to stop?"

"Yes. Please. I can't go on," she said. "I'm sore all over, and I think I've swallowed a gallon or two of salt water."

"You did good."

"I fell off every time."

"Yes, but each time you did it a little more gracefully."

Emily laughed. "Well, this graceful lady is done for today." She lay face-down on the board and paddled toward shore.

"Ah, you said 'for today.' That's a good sign." Will kept pace beside her.

"Maybe. I'll have to get over this first."

Beside the truck, they peeled off the suits and ran towels over their hair. Emily admitted the experience made her adrenaline pump, and her mood was positive.

"Thanks for thinking of me today. It did me a world of good."

Will smiled at her. "I think of you every day," he said with a glint in his eye.

"Yeah, I bet," she said, heaving herself up into the passenger seat of his truck.

When they pulled into Emily's driveway, Dustin stood on the porch, his legs apart and his hands on his hips. The expression on his face did not bode well.

"What's he doing here?' Will said. "Is he always here?"

"Of course not."

Emily didn't know the reason behind Dustin's angry expression. Something told her not to look forward to finding out. Nevertheless, she slid out of the truck with a smile on her face and hoped to defuse the situation.

"Hey, guess what. I went surfing."

Dustin walked down the steps to meet her at the bottom. His angry glare shifted from her to Will and back again.

"Don't you think you should've let me know where you were?" He didn't give her a chance to answer. "I was worried about you," he said. "I came over here, and you were gone. Your truck's here, the dog's here, but you're not."

Emily realized he had a good point, and she intended to apologize, but Will stepped into the fray and didn't hide his irritation.

"She was with me. There was nothing to worry about."

"First of all," Dustin said, holding up his index finger. "I didn't know she was with you. Second of all," he said as a second finger came up. "How do I know there's nothing to worry about with you?"

That remark drew a reaction from both Will and Emily. "Hey!" they said at the same time.

"How do you know he's safe?" Dustin glared at her. "How do you know he's not the one?"

Will stepped toward him, his right arm raised, but Emily anticipated the move and caught him by the wrist.

"Hang on, Will," she said with a calm she was far from feeling.

"Who the hell do you think you are? You're accusing me of being a murderer?" her friend shouted at Dustin. Will's body trembled with rage.

Emily was alarmed by the expression on Will's face. He looked like he could commit murder at that moment, and he had Dustin in his sights as his victim.

"I'm saying it's not safe for her to take off alone with anyone."

Dustin's words may have bordered on being conciliatory, but his tone was anything but. It dripped ice.

"I should rip you to pieces," Will said through gritted teeth. His face was beet-red, and his breath rasped with anger.

"No one is going to rip anyone to pieces. This is crazy. Will is my friend. He has been for years. He'd never harm me."

Dustin tore his cold gaze away from Will and directed it at Emily. "How can you be sure?"

"What the...? How can she be sure it's not you, for Christ sake?" Will took two steps toward Dustin before Emily wedged herself between them. That didn't stop Will from reaching a long arm over her shoulder to point a finger in his adversary's face. "How long has she known you? You just breeze into town and, all of a sudden, you're her savior?"

"Stop this," Emily said. "I'm my own savior, and I'm not worried about being harmed by either of you. You guys can tuck your testosterone away for now and go home. I'm not impressed."

Emily stepped around Dustin and walked toward the house. She hoped they wouldn't throw punches at each other the moment her back was turned to them. She would have no choice but to break it up. She didn't know if the heated silence behind her was a good sign or not.

The last thing she heard before the door closed behind her was Will saying, "I'm not leaving until you do."

Once inside, Emily pushed aside the curtain a fraction of an inch to keep an eye on the action. The two men faced each other for several more seconds before Dustin walked toward the beach. He was almost at the tree line when he turned around to glare at Will. Her old friend swiveled toward his truck, climbed in, and drove away, but not before he cast a frustrated glance toward the window where she stood.

With the two men out of sight, Emily went to the kitchen. She had trouble wrapping her thoughts around what had just happened and her own part in it. Guilt nagged at her. *Shouldn't she have sided with Will, one of her oldest friends? Why had she taken a neutral position? Should she have sent Dustin away?* Emily didn't agree with Dustin's methods, but, deep down, she must agree with him in principle. Otherwise, her conscience wouldn't have allowed her to stand aside and let an old friend be hurt.

As she poured hot water over the calming lavender leaves in her teacup, she heard heavy footsteps on the wooden boards outside.

She glanced out the window, but she didn't see a vehicle in the driveway. She grabbed a knife in one hand, her cell phone in the other, and crouched as low as she could to make her way to a window that would give her a full view of the porch. She made it halfway across the room when knuckles rapped on the door, and she saw the outline of the person on the other side. She stood to her full height, dropped the knife on a side table, and crossed the room.

"What are you doing here?" She pulled open the door and set her hands on her hips.

"We need to talk," Dustin said.

"I don't think so. I'm too angry to talk now."

"You're angry? How do you think I feel?"

"I don't know what you have to be angry about?" she said.

"How about the fact you did a disappearing act without letting me know?"

He brushed past her. Emily swiveled to follow him to the kitchen.

"I admit I was wrong to not let you know I was leaving. In hindsight, I can see that. But you're not my big brother or my father. I didn't realize I had to answer to you. Will suggested a fun activity, and I said yes. It's as simple as that."

"And what if that fun activity ended in you being murdered?" he said with his back to her as he helped himself to a cup of coffee.

"Are you crazy? Will isn't a murderer."

"How do you know?" He glared at her over his shoulder.

"I know him. We've known each other since we were children. He's a nice guy, and he wouldn't hurt me or anyone else."

"Do you know how many murders a year are committed by nice guys? That's how these people pull off their crimes, by seeming to be nice people. And they prey on people like you, who are too trusting and too gullible."

Emily's blood boiled.

"I am not too trusting nor gullible. I can read people. I know who I can trust and who I can't. And right now, I wonder if you're the guy I shouldn't trust. You come in here accusing my friends - people I've known for years - of being killers. That's insane."

"What's insane is your behavior. How am I supposed to protect you if you act like that?"

"I didn't ask you to protect me." Her voice rose in volume.

"You landed at my door the other night, needing a place to sleep because some guy tried to attack you."

"That didn't mean I elected you for the role of bodyguard."

"Fine. I'll leave." He turned toward the door.

"Good, because I can't handle any more of this."

"Lock the door behind me."

"Of course, I'll lock the door. I'm not stupid."

He gave her a doubtful look before he disappeared from view.

CHAPTER 20

A headache pounded in Emily's head the next morning, the same one that had prevented her from going to sleep until well past midnight.

She had not been productive at the wheel the previous night. The altercation with Will and Dustin weighed on her mind. Everything about it bothered her. Her neighbor made her doubt her friends, something she had never wanted to experience. They had been with her through many of her hardships. In her heart, she was certain she was safe with them, but Dustin had succeeded in planting a tiny seed of doubt, and that seed nibbled away at her normally trusting nature.

By unspoken agreement, Dustin hadn't spent the night in her spare bedroom. She had made it clear enough she didn't want him there anymore, but she was surprised by how she had grown accustomed to someone being in the house. Her spirits dipped a little when she entered an empty kitchen in the morning, and she wondered why it would matter. She had lived alone for years, and she didn't have any plans to make a change.

A glance through her fridge told Emily she needed to get into town to buy some provisions. At least it would give her a much-needed excuse to get out of the house.

At the grocery store, her thoughts returned to the previous day. *Why did Will have a sudden desire to take her surfing? On the other hand, why did she question it? A month ago, it would have seemed normal to her. Now, she doubted everyone and everything.*

Emily turned at the sound of her name as she placed a watermelon in her grocery cart.

"Hey, Rob," she said, as she greeted the cop. He was a young man, a little intense and over-eager, but likable, in a puppy-like way.

"Ted talked to IHIT this morning. I hear they haven't made much progress in the case." He pulled his cart alongside hers. It seemed to contain a lot of junk food.

"No, they haven't." Emily's spirits plummeted. She didn't need to be reminded the killer waited out there somewhere, and no one seemed to be able to find him.

"You know, everybody says that nothing like this has ever happened around here, but I told Ted that wasn't true."

Rob had Emily's full attention. If they could link this to another crime, it could be an important step toward the discovery of the killer.

"What do you mean?" She turned and faced him full-on.

"I remember my grandpa told me about the same thing happening in his time. He was a cop too, you know. I come from a law enforcement family," he said with a proud smile.

Emily remembered Rob's father worked as a security guard in a neighboring town, but she didn't want the conversation to be sidetracked with the details of his family tree. Although, the fact the crime happened a long time ago dimmed its importance significantly.

"So, what was that about your grandfather?" she said.

"I remember him telling me about a woman who was attacked while walking on the beach, someone else was killed, and they never caught the guy. It was the same situation as yours."

"That's interesting." Thoughts whirled through Emily's head. "How did Ted react when you told him?"

"He said it had to be a coincidence. He said it was too long ago to be connected. He's right, of course. I just wanted to correct people when they say nothing like this ever happened in Clear Point."

"Yes, of course," she said, her voice soft and thoughtful. "Crime can happen anywhere. That's what they've been telling me."

Emily finished her shopping as quickly as she could. Despite the agreement between Rob and Ted that the previous crime wasn't connected to the present one, the coincidence intrigued her.

At the police station, she pulled her truck into a spot next to Ted's cruiser.

"I ran into Rob earlier." Emily got to the point as soon as she sat in the chair facing his desk. "He told me about a murder that happened in his grandfather's time. He said it was the same as this one."

"Yeah, he told me about that." Ted leaned back in his chair and linked his hands across his stomach. "I don't see how it can have any connection to this case. It happened sixty years ago. I think the suspect would be a little on the old side to attempt to do it again. And I wouldn't call two crimes sixty years apart the work of a serial killer."

"I realize that," Emily said, put off by his attitude. "But I wonder if there could be some significance. Have you read the case file?"

"I looked at it, but it's pretty slim." He opened a desk drawer and removed a file two inches thick. "There were no clues, nothing to go on."

"Could I take a look at it? Just to give me something to do?"

"I can't do that. This is a confidential police file," he said. He dropped it back in the drawer and slammed it shut. "Besides, even if I could let you see it, it wouldn't be a good idea. It might upset you more than anything."

"How could it do that? I think it'd make me feel useful." Emily hoped to appeal to Ted's soft heart, but success seemed unlikely.

Emily couldn't explain why she wanted to see the file and study the old case. Of course, it was too old to be connected, but it felt important to her.

"I'm sorry," Ted said. He must have seen the disappointment on her face. "You'll have to rely upon the authorities to take care of your case, and you'd be better to put the old one out of your mind."

"Thanks, Ted, I'll do that," she said, sarcasm evident in her voice. *Why did everyone think she could just erase things from her mind?*

Emily returned home. Her spirits dropped even lower when she found her neighbor perched on her front porch. He sipped from a bottle of beer.

"What are you doing here?" she said, as she watched Max greet him with enthusiasm. "And why are you drinking beer? It's not even noon yet."

Dustin glanced at his watch.

"Yes, it is. It's twelve-oh-five. There's no problem."

Emily rolled her eyes. "What are you doing here?" she said again.

"I had nothing else to do, so I came by to see what was up."

"When you saw I was gone, you could've left."

"No, all the more reason for me to stay and keep an eye on the place."

Emily suspected he was an unemployed, borderline alcoholic. Yet he had paid a lot of money for his house along with the renovations. *Where did his money come from? And why did he have an interest in her and her problems?*

Emily shook her head to clear it. She didn't want him here now. She wanted to lick her wounds in peace.

"What's wrong?" he said.

"Nothing. You can go home now." She stepped onto the porch.

He had the nerve to laugh at her. "What's bothering you? You can forget it if you think you're going to get rid of me so easily."

Emily dropped into the chair next to him and took a deep breath. She gave in and told Dustin about meeting Rob in the store and his revelation about the old case, followed by her visit to see Ted.

"I want that file. I don't understand why Ted wouldn't let me see it. What harm would it do?"

"He's a cop. It doesn't work that way. Do you think he'll hand out case files to every Tom, Dick, or Harry that walks through the door?"

"He knows me. He's known me for years."

Dustin shook his head. "It doesn't matter. You could be Mother Theresa; he wouldn't let you see the files."

"I have a feeling they're key to this case. Ted doesn't seem to think so."

"I agree with you. That's why I think we should intervene," he said, as he took another sip from the bottle.

"What do you mean by 'intervene'?"

"We should borrow the file."

"You mean...steal it?" Emily's voice rose.

"Borrow it. We'll give it back when we're finished."

"You're suggesting we steal a file from the police station?" Emily couldn't believe what she had heard.

Dustin sighed before he locked his gaze on hers. "Do you want to get to the bottom of this, or not?" he said. "Do you want to live your life in fear, or do you want it to return to normal?"

"Of course, I want it to return to normal. But..." She turned her face toward the ocean. All she saw in her mind's eye was a vision of herself behind bars in the local jail. "It wouldn't be right."

"What's that saying? Desperate measures for desperate times?"

Emily's thoughts strayed to the attack, the sleepless nights, the distrust of her friends and neighbors that grew like a bad weed inside of her. She turned her gaze to Dustin.

"Of course, I would never do it, but hypothetically, if I did agree, how would it happen?" she said.

"We know where the file is. All we have to do is provide a distraction for Ted and his little friends, and we take it."

"He'll notice it's gone."

"Maybe. Maybe not. We'll come up with a suitable substitute, and before you know it, we'll return the original."

"This is crazy. I can't believe I'm even listening to this."

Dustin smiled.

CHAPTER 21

Emily's stomach churned. She prayed she wouldn't throw up. She glanced to her left and searched for a glimpse of Dustin, to no avail. *How had he convinced her to go through with his scheme? This was not her. She always prided herself for being honest and transparent with people. What had happened to her principles?*

She flicked a glance at her watch and took a deep breath.

"Oh my God! It's him. I think it's him!" Emily yelled. She knew the windows were open, and her voice would carry to the ears she aimed for.

Within seconds, the two police officers, followed by their chief, hurried out of the police station. Ted's gaze swept over the surroundings until it settled on Emily.

"Are you all right? What the hell happened?" he said, hurrying to her side.

She pointed toward a grove of trees to the right of the building.

"It was a man. He went in there. There was something about him that was familiar. It brought back terrible memories."

"Rob, stay with Emily. Ralph, you come with me."

Ted and his deputy struck off in the direction Emily had indicated. The other young cop gritted his teeth and remained by her side, his gaze glued to the trees, and his right hand on his sidearm. He was prepared to serve and protect.

Emily pretended to glance around her in fear. She spotted Dustin's form skulking into the front door of the police station. The few bystanders who gathered didn't seem to notice. If they did, they were far more interested in the action they hoped to witness on the other side of the building.

"They got him," the officer beside her said, and Emily's heart skipped a beat, certain he referred to Dustin.

Instead, she watched as the two police officers led a man out of the trees, each of them holding one of his arms. The man's shoulders were stooped, and his eyes were wide. Emily's mouth dropped open, and her gaze flickered to Ted's face. With his brows lowered, his expression was a mixture of dismay and confusion.

"Is this the man you saw? The one you think resembles the killer?" Ted asked as the three men stopped in front of her.

"I...I may have made a mistake," Emily said. She was horrified by what she had initiated. "I'm sorry, Mr. Bennett. Are you all right?"

"I was just looking for some shade while I waited for my daughter," the man said, his voice trembling. His gaze flicked from Emily to Ted.

John Bennett, a kindhearted ninety-year-old resident of Clear Point, lived with his daughter and often strolled the streets during the day while she did her shopping. Emily couldn't believe she was not only complicit in the break-in of a police station, but she had upset this mild-mannered man while doing so.

"I'm so sorry," she said again. "I made a terrible mistake."

"That's all right, my dear. It's kind of exciting to be arrested. That's never happened to me before," he said with a smile. Emily knew he made a special effort to reassure her, making her feel even worse.

"We're not arresting you, John," Ted said. "We just needed to check with Emily to clear up the misunderstanding." His last words were delivered with a disapproving frown aimed at Emily.

"Everything okay here?" a voice said from behind Emily's right shoulder. She turned to see Dustin's smiling face observing the small crowd of people with curiosity. Her gaze dropped to the shopping bag in his right hand before it lifted to catch the slight nod of his head.

"Everyone can go about their business now," Ted said in a loud voice. He waved his arms in an effort to disperse the group. The cop turned to Emily and lowered his voice. "I hope you think before you do something like that again. I'm disappointed in you."

Not as much as I'm disappointed in myself, she thought, as she watched him stalk into the police station.

"That went well," Dustin remarked.

Emily whirled on him.

"That was horrible," she said through gritted teeth. "They were supposed to come out of the bushes empty-handed. I never thought anyone would be in there, least of all Mr. Bennett. I feel terrible."

"At least I got the file." He took her arm and led her back to the SUV.

"Did you leave the other one?" she said as she climbed into the passenger seat.

"Yes. Ted has a nice file of healthy recipes he can browse through if he has a chance."

Emily concentrated on the documents in front of her. So far, she had read about the basics of the attack, which were indeed similar to the attack on herself. A woman had been walking on the beach when someone had jumped out of the bushes and tried to strangle her. Another woman, a stranger to the victim, had come upon the attack and intervened, losing her life in the process. The perpetrator had escaped and never been found.

Emily sat cross-legged on the bed, hunched over the file, embroiled in the details of the forensic analysis, when she jerked and squelched a scream. Something had brushed against her back. Her surprise and fear turned to anger when she discovered Dustin peering over her shoulder at the file.

"Found anything so far?" he said, seemingly unaware he had startled her.

"None of your business," she said. "Who told you that you could just walk into my bedroom unannounced?"

He grinned. "We're a couple, remember? I'm supposed to be familiar with the inside of your bedroom. I can't maintain my role as boyfriend without doing a little research first, can I?"

"Get out," she said, pointing at the door.

"Are you still angry about Mr. Bennett?"

"I'm upset about the whole thing. The break-in, Mr. Bennett, everything."

"It wasn't technically a break-in. The door was open. The building just happened to be empty at the time. And, might I remind you, you agreed to it. We discussed it, and you said yes."

"I'd like to be alone right now." Emily gritted her teeth and tried to be patient. Her nerves were frayed. She was angry with Dustin for getting her into this, and she was angry with herself for letting him do it.

In response, he climbed onto the bed beside her, forcing Emily to scoot over farther. Distracted, she didn't have time to pick up the file before it was in his hands.

"Let's see this," he said.

"No. It's mine. It's none of your business. Nothing about me is any of your business. I want you out of my house and out of my life. I've had it with you."

When they returned from town, she told him she was going to her room and didn't want to be disturbed. She wrongly assumed he would respect her wishes.

"I have to remind you, no matter how you feel about it, if it wasn't for me you wouldn't have this file right now," he said, a smug smile on his lips.

"Which leads me to wonder why you're so good at illegal and underhanded stuff."

"I'm creative and open-minded." He didn't lift his gaze from the file.

Emily rolled her eyes, put both hands on his shoulder, and shoved. He didn't budge.

"Rob was right," he said. "This sounds like your attack, but sixty years ago."

"First, I don't like it referred to as 'my attack.' Second, it's none of your business."

"You know, you're starting to sound like a broken record," he said. "You lack originality."

"You lack a brain."

"There you go. That's a new one. I like to see progress."

Emily flopped back on the pillows in frustration. She closed her eyes and wondered what she had done to deserve this man.

"Oh, you want to move onto the next phase of familiarization, do you?"

Her eyes flew open to see a grinning Dustin leaning over her. His face moved closer. She rolled to the left a second before his lips would have landed on hers.

"Oh no, you don't." She pointed a furious finger at him. "That is not going to happen, and if you think it will, you can walk out that door right now. I'm still angry with you."

He laughed. "Don't worry. I'm just teasing you. You're far from being my type. I prefer buxom women," he said with a wink. "Although you do have a lot of other things going for you."

Emily flinched but recovered in an instant.

"You can leave all of my 'things' out of this. I'm not happy with our arrangement. I think it's time for a breakup."

A hand settled on her wrist.

"I'm just kidding. Let's call a truce. Let me look at this with you. I can be a sounding board. I won't say a word unless you ask," he said, his tone soothing.

The wind died out of Emily's outraged sails. She needed help with this. She couldn't call on Francie for help. Her friend repeatedly urged her to put the murder behind her and move on. Emily would be discouraged from taking an interest in an ancient case.

She also did not want to involve Will or Trevor at this point. Tensions were already high between Dustin and her friends. There was no need to put them in each other's paths.

Her neighbor, for all his ability to irritate, was an outsider. He also struck Emily as being intelligent. It was possible he would make a good sounding board. If not, she would boot him off the bed and out of the house.

"All right, but let's get a few things straight. I am not now, and never will be, interested in you in a romantic way. I will take you up on your offer as a sounding board, but I don't need to hear unnecessary commentary. This is something I'm interested in, something I'm looking into, and if you're going to tell me to keep my nose out of it, you can leave right now."

Dustin pressed his lips together and made a zipping motion in front of his mouth.

"Good. Keep it that way," Emily said. Her gaze returned to the file. "I've skimmed it so far, but the basics seem to be much the same as what happened to me, even down to the second witness who scared him off."

Dustin raised his hand. "Permission to speak, sir," he said in a pseudo-military voice.

Emily rolled her eyes. "Yes?"

"Were the witnesses also men, as they were now?

"The first one, the one who was murdered, was a woman. The second witness was a man."

"Who was the initial victim?"

"You mean the one who survived?"

Dustin nodded.

Emily glanced down at the folder. "Her name was Elizabeth Wheaton."

"Does that name mean anything to you?"

"No. There's nothing here that rings any bells. I've never heard anyone talk about this, even years ago when I used to spend time with my grandmother."

"There must be someone around here who can tell us more about it."

"So, you agree with me it's something to look into?"

"Yeah. I think it's worthwhile."

"It's so strange, though. How could some random act of violence sixty years ago have anything to do with another random act of violence today?"

"I don't know, but I think it'd be a good idea to find out."

Chapter 22

"Ugh, my head is spinning. I can't stare at this anymore," she said.

Emily glanced at Dustin. The file in front of him seemed to draw his full concentration. "You look enthralled."

"I am," he said without lifting his head.

They had divided the pages between them, and Dustin retreated to the chair in the corner, while Emily remained on the bed.

"You don't find it gets to be too much? All that forensic detail?" she said.

"Not at all."

"Dustin, what did you do before you became a writer?" Emily set down her share of the papers. The more time she spent with him, the more of an enigma he became. He vacillated from grumpy to helpful, from annoying to charming. The details about his life, his career, and his past were kept hidden away. Yet, he seemed to enjoy sticking his nose in other people's business. At times, she detected a sense of loss or sadness in him. Yet he gave the impression of being in control and confident of his place in the world. Definitely a man of contrasts.

"Why do you ask?"

"Because I googled holobiont, and I can't picture you as a botanist. From what I can see, you don't like anything plant-related."

"Not true. I like corn on the cob." He continued to flip through the papers.

"Spill the beans."

He sighed and set down the file.

"Why is it so important to you?" he said.

"Because it's part of who you are. Because I'd like to know who I'm dealing with."

"Is this about trust? You're not sure you're safe with me? I'd think by now you would've figured that out."

"I sense I'm safe with you. But I like to know people, especially someone I spend a lot of time with. And now I know you lied about all that botany hoo-ha, I wonder if I can feel comfortable with you."

"It wasn't a lie so much as an evasion."

"Semantics."

"Not at all. You tried to force yourself into my bubble, and I had a classic fight-or-flight reaction. It's the result of psychological childhood trauma." He stretched his legs out in front of him.

"You're such a bullshit artist."

"There you go. We have something in common, after all. We're both artistic."

Emily glared at him.

"All right. I'll spill. I was a journalist," he said.

"You're kidding."

"You're surprised?"

"It's unexpected. Who were you with?"

"The Globe and Mail."

"Oh, the big times. You lived in Toronto?"

"No, Calgary. Welcome to the modern world. With the wonders of something called the internet, not to mention the cellular phone, you can work from anywhere."

"What kind of stories did you cover?" she said, intrigued.

"Predominantly crime."

They stared at each other for several moments before Emily spoke again.

"That explains your intense interest in my drama. It brought back memories of your heyday."

"What makes you think it was my heyday? It could have been the worst time of my life. Maybe that's why I'm not doing it anymore."

"Is that it? Was it the worst time of your life?"

"Never mind. Pretend I didn't say anything."

"What happened? Why did you leave it?"

"I didn't leave on my own. I was asked to leave." His gaze returned to the file in his lap.

"Why?"

"Emily, I don't want to talk about this right now."

"I get that. But wanting and needing are two different things. I think you need to talk about it."

"You can forget the psychobabble."

"This isn't psychobabble. It's two friends talking, and one of the two has to get something off his chest."

"Friends?" he said, lifting his head, his eyebrows raised.

"Sure, why not?" she said. She could live with that definition of their relationship. "Was it because of your drinking?"

"I don't have a drinking problem."

"Come on. Are you going to make me pull teeth?"

He pinned her with a lengthy glare before giving in. "I went through a bad time, and I may have been a bit bad-tempered."

Emily couldn't hold back the laugh. "You may have been bad-tempered? I can't imagine. You're so Zen."

"Very amusing," he said.

"Why were you bad-tempered? Too many paper cuts?"

Emily's laughter stopped when she saw the expression on his face. He had dropped his facade long enough to reveal a layer of anguish.

"What was it, Dustin? What happened?" she asked.

"My wife left me." He turned his head to stare out the window, grief etched on his face.

"I'm so sorry. I shouldn't have made a joke of it."

"It's okay. You didn't know," he said with a shrug of his shoulders.

"What happened?"

"Emily, please, I think that's enough for today. My hour must be up."

"Sorry. Of course. Would you like a cup of tea? Lavender?"

"Coffee, black, would be fine, thanks."

CHAPTER 23

Emily hit the power button on the computer on her way to the kitchen the next morning. The sight of the grey, wet weather made her grimace as she filled the coffee pot with water and gazed out her kitchen window. The animals would be cold and miserable. She would feel the same when she went out to take care of them.

A few minutes later, her eggs cooked slowly in the frying pan, and she settled in front of her computer screen to pull up her e-mails. Her routine began by deleting the accumulation of promotional items in her inbox, leaving her to concentrate on the useful e-mails.

Layla had sent her a message with a list of items that needed restocking at the shop. Emily confirmed she had some already made and would work on getting the others done as soon as possible. The e-mail was sent to the printer to be posted on her bulletin board in the workshop.

Her sister had sent a query about how things were going, and Emily returned a quick, upbeat response she hoped didn't reek of insincerity. The lack of progress in the case discouraged her. She wanted her life to return to normal, without doubts or fears about the people among whom she lived. She also didn't want to discuss those fears with her family or close friends.

A third e-mail drew her attention. The sender appeared as 'Nitotem.' The name was unfamiliar to her, and the subject line said, 'How was your run?' Emily's brows drew together.

She double-clicked to bring up the text.

Hey Emily,

How was your run that day? I hear you've given up running on the beach at dusk. Will you be safer during the day? Some days, the beach is deserted even in broad daylight. Will you stay at home then too? Will you ever feel safe?

Maybe next time it won't be anywhere near the beach. Maybe it'll be on your way to Clear Point. Maybe you'll get a flat tire, and when you get out to change it, someone will come at you from behind.

Maybe you'll step out of the pub at night by yourself after having a few drinks with your friends, and somebody will grab you and drag you away.

You never know when or where it'll happen next time. Maybe running on the beach is the least of your worries.

Emily couldn't tear her gaze from the screen. It paralyzed her. Her brain could not wrap itself around the words. *This had to be from the person who had attacked her, didn't it?*

Whether she sat there five minutes or an hour, she couldn't say, but a loud rap on the door startled her. Standing, her chair fell over with a crash and she stifled a scream. Max gave a loud bark and headed for the door as Emily looked around her for a nearby weapon. A table lamp stood close at hand. She yanked the cord out of the wall and carried the lamp high above her head.

Dustin stood on the other side of the door, his shoulders hunched, and the collar of his jacket pulled up to protect his neck from the sleet. All she saw of his face through the window was his deep frown. Without waiting for an invitation, he stepped inside as soon as she opened the door. He glanced around the room before he turned to face Emily. His gaze went to the lamp in her hand and returned to her face, his eyes narrowed.

"Trying to throw some light on the situation, are you?"

"Um, I wanted to move it to another spot." Emily carried the lamp back to its original corner but didn't plug it into the socket. "What brings you here?"

He shrugged and glanced around the room again before he looked her in the eye. "I'm just checking in, making sure everything's okay."

Emily's gaze shifted to her computer screen, where the e-mail remained open. "Thanks. That's nice of you," she said, absentmindedly, forcing her gaze back to his.

"You seem a little shaky."

Again, she couldn't stop herself from glancing toward her computer before she stammered another half-hearted reply. "I'm fine."

With a frown once again pasted on his face, Dustin crossed to the desk and leaned over the computer.

"That's private." Emily grasped his arm.

"This doesn't sound good," he said, ignoring her. "This doesn't sound good at all." He lifted his head and gazed toward the kitchen. "Do I smell something burning?"

"Oh, damn." Emily let go of his arm and ran to save her eggs. Seconds later, they were dumped in the garbage bin. She returned to the desk, stared at the screen with dismay, and re-read the e-mail before turning to Dustin.

"I know," she said. "I don't know who it could be, or why they're doing this."

"You have to show this to the police."

Emily nodded. "Yes, I'll call Ted, but I don't know what he's going to be able to do."

"He'll send it on to IHIT, and they'll investigate," Dustin said.

"What if...what if he plans to try again?" she said, her voice low and trembling.

"We'll deal with it."

•   •   •

Emily's meeting with Ted underwhelmed her. She had printed the e-mail for him, and he stared at it as if she had handed him her grocery list.

"It could be just a prankster, someone local who knows what happened and wants to play on your fears. Nitotem. That's a strange name."

"I googled it. It means 'my friend' in Cree," Emily said.

Ted's eyebrow lifted.

"What if it's not a prank?" she said. "What if it's from the guy who tried to kill me?"

"It's unlikely, but I'll send it to Humble. They have people who specialize in this kind of thing. They may be able to trace it."

"I don't want to wait too long."

"Don't worry. I'll send it to him right away. Forward me the original."

"Will do. Thanks."

She left the police station feeling deflated, with a sense nothing would come out of this new development. She left her truck in the lot, turned right, and walked toward the water. Another right took her along the dock to a whitewashed building with dark blue trim. The sign along the eaves said 'McCade's Fishing Tours.'

"Hey, Joyce. Is Will around?" she said to the older, dark-haired woman behind the counter.

"He's working on the small boat. Minor repair to do."

"Great. Thanks."

Emily made her way down to the pier toward the fishing boats that bobbed side-by-side at their moorings. She was familiar with the trio of vessels, having spent time on them with Will over the years. In his father's day, there had been one boat, but Will had built up his small fleet and now owned two boats dedicated to fishing tours and one for whale-watching. He had told her he planned to add another in the near future.

She spotted his back as he knelt beside the engine. His head hung almost upside down, studying something. A rag peeked out of his back pocket, along with a couple of wrenches. She grabbed the railing and stepped aboard, making the boat dip slightly to one side. Max followed behind. Will straightened and twisted around. Instead of the smile she had hoped to receive, his expression remained bland as he returned to his work.

Emily sighed and forced a smile to her face.

"Hey, how's it goin'?" she said, coming up behind him.

"I'm fighting with this damn motor," he said without looking at her.

She sat on a bench on the other side of the engine to get a clear view of his face. The sight wasn't encouraging. His scowl was deeper than the 'damn motor' warranted, which meant the rest of his bad mood was directed at her.

"Will, we need to talk."

"I don't have anything to say. And, apparently, whatever I say or do has to be approved by your new friend," he said with a sneer.

"That's not true."

"It sure seemed true to me." He threw down his wrench. He looked like he had plenty he wanted to say, and it wouldn't be good. "How long have we known each other? Twenty years? Probably more than that. This guy comes waltzing into my town – our town – and decides I'm a murderer, and he's going to be the one to protect you from me. From me? Are you kidding?"

His arms were at his sides. His face was reddened with fury, and his eyes bulged.

"Look, I know it's ridiculous," Emily said. "I know it's impossible you or anyone else in this town is a murderer. I get that. He doesn't. He's from the city; he doesn't know our town yet."

"And, because of that, we have to bow and scrape and let him get away with tossing around accusations? Against me and your friends?"

"I'm not letting him get away with anything of the sort."

Will released a breath, and his shoulders slumped.

"Are you serious about this guy?" he said, his eyes filled with pain.

Emily had a decision to make. *Did she confide in Will that her relationship with Dustin was a sham, all for the sake of protection? Or, did she continue the charade for a while longer?* It wasn't that she didn't trust Will, but she knew he, in turn, would confide in Trevor, who was not known for his discretion. On the heels of the threatening e-mail this morning, she decided to keep her secret to herself. Will would be furious when he found out she had lied to him, but she would deal with that when the time came.

"I think I may be," she said, hedging her bets. "He's not as bad as you think. Right now, he's overprotective, but I'm working on that."

Will turned away from her and returned his attention to the motor. Emily's heart twisted. His hurt feelings were obvious but telling him the truth wasn't an option now. She had made her decision and would stick with it. Anyway, even if she confessed, it didn't mean she had romantic feelings for Will either. He had only ever been a good friend to her.

Emily went to his side. She placed a gentle hand on his back, leaned over, and gave the back of his head a kiss.

"I'll see you later," she said before she stepped onto the dock and encouraged Max to follow her.

At home, she parked her truck in the driveway and gazed around her, peering into the bushes. It was a habit she had developed since the murder, and it had gained importance since receiving that e-mail.

About to open the door of the vehicle, she caught sight of movement on the path from the beach. Max also picked up on it, a low rumble of warning in his throat. Emily hit the automatic door-lock button and had her hand on the keys in the ignition when she recognized Dustin as he emerged from the trees. Her breath left her in a whoosh, and she unlocked the doors.

"How did it go with Ted?" Dustin said as she and Max climbed out of the truck.

"He'll send it to IHIT. Maybe they'll be able to trace the e-mail to someone."

"That might take a while."

"He said he'd put a rush on it."

The sour expression on Dustin's face made it clear what he thought would come out of it.

Chapter 24

The phone jangled beside her and jolted Emily out of her reverie. The bowl she worked on had been forgotten as her thoughts strayed, and she gazed unseeingly out the window. She set her brush in the tray before she reached for the receiver.

Lisa's voice greeted her. "How's my baby sister?"

"Perfect timing. I needed a distraction," Emily said.

"I'm glad I can help."

"You're always helpful."

"Tell me the truth. How are you? Are you getting enough sleep?"

Emily thought of the restful nights she'd had since Dustin had decided to move back into the spare room. "Yes, I'm sleeping well."

"You're not nervous all alone in that house?"

Emily didn't want to share the fact she was not alone anymore. She would have to answer too many questions and listen to the speculation in her sister's voice.

"No, it's all good," she said instead.

"Any more news on the investigation?"

Emily filled her in on how she had found out there had been another incident sixty years ago that was eerily similar. She didn't tell her about breaking into the police station to get the file.

"Wouldn't that have been around the same time as Gran lived in Clear Point?" Lisa said.

"I suppose," Emily responded, doing the math in her head. "You're right. It could have been around that time. Too bad she's not around to fill me in on what happened."

"Yeah. Although, maybe she left something behind."

"What do you mean?"

"Dad has a box or two of her stuff. It could be a long shot, but maybe there's something in there."

"You're right," Emily said, excited at the thought. "I'll give Dad a call and ask him. By the way, you didn't mention anything about the incident to him, did you?"

"Not a word, just like I promised."

"Good. I don't want him to worry."

The two women talked for a while longer before they said their goodbyes. Emily promised to keep Lisa updated on how she progressed in her own little investigation.

•   •   •

The sky was steel gray, and a fine mist settled on the windshield. They were in Emily's truck and the back seat was filled with pottery to drop off at a shop in North Vancouver. She made the trip every five or six weeks during the year, more often during the busy summer season. Most of the time she drove the extra hour to go to Abbotsford and visit her dad, but rarely stayed overnight, unless the weather worked against her.

The previous day, Emily told Dustin they wouldn't need to book a hotel; they could drive back the same day. He insisted they stay over, claiming the talk with her father might lead them to someone else. She admitted he might have a point.

The store on 32nd Avenue carried craftwork from British Columbian artists. It wasn't large, but they had been in business for more than fifteen years, so they were doing something right. Emily had a friendly relationship with Karen, the owner, and they often sat down for a cup of tea when she made a delivery. This time, Emily knew it would be a quick drop-off before they went to visit her father. That didn't mean she escaped the speculative looks from the owner and shopworkers when Dustin appeared, loaded down with a box of pottery.

"Who is *he*?" Karen whispered in Emily's ear when Dustin passed them on his way to the back room.

"A friend, that's all." She couldn't meet Karen's eye.

"Hmm. A friend, eh? You know how to pick 'em," Karen said with a raised brow.

"It's not what you're thinking."

"Yes, and you know exactly what I'm thinking." Her sarcasm was difficult to miss.

"I can see it in your face. We're working together on a project, nothing more."

"He doesn't look like a potter to me."

"He's not," Emily said. A thought occurred to her. She turned to her friend. "What does he look like to you?"

"I don't know, but not an artist. He seems a little too…I don't know…would dangerous be a good word? Maybe mysterious would be a better choice," Karen said, her gaze glued on the door to the back room as if she had x-ray vision.

Emily wished she could make a witty comeback, but her mind was blank. Karen's description hit the nail on the head, the elusive nail for which she searched. It was food for thought, but she wouldn't be able to digest it until later. Dustin emerged from the room and caught her eye. She knew they had to move on.

As they fought their way through mid-day traffic on the Lion's Gate Bridge, which would take them through beautiful Stanley Park and onward to Downtown Vancouver, Emily observed the harbor district and the view of the cityscape in the distance. She never ceased to marvel at the difference in her present existence compared to that of six years ago.

Back then, she had lived in the vacuum of her fast-paced career as a graphic designer. She had juggled her needs and the needs of her husband amid the skyscrapers, traffic jams, and the stress of schedules. At the time, she had everything she had ever dreamed of. After all, she lived in one of the best metropolitan cities in the world. Vancouver was varied in culture, scenery, and available activities. Everything anyone wanted could be found there. In the end, Emily found unhappiness.

In her present life, she worked hard, but her schedule was her own to make. The highest building in Clear Point was three stories high, and the traffic jams were found in the peak of the summer by excited surfers and outdoor enthusiasts. And, up until a few weeks ago, she had been happy.

Life could change in a heartbeat.

Harry Burton lived in a small condo in a building designed for elderly people. He was seventy years old but appeared ten years older. Over time, he had shrunk from an imposing figure to a man who looked like a brisk wind could carry him away.

His disposition had undergone a change too. His jovial, laid-back attitude had all but deserted him after her mother's death. His aches and pains robbed him of what remained of those characteristics and turned him into a grump.

Nevertheless, her father was happy to see her and returned her hug and kiss while he stared over her shoulder with curiosity.

"Who's this?" he said.

"This is Dustin. He's a friend." Emily hadn't thought about how she would introduce her neighbor until Karen's comments had opened her eyes to the problem. Karen was a piece of cake compared to her dad.

"I hope he's better than that last one. What was his name? Alan? You don't need to go through that again."

"Dad..." Emily knew where this would lead, and she tried to interrupt him. But her father had already rounded on a wide-eyed Dustin.

"I hope you're not like that other lad. You know there are a lot more important things in life than looks. My girl has got plenty of good qualities, and anybody'd be lucky to have her."

If she hadn't been so humiliated, she would have laughed at the expression on Dustin's face. His mouth had dropped open, and anything he may have wanted to say was firmly lodged inside of him. Emily realized she would have a lot of damage control on her hands later, trying to fob off his questions.

"Dad, I swear Dustin and I are just friends. He came with me to do my deliveries because I had such a heavy load."

The older man frowned at Dustin as if he dared him to contradict her. Dustin smiled at her father, but he looked unsure of himself, something Emily was not used to seeing.

"How about I make us some coffee?" Desperate to change the subject, she thought they could talk easier over coffee and cookies.

"Did you make these?" her father asked, pointing at the sweets she had set out on a plate.

"I did, like a big girl."

He bent over to peer at them without touching them. "What's in them? Not some of that new stuff you always put into things, I hope."

"What new stuff, Dad? They're just cookies, not nuclear bombs."

"They're full of... stuff."

"Yes, they are," she said. "They're full of oatmeal and nuts and raisins, all things that are good for you."

"None of those other things? Those little balls?"

"You mean quinoa? No, there's no quinoa, only ingredients you like."

"She always tries to sneak healthy crap into me," he grumbled to Dustin.

"I know what you mean," Dustin said. "Did you ever see the green stuff she drinks?"

"No." Her father's eyes widened, and he glared with suspicion at his daughter as if she intended to force him to drink the dreaded concoction. Emily rolled her eyes at the two of them.

"Dad, I thought about Gran the other day," she said, in an attempt to turn the conversation in the right direction. "She lived in Clear Point a long time, didn't she?"

"Yep, a good chunk of her life," Harry said around a bite of a cookie.

"Why did she leave? Was it to get married?"

"I think that could have been a big part of it."

"What was the other part?"

He shook his head and reached for another cookie. "There were problems in Clear Point."

"Problems? Like what?" Emily's heart rate quickened, certain they would have answers to some of their questions. She threw a glance at Dustin. A blank expression masked his thoughts.

"Just problems," her father said with a shrug. "I don't know the details. This happened before your mother was born, you know. And I married your mother twenty or so years later." He peered over his glasses at her.

"I heard there was a murder in Clear Point." Emily watched his face for a reaction. Her father frowned as he took a sip of his coffee.

"There was, but I don't know much about that," he said.

"But you remember? Did Gran talk about it?" She leaned forward in her chair.

"No, she didn't. I don't remember how I heard about it," he said before he focused on Emily. "Why're you so interested?"

"I heard about it, and it made me curious." She forced herself to sound casual.

"You had your own murder over there," he said with an accusing tone.

"That's what made me curious about what happened back then. I thought maybe Gran had talked about it."

Harry Burton leaned back in his chair and sighed. "To tell you the absolute truth, there was something fishy about it. Like I said, I don't know all the details. It was before my time. But, at one point, your mother got wind of it – we were married then, but we didn't have kids yet – and she asked Betty about it. I was there. I saw her reaction. She turned white as a sheet and said she couldn't talk about it. Your mom, bless her heart, wanted to look into it, but I discouraged her. She finally agreed to leave it alone."

"What do you think happened? Why would it have disturbed Gran? Do you think she was involved somehow?"

"I wasn't there." Her father lifted his hands, palms up, by his side. "I don't know. I didn't even grow up on the island."

"Was there anyone she would've talked to about it?"

The older man's forehead creased as he gazed upward. "She might've told her husband, but he died fifteen years ago," he said. "I'm sure she had some close friends at the time, but I don't know who they were, and they'd all be dead by now."

"Lisa told me you have a box of things that used to belong to her."

"Yeah, a couple of boxes were left after she died and the furniture was sold off. Since your mom was gone, they came to me. I didn't know what to do with them. I always intended to give them to you girls to go through them someday. Do you want them?"

"Of course, I do."

"Well, you got yourself a fine young man here who can carry them out to the truck for you."

Chapter 25

By nine-thirty it was too late to consider making the trip back to Clear Point. Both Emily and Dustin were tired and decided they would make an early start in the morning.

"One room? I thought you booked two rooms."

"No, I said I'd take care of getting us a hotel for the night. What's wrong with one room? It has two beds. Are you worried you'll give in to temptation and get into bed with me?" Dustin said.

"No, that's not something I'm worried about. I just wanted to have some time alone, that's all." She dropped her overnight bag onto one of the double beds. Her gaze swept the room. Renovations would be a good idea, she thought, but it didn't smell musty, and it fell within her budget. She could handle it for one night.

"You won't even know I'm here," Dustin added. "Where do you want me to put this?"

"The table will be fine."

There had been two containers in her father's storage locker. One was a plain cardboard box that pulled away at the seams. The other container was a small trunk. It reminded Emily of an old-fashioned treasure chest from a pirate movie. At her request, Dustin had carried the box up to the room.

They had spent a lot of time with her father, going to a restaurant for dinner, and returning for coffee at his condo. Most of that time, Emily's mind was on what she might find in the boxes of her grandmother's belongings. The mystery of what had happened sixty years earlier had become an obsession for her. *Was it because it made her feel useful? Or, did she search for a connection with someone else who had experienced the same terror she had?*

Dust particles shimmered in the air-conditioned air of the hotel room as Emily loosened the top of the box and peered inside. She felt the heat from Dustin's body as he looked over her shoulder.

"Hmm. Looks interesting." He left her side to pick up the TV remote control and settle onto the bed.

It may not have been interesting to a casual observer, a non-relative, but it fascinated Emily. These objects had been owned and handled by her grandmother. They had been a part of her ancestor's life and were important enough for her to have kept them.

She removed vases, tiny porcelain bells, and decorative bowls. There were a few framed photos she lingered over, straining to recognize the people. She could distinguish her mother and grandmother. A man she thought could be her grandfather appeared in one, but others were unrecognizable to her.

Each breakable item in the box was wrapped with clothing, rags, or pillowcases. There were old blouses, aprons, even a couple of dresses.

"Find anything worthwhile?" she heard over the noise of a ball game on the television.

"I don't know. Some pictures, but I doubt it's anyone important or relevant to what we need."

"Mmm." His attention reverted to the game. It would take something more significant to capture his attention.

As she neared the bottom of the box, she thought she may have found that something. Her hand brushed across a book with a worn black cover. With reverence, she lifted it and thumbed through the pages. She had fallen upon her grandmother's diary. Betty's elegant slanted handwriting filled the sheets of paper.

"Ohhh," she said on a breath.

"What?" Dustin straightened and swiveled his gaze toward her.

Emily closed the book and hugged it to her chest as she turned to face him.

"A diary. I found her diary," she said, her voice hushed.

"That could be the motherlode."

"I hope so."

Emily sat cross-legged on the bed and laid the book in front of her. She looked at Dustin and grinned. "It's like I've found a treasure."

"Maybe there'll be a map with a big X on it."

She laughed. "That would be exciting."

"Do you want me to shut off the TV?"

"No, go ahead. I'll let you know if I find anything interesting."

Later, Emily lifted her head and realized the television was off. Dustin was no longer in the room, but a sliver of light snuck out from under the bathroom door. A moment later, the door opened, and he came out wearing a loose pair of shorts and nothing else. Emily blinked twice.

"What are you doing?" She tried to temper the alarm in her voice.

"What do you mean? I'm going to bed," he said with a puzzled frown.

"What time is it?" She grabbed the clock on the bedside table and turned it toward her. "Twelve-thirty? I didn't realize it was so late."

She set aside the diary, pulled a pair of pajamas from her bag, and headed to the washroom. When she came out, she found Dustin flipping through the book.

He glanced up at her. "This isn't easy to read. I mean her handwriting's neat enough, but there are a bunch of words that are hard to make out."

"It's because we're not used to reading actual handwriting. We've become so used to typed words it throws us off to see something different."

Emily settled under the covers and propped her back against the pillows.

"What have you read so far?" Dustin said.

"Not an awful lot. It's hard to pinpoint the time she's writing in. She only noted the month and day, not the year. I don't remember the exact date of the other attack, although I think it was in May. I may read the whole thing and not find any mention of the murder."

"Are there more journals in the box?" He handed the diary back to her.

"No, just the one."

"Then it has to be the right one. Let's hope."

CHAPTER 26

After a quick breakfast – Dustin grabbed something from a drive-through, while Emily ate one of her own muffins she had brought along – they started on the journey to Clear Point. Since it was Sunday, the traffic through Vancouver wasn't heavy. They crossed the bridge and made it to Horseshoe Bay and the ferry-crossing in good time.

During the ninety-minute ferry ride, they watched the news broadcast on the big-screen TV in the lounge and wandered around the upper deck, admiring the view.

Once the ferry reached Vancouver Island, they were back in the truck and moving through Nanaimo and Parksville to get on the road that would take them to the opposite side of the island.

"So, tell me what the hell your dad was talking about yesterday." Dustin merged onto the main road.

"What do you mean? He talked about a lot of things. We were there for hours. By the way, I have to say, you're surprisingly patient."

"Patient?" he said with a chuckle.

"Yeah, my dad can be a bit much to handle sometimes, but you weren't grumpy with him at all. You handled him perfectly."

"I figured he was grumpy enough for both of us, so I played it cool. Besides, he kept calling me 'a fine young man.' I didn't want to make him change his mind."

Emily laughed. "He's turned into an old grouch. I know he's lonely, but he won't admit it. I've asked him to come and live with me. I've got plenty of room, but he won't hear of it. He says he's happy where he is. According to him, he has lots of friends, although I've never seen any of them hanging around. I think he's happy being bad-tempered."

"It can be fun from time to time," Dustin said.

"You should know."

He ignored her wry remark. "So, back to my question, which I will clarify, what was he talking about with all that Alan business and whatnot?"

The smile left Emily's face, and she waved her hand in the air, dismissing his question. "That was nothing. He just didn't like Alan."

"It sounded like something. You and Alan broke up because you weren't good-looking enough for him? Did I understand that right?"

"It was a bit more than that."

"He left you because of something you did?"

"I didn't do anything. It was complicated." Emily hoped her tone was indifferent enough for him to get the hint.

"But your dad said Alan found you lacking for some reason. He didn't think you were good-looking enough, was that it? What's wrong with him?"

Emily cast him a sideways glance.

"I'm serious. I say it like it is. You are a very good-looking girl. As a matter of fact, at times, you could even be described as gorgeous. I have a hard time believing some guy left you because you didn't reach his standards."

"Some people have certain...requirements, and I didn't fill them. Anyway, I don't want to talk about this anymore. Dad should never have started going on like that. Sometimes he's like a freight train, and he's hard to stop."

There were several minutes of silence, and Emily sighed with relief.

"How long had you guys been together?" Dustin said.

She turned her head toward the window, closed her eyes, and offered up a silent prayer for salvation. "What is it you don't understand about my not wanting to talk about it anymore?" she said with a pleading look.

"It'll do you good to talk about it. Think of it as therapy."

"I have a therapist, thank you very much."

"You do? You go to see a therapist because of Alan?" His gaze left the road to stare at her.

"Not anymore, but I think I'll have to go back to see her after this little road trip with you."

"Now look who's grumpy. I want to make conversation. I thought it'd be good to spend some time getting to know each other."

She swiveled to face him. "Okay. So, tell me about yourself."

"You know everything already."

"No, I don't. Why don't you tell me about your wife?"

Dustin pursed his lips, narrowed his eyes, and concentrated on the winding road in front of him.

"Oh, you don't want to talk about it," Emily said. "What's good for the goose isn't good for the gander after all, is it?"

"I thought I was being nice telling you you're good-looking enough for any guy. I'm just curious about who could dump you because of your looks. Your character, I would understand, but not your looks."

Emily stared at his profile for several moments until he glanced over at her and gave a little smile.

"I had a double mastectomy."

The words hung in the air, and it was too late to pull them back. Dustin had been added to the short list of those who knew of her past. It was less painful than she had expected. *Was it because time truly healed all wounds? Had she finally come to terms with it?*

The car jerked to the right and back again. Dustin stared at her with wide eyes before he swung his gaze back to the road.

"What? When?" His gaze flicked to her chest.

"About eight years back. Since my mother died of breast cancer, I had some tests done, and it turned out I was at a very high risk of developing the disease," she said, her voice monotone. Memories flooded her mind, none of them good, most of them horrible. "The doctors recommended I have my breasts removed. I agreed."

The car bounced onto the gravel shoulder before it came to a complete stop. Dustin twisted to the side, one arm on the steering wheel, the other across the seat back between them.

"And Alan left you because of it," he said.

"Not initially. He told me he respected my decision, and he'd stand by me and love me, no matter what."

"So, what changed?"

"His mind," she said with a shrug she struggled to keep casual. "He decided my breasts were more important than the rest of me."

The silence hung in the air like a thick, black cloud until Dustin shoved it aside. "I don't know what to say. It must've been a terrible decision for you to make."

Emily remained face-forward and stared at the tops of the trees swaying high above them.

"Strangely enough, it wasn't that difficult for me. I'd seen what the disease did to my mother in such a short period of time. I didn't hesitate at all. If there's something in or on my body that can cause that amount of pain and misery, I don't want to have anything to do with it. Get rid of it, or in this case, them. The downside was, of course, a lot of my attractiveness left with them."

"That's not true. Didn't I just tell you you're very attractive."

"Yes, with my clothes on." She remembered the expression of distaste on Alan's face when he had seen her naked.

"Well, I wouldn't know, would I?" His eyes widened in horror. "Oh Christ, I just remembered. It was a stupid joke, okay? I would never have said it if I'd known."

"What are you talking about?" She turned to face him.

He ran both his hands over his face and grimaced. "My stupid remark about preferring buxom women. Oh God." He banged the back of his head against the headrest.

She laughed. "That'll teach you."

Dustin was solicitous for the rest of the trip home. Emily enjoyed it for a while, but it eventually wore thin.

"Cut it out," she said.

"Cut what out?"

"Stop being so nice to me. I'm not made of china, you know. My feelings aren't hurt. I won't go home and cry for hours alone in my room. I'm a big girl. I made a life-changing decision, fully aware of all the consequences, and I have no regrets. So, you can go back to being a rough, tough cream-puff."

"Rough, tough cream-puff?" he said, his brows raised.

"Yeah, all full of bluster, but soft and gooey on the inside."

"I'm not soft and gooey, I'll have you know. I'm made of steel inside and out."

"I don't believe you. You're sensitive enough to have suffered some kind of breakdown when your wife left. It obviously affected you."

Emily waited for a reaction, but all she saw was a slight tightening of his jawline. Several seconds passed with no rebuttal from Dustin.

"So, how long were you together before she left?"

His eyes stared straight ahead with no change of expression, but the hands that gripped the steering wheel in a ten-to-two formation had developed white knuckles.

"Did you have any kids?" she persisted.

"No."

She was grateful to have some sort of response. "There was no peripheral damage for young children, which is a good thing, but it was difficult for the adults in the equation," she stated, watching him.

"You got it."

"It must have been messy if it led to you losing your job."

"How did you react when Alan left you?"

He had turned the tables on her, and it didn't feel good.

"It changed my life," she said with honesty. "I experienced two devastating blows, one after the other. It made me rethink everything about my life. I'm not the same person I was before."

"There you have it."

Emily looked at him, thinking they had a lot more in common than she would have guessed.

"Yes, you're right. There you have it. It explains a lot for both of us."

Chapter 27

The vistas of Clear Point were in view when Emily's cell phone rang. The loud buzz echoed through the car and jarred them out of their thoughts. Her sister's number appeared on the screen.

"Hey Lisa."

"What's this about a new beau?"

Emily glanced over at Dustin and hoped he couldn't hear the conversation. His gaze was fixed on the road.

"Don't believe everything you hear, that's all I have to say."

Lisa laughed. "I expect more details than that, but I understand if you can't talk right now. It was nice of you to go see Dad. He loves the visits."

"I know, and I'll try to go more often," Emily said. "He didn't waste any time calling you."

"He was thrilled to tell me you'd been there and to remind me how long it's been since I've gone to Van."

"Yeah, he likes to rub it in."

"He also went on about Gran being tied up in some murder in Clear Point. Is he confused or what? I thought you weren't going to tell him about the murder."

"Did you say anything about it?" Emily said, worry creasing her brow.

"Not at all. I let him ramble on, but I'm worried about him, Em. He was always so lucid."

"And he still is. It's a long story. I'll call you tomorrow, and we'll talk, okay?"

"You're scaring me."

Emily knew how little it took to scare her sister. "Don't worry about it. It's strange, but it's nothing to be afraid of."

"We have a lot of catching up to do. I wish I could get away to go see you, and I can't wait to meet your new guy."

Emily groaned into the phone. "Stop it. I'll talk to you later, Sis."

"News travels fast," Dustin said, as she ended the connection.

"Sometimes it travels at the speed of light, and other times, it takes years and a hell of a lot of digging to find it."

•　　•　　•

"Where do you want me to put this?"

Dustin stood in her living room, Max by his side. They had stopped by Will's house to pick up the dog before they returned home. Dustin waited in the truck while Emily went inside to collect her pet. When she noticed her friend's disgruntled stare out the window, she kept the visit brief.

"On my desk, for now, I guess," Emily said. She stood aside as Dustin placed the heavy chest on her rickety desk. She slid the lighter cardboard box into a corner of the room. Before they had left the motel, Emily placed all the trinkets and keepsakes back into the box, along with the diary she had read the night before. The time to investigate the chest was here.

Rust and dents decorated the outside of the trunk, but it appeared to be solid. The lock was no longer functional and saved them the bother of needing any special tools or locksmiths. Emily reverently lifted the lid as if unveiling a long-lost treasure. Perhaps she was, she thought.

She stared at the contents for several moments before she extracted a dusty photo album. It was the old-fashioned type with thick black pages, and black-and-white photos glued side by side. Her fingertips glided over the images.

"Wow. I don't know what I expected to find in here, but it wasn't this," she said, her voice hushed.

Emily looked at Dustin, her face lit with wonder. She set the old photo album aside and returned her attention to the contents of the chest.

"There's one other photo album in here. The rest seems to be made up of papers and documents."

"That'll keep you busy for a while," Dustin spoke over his shoulder on his way to the kitchen. The coffeemaker gurgled, and mugs clattered.

Emily placed the two albums on her desk before she sifted through the balance of the contents. Documents that resembled deeds and other legal papers were stacked in one pile. Recipes were put into another stack. There were several clippings from newspapers, the majority of them obituaries and birth notices. They were assigned to their own pile.

Novels by Jane Austin, Agatha Christie, and Charles Dickens made up the rest. They were dog-eared and well-loved. Emily resolved to handle them with the care they deserved.

She stepped back and surveyed her bounty, her smile wide. "This will be fascinating. I can't believe Dad didn't tell me about this sooner. I would've loved to go through it."

"He might have thought it was a pile of junk." Dustin came into the room carrying two mugs of coffee. "At any rate, now you have your chance. Enjoy it."

"I'll start with the photo albums."

Emily sprawled on the couch with Max curled up beside her and an album on her lap. Dustin grabbed the other one and settled into the armchair, his right ankle crossed over his left knee.

"This has to be a photo of your grandmother. You're the spitting image of her."

Emily scrambled off the couch, ignored Max's grumbling, and peered over Dustin's shoulder. "You think so?"

"Definitely. Of course, the hairstyle and clothing are different, but your facial features are the same."

She smiled with pride. "I'll take that as a compliment."

"You should. She was a beautiful woman."

Emily returned to her couch and original position. "There are so many people in these pictures. I wish I knew who they were," she said.

"Pull them off the page and examine the back. Maybe she wrote something on them."

Emily hated to risk damaging the photos, but she knew Dustin had a point. With care, she removed one of them. As he had guessed, her grandmother had inscribed the names of the four people in the photo, herself included. The names were unfamiliar, but at some point, she thought they might prove useful.

She examined the images and searched for a resemblance to one of her friends. Francie, Trevor, and Will were all third or fourth generation Clear Point residents, so it was possible Emily's grandmother had known or perhaps been a close friend of one of their ancestors. However, the age and the quality of the photos blurred the features of the people in them and made it difficult for her to recognize anyone.

"There are pictures of people who must be my great-grandparents. They look so stern, like their faces would crack if they smiled," she said, laughing.

"They had to sit still for quite a while to get those pictures taken," Dustin said. "And they didn't like to waste film. Today, people take hundreds, even thousands, of digital photos, knowing they can delete the ones they don't like. Back then, film and picture development were expensive. They didn't trivialize it."

"You're right. It just makes me wonder what they were like and how they lived."

Engrossed by the pictures, she tried to piece together her grandmother's past. "Hmm. All of a sudden, there seems to be a new man showing up in the pictures. I wonder who he is."

Emily glanced over her shoulder to see why Dustin hadn't responded to her comment. The room was empty. She set aside the album and went to the kitchen in search of her houseguest. The screen of his laptop was the solitary light in the room, and it accentuated the expression of concentration on his face.

"Both of you were bored by my company?" Emily nodded at Max, sound asleep at Dustin's feet.

"I thought I'd get some other stuff done. You didn't even notice I was gone, so you didn't need me there."

"You're working on your book?"

He closed his laptop as Emily circled behind him.

"Why can't I see it?" she said.

"No one will see it until I'm ready. Did you find anything interesting?"

"A new man turned up, but she didn't write any names on the back. She wasn't consistent."

"He doesn't look familiar to you?" He swiveled to face her.

"Not really. The images are grainy. It's difficult to recognize him from one photo to the next."

"Don't worry. We'll figure it out."

Emily plopped onto the chair across from him and leaned her elbows on the table.

"Why are you doing this, Dustin? I mean, what's in this for you?"

He shrugged. "Nothing, I guess. Maybe I just find it interesting and challenging. I always loved mysteries, and I don't want to stand by and do nothing while someone is threatened."

"So, it's a combination of curiosity and heightened protective instincts?"

He snorted out a laugh. "Yeah, I guess you could sum it up that way."

"It seems like an awful lot to do for someone who's basically a stranger to you."

"I suppose, but there are a lot of things you don't know about me. And one of those things is I like helping strangers."

"Funny, that's not the impression I first had of you." She leaned back in the chair.

"First impressions are useless."

"Are you saying you used to be a Good Samaritan?" she said.

He laughed out loud. "I wouldn't put it quite that way."

"How would you put it?"

He leaned toward her, a smile on his face. "I'd say I have my reasons for wanting to help you, and I don't need to share them with you."

CHAPTER 28

Emily sat upright so quickly tea sloshed over the side of her mug.

"Dustin, come here!"

"What is it?" He appeared beside her. His head pivoted from side to side, searching the room.

"Listen to this," she said.

I've had the most horrible experience, something I never would have imagined in my beautiful town of Clear Point. It's been more than twenty-four hours since it happened, but my hands have just now stopped trembling, allowing me to write.

I went for my usual walk on the beach last night, just after dinnertime. I was walking through the narrow section when someone jumped out of the bushes and knocked me down. He put his hands around my throat and tried to strangle me! I couldn't believe it. Someone tried to kill me. I didn't recognize him. He was dressed entirely in black with a covering over his face. I struggled, of course, but he was much stronger than me, and his hands were so tight around my throat I lost consciousness. My last thought was of my parents. I was sure I would never see them again.

Obviously, I survived, but that brings me to the next horrible part of my story. Someone came along and saw what was happening. She tried to intervene, to save me. And she was killed. Yes, murdered by the same man who tried to kill me. I feel terrible. That poor woman is dead because she saved my life. How horrible it must be for her family. I'm sure they don't think it's a fair trade. They would rather I be dead, and her alive. I don't blame them for feeling that way.

Emily's voice was low and breathless as she read the passage written by her grandparent. She turned to Dustin with wide eyes.

"Your grandmother wrote that?" He lowered himself into the armchair across from her.

"Yes. It turns out not only did she know about the murder, but she was involved, the same way I was."

"Elizabeth Wheaton."

"Betty is short for Elizabeth. It never dawned on me. And Wheaton must've been her maiden name. I never knew what it was." Emily glanced at the clock. "I could call my dad to ask him. What kind of coincidence is that? That I lived through something so similar?"

Dustin remained silent as she grabbed the handset.

"Hey Dad, how's it going?"

They chatted for a few minutes before Emily got to the point.

"I have a question for you. I went through Gran's stuff, and I realize I never knew her maiden name. Do you know what it was?"

Emily's gaze met Dustin's as she listened to her father on the other end of the line.

She said her goodbyes and hung up the phone, her mind reeling. Her own grandmother had been the mysterious victim so long ago, and Emily had relived her experience sixty years later. She lifted her head to see Dustin looking at her with raised brows.

"She was the one," she said. "I have trouble believing it."

"Are you sure?" It was obvious he was struck by the same problem. "Maybe this is someone else's diary."

"Elizabeth Wheaton. That was my grandmother's name. Back in 1959, this woman was twenty-five years old, and that would coincide with Gran's age. How can this be? It's like history repeating itself."

"It's definitely weird." Dustin stared across the room, his eyes unfocused.

"I can't wrap my mind around it."

"The good news is we have more information now. And we have better access to people in the know," Dustin said.

"What are you talking about?"

"It's your family." He turned to her. "There's got to be someone who can tell us more."

"I suppose there's my dad, but he came into the picture long after any of this took place. Besides, we already spoke to him about it, and he didn't seem to know much more than the fact it had happened and my grandmother didn't like to talk about it," she said. "I assumed it was because of the trauma of having a murder happen so close to her. I never imagined she was one of the victims."

Emily shook her head and ran her fingers through her hair. "I can't believe I didn't know anything about it. Surely, it would've come up at the dinner table at some point. 'Oh, by the way, did I mention your grandmother was involved in a murder in Clear Point years ago?', or something along those lines."

"Maybe they were all as clueless as you were. This happened before your grandmother married. Maybe she never shared it with anyone."

"That's got to be it." Emily chewed on her lip and wondered what the next step should be.

"Let's go over the facts. Your grandmother was born here, in Clear Point."

"Yes, and she grew up here. She left and moved to Kamloops after she got married."

Emily paced the floor as she talked until she couldn't stand the confines of the room any longer. In the kitchen, she pulled two mugs out of the cupboard and measured green tea leaves into strainers. Her mind whirled with so many thoughts she didn't realize what she had done until she set a cup of hot tea on the table in front of Dustin.

"I'm sorry. Did you want a tea?" she said.

He shrugged and sniffed at the concoction before he took a small sip.

"I guess there's a first time for everything," he mumbled.

"This is too weird. Don't you think it's weird my own grandmother lived through the same experience I did?"

"Yes, I do."

"It's a coincidence, don't you think?" she said. She grabbed a damp dishcloth and scrubbed the already-clean counters.

"I suppose it is."

"You don't sound sure. What else could it be, other than a coincidence? Planned? How could that be? How could someone plan two events sixty years apart?"

"Why don't you sit down, and we'll go over the facts? I brought out the file..."

"I can't sit down. I just...I don't know what to do...I don't understand."

Emily filled the kettle and put it on the stove before she removed a mug from the cupboard. Dustin shook his head as he turned off the stove and took her by the arm.

"Come sit down. Your tea is here." He pulled out her chair. "Emily, if it's any consolation, I think it has to be a coincidence. It can't be anything else."

"Okay, so it's a coincidence it was my grandmother, but something tells me the two murders are connected."

"Explain," he said.

"I can't. I just don't know. It's nothing specific; it's an impression I have," she said as she resumed her pacing.

"Okay, we can start with an impression, but then we're going to have to find something more concrete."

"Like what?" She swiveled to face him.

"I don't know. How about I start with questions and we'll see where they lead?"

"Good plan." Emily sat on the edge of a kitchen chair facing Dustin, her hands clasped between her knees. "Okay, shoot."

"When did your grandmother pass away?"

"She died when I was twenty-seven."

"You spend a lot of time with her?"

"Yes, we spent our summers here at Clear Point, and she would come and stay with us. I didn't see her as much once I started university."

"Did she talk to you about her life here as a younger woman?"

Emily stared out the window, the blossoms on the fruit trees in front of her eyes, but summer days spent with her friends filled her vision, her grandmother in the background, handing out lemonade and snacks.

"Sometimes, but only happy things. She never mentioned anything about a murder, that's for sure."

"Did she explain why she moved away from Clear Point?"

"She said it was because she got married, and her husband worked in Kamloops."

She stared at Dustin while he sipped his tea. After a few moments, he lifted his head and looked at her. "I'm at a loss right now. I don't know where else to go with this," he said.

Emily jumped to her feet and went to stand in front of the window. When she switched on the kettle again, Dustin spoke up. "You should maybe think about going decaf."

"I'm fine. I have to figure this out. I have to come up with a plan. There's a connection, I'm sure of it."

"Possibly."

"If I solve the crime from sixty years ago, I'll know who's responsible for this murder."

"How can you be so sure?"

"I don't know." Emily gazed at him without seeing him. "I just am."

"Then we have to start with your grandmother or people who are still alive who were acquainted with her."

"You're right. There's got to be someone we can talk to," Emily said.

"What about your mother's family? Did she have any brothers or sisters?"

"No, she was an only child."

"It seems strange something so dramatic could happen in your grandmother's life, and no one talked about it."

Emily's laugh was laced with bitterness. "Not in my family. The goal seemed to be to protect the children from drama at all costs."

At the window, Emily cleared her throat twice to remove the lump. Yet, she heard the tears in her voice when she spoke again.

"Her hair was gone, and she'd lost so much weight. It killed me to see her like that. She insisted she'd beat it, and she'd be fine." Emily bowed her head. "I should've known she was lying. I went back to university. She died three months later. I only saw her a couple of times before she died.

"My dad said they didn't want us to worry. They wanted us to concentrate on our studies, and they didn't want to fill our young minds with negative thoughts. So, you see," she said, turning to face Dustin, "we were protected from all the bad things."

"They loved you."

"Yes, but shit happens in life, and if you're always protected from it, it becomes hard to deal with on your own when it hits the fan. Sometimes, you have to learn how to deal."

"Good point."

"The real point is I need to find someone who can help me." She shoved painful memories aside. "And the sole person I can think of at this point is Rob's grandfather. He was in charge of the case at the time."

"That's a good call. I'll go with you."

"Are you sure? I'm taking up a lot of your time. You could be working instead."

"Exactly. And what kind of fun is that?"

CHAPTER 29

Fred Abbott, the ex-police officer, lived in a retirement community in Nanaimo. Now eighty-eight years old, he had left Clear Point almost twenty-five years earlier. Despite his age, he seemed to be in good physical shape – he had just returned from eighteen holes of golf – and his mental acuity was still sharp. He remembered the case well and recognized Emily right away.

"You look exactly like her," he said. "She was a beauty."

"My grandmother?"

"Oh yes, a lot of men had their eye on her, me being no exception. Unfortunately, she was lured away by a landlubber."

He eyed Dustin with suspicion as if to gauge how well he would survive on the open seas.

"You were a police officer at the time of the murder in which my grandmother was involved?"

"I was. You have to understand we'd never had a murder in Clear Point, or anywhere within hundreds of miles of us. And I never had one since. It was special, all right."

"Can you tell us more about it?"

"Your grandmother, Betty, was walking on the beach, as she did most evenings, and someone leaped out of the bushes and tried to strangle her to death. Luckily for her, someone came along. Unluckily for that woman, she was killed in the process. Now I heard it's happened again. The damnedest thing," he said, shaking his head.

"I read the police report from my grandmother's day, but it wasn't conclusive."

"That's because we never reached a conclusion with that case. I'll tell you though," he said, wagging a finger at Emily. "I never gave up. Even after they told me to move on, I kept plugging away at it whenever I could. It was a big thing for me. It was the one and only murder case I'd ever worked on. The problem was we couldn't make anything stick. We didn't have the fancy things they have now, DNA analysis and stuff. Although, from what Rob told me, it doesn't seem like it's getting them much further with this case."

Dustin leaned forward and drew the man's attention from Emily. "When you say you couldn't get it to stick, does that mean you had a suspect, but you couldn't prove it?"

"I wouldn't go so far as to say we had a suspect, but we had a suspicion, and your grandmother did too." He nodded at Emily.

"Who was it? Who did you suspect?" She moved to the edge of her seat.

"It wasn't so much a 'who' rather than a 'what.' I'm sure you know Clear Point is not as white as the driven snow. Like it or not, it's in a prime spot for smuggling. It has been for a long time. It's been used for bringing in everything from bootleg liquor to drugs to illegal immigrants. But, back in those days, we went through a rash of weapons smuggling. The ocean liners brought them over from Asia, and they were offloaded in the middle of the night onto smaller fishing boats. They were brought through Clear Point to hit the mainland, avoiding customs inspectors and coast guards. Now, they tend to use the seaplanes for their activities.

"We had the damnedest time catching them. They were smart, and they were sneaky, but we knew they were there. We broke up the ring, after the murder, and after your grandmother left the island. I suspected they were involved in the killing somehow, but I couldn't prove anything."

"Did my grandmother suspect the same?"

"I don't know. She was close-lipped about it all. She up and left pretty fast. One day, she was there and the next, she was gone. Then, I heard she'd married some guy from Kamloops."

Emily's brow creased. She found it difficult to reconcile this mysterious, spontaneous Elizabeth with the quiet, reserved woman she had known for the first part of her life.

"You never heard from her since?" Dustin asked the retired cop.

"I contacted her once to see how she was, and I have to admit, to see if she had found anything interesting about the case. She said she'd forgotten all about it. It was in her past, and it was going to stay there."

"How bizarre," Emily said. "I don't think I'll ever be able to forget about it."

"To tell you the truth, young lady, I doubt your grandmother did either. For some reason, she was scared." He stared at her for a moment before he continued. "You know, you remind me a lot of her, and I don't mean just your looks. She had that gleam in her eye too. She wasn't going to back down. But, for some reason, she did."

•   •   •

The drive back to Clear Point from Nanaimo, a two-hour trip on the narrow, winding road, began in silence. Emily always enjoyed the scenic drive, but, today, her thoughts churned along with her stomach. It seemed like her entire childhood had been a farce.

The memories of the good times they'd had during her summers on Vancouver Island were now clouded with visions of a murder and her grandmother's involvement. *Why did Betty Wheaton give up the search for the killer? Was she implicated somehow? Had she been blackmailed into silence? What about Emily's grandfather? She remembered him well. He had been a warm, loving person, at least in her young eyes. Had he somehow threatened her grandmother and forced her to marry him?* So many questions ran through her mind, and she had no answers for any of them.

Emily slouched on the passenger side of the truck, hardly aware someone sat in the driver's seat beside her. A throat-clearing startled her. She turned her head to see Dustin sneak a glance at her.

"You've had enough time to gather your thoughts. What do you think?" he said.

"My thoughts are all over the place on this one. It's as if someone told me pigs had wings."

"What bothers you the most?"

"So many things. My grandmother being tangled up in that murder, as I am with this one. The fact she tried to solve it, as I have this one. The fact she left Clear Point without any real explanation..."

"I know what you're thinking, but it doesn't mean it's going to happen. And, if you want to think that way, you can consider your grandmother lived a long and happy life after she left Clear Point."

"She lived a long life, but was it happy?"

"That's what we have to find out."

Emily shifted sideways and focused on Dustin's profile. "You keep saying 'we.' Why are you doing this? Why are you helping me? You've never given me a straight answer to that question."

"Why not? It's stimulating. I want to be a hotshot detective," he said with a grin.

"Hotshot? It's yet to be seen if either of us are hotshots, but you must have better things to do with your time than follow me around the west coast talking to people."

"I can take a bit of time off from my work."

"Your writing?"

"Yep."

"You have no other motive?"

"Nope."

"All right, Hotshot, share your thoughts with me." She leaned back and crossed her arms.

"I think your grandmother knew a lot more than she told people. I think she hid something; I don't know what. I think she left with her secret and never revealed it to anyone."

"Do you think my grandfather was involved in the murder and forced her to marry him?"

"That's an interesting theory. No, it hadn't occurred to me. I suppose it's possible, but you're the best person to answer that question. You knew them. What were they like together?"

"They were like an old married couple. They seemed content with each other...no, more than content. They seemed to love each other. But after today, I wonder how much real, and how much was staged."

"Your father may be able to help us answer that question, or if not, he might know someone else who can."

"I'll go down on the weekend."

"Fine. I'll book a hotel."

"You're coming with me?" she said, her eyes wide.

"Hotshot, remember?"

"It's not necessary..."

"I know it's not, but I'm coming with you anyway."

Chapter 30

"I need a break." Emily set down the journal and stretched her arms above her head. She glanced over at Dustin, his concentration trained on his computer screen. "What are you doing?"

"Working."

"On what?"

"I'm writing. Stop being so nosy."

Emily circled behind him and gazed over his shoulder. He lowered the screen on the laptop.

"Oh no, you don't. It seems to me I already told you no one reads my writing until it's finished."

"I could be a great sounding board for you. I could read through it, tell you how it sounds."

"In other words, you want to be a beta reader."

"Sure, if that's what it's called, I'll do it."

"That's what it's called, and you're not going to do it."

"You're no fun." Emily threw herself into a chair. "Let's get out of here for a while. I need to move around."

"Where do you want to go?"

"We could go to the ridge, hike along the trail. It's a beautiful day. We shouldn't waste it. The diary and the computer will be here when we get back," she said.

"Sounds good." Dustin shoved back his chair.

Emily tugged on her sneakers and glanced at Max, who returned her look with a question in his eyes. "I think you should sit this one out, old boy. It'll be too long for you to handle."

The dog lowered his head onto his paws. He didn't seem disappointed to be left behind.

The drive to the trail took ten minutes, and Emily smiled as they pulled off the road to park. This was her favorite spot for hiking. It lay on a peninsula with a steep climb to the peak. The view from the top always took her breath away, but the route to get there provided some stiff competition in terms of superb views.

"Have you been here before?" she asked Dustin as they ventured onto the trail.

"A few times. It's got some nice challenges."

The first section of the trail was effortless and allowed them to enjoy the sights and sounds of the ocean not so far below them. As the degree of the slope increased, the trail zigzagged through the wooded areas, often winding into the open to show off the ocean vistas. Emily led the way, while Dustin followed behind, his hiking boots crunching the gravel underfoot.

They exchanged greetings with people they came across. Some made the return journey, while a few passed them as they jogged toward the summit. Emily was content to keep a steady walking pace, preferring to jog on flat, smooth terrain. She breathed the fresh mountain air, and the tension eased from her body with each step she took.

As she negotiated around a sharp corner, she glanced over her shoulder to discover Dustin was out of her sight; they were separated by a dense growth of trees. Emily barely had time to register that fact before she lay flat on the ground. A heavy human weight bore down on her back, knees crushing her ribs. A leather-gloved hand shoved her face into the damp moss beneath her.

Emily struggled and managed to lift her head enough to inhale a breath of air before her face was forced downward again. The person was strong. She knew she wouldn't be able to fight him much longer. Her right hand brushed against something that felt like a branch. She wrapped her fingers around it and thrust it blindly at the person on her back. A grunt of pain told her she had made contact. She stabbed again, certain the branch would soon be ripped from her grasp.

The weight left her. She heard something crash through the woods, seemingly running away. Emily shoved herself up onto her elbows and gulped in much-needed air. She heard voices come from two directions. In front of her, several young chattering voices approached, and from behind, she heard Dustin call her name.

They all arrived in the clearing at the same time. The three teenage girls were silenced by the sight of a woman picking herself up out of the dirt. The man rushing up to her in concern added to the mysterious sight.

"Emily! Are you all right? What happened?" Dustin said as he fell to his knees beside her.

"Where were you?" She turned to face him and gasped in shock. "What happened to you?"

A streak of red ran down his cheek from a small gash beside his eye.

"Somebody took me out back there?" He waved toward the trail. "Pitched me over the bank. Are you hurt?"

"I don't think so, but someone tried."

The three girls eased their way around the couple.

"Do you guys need help?" one of them asked, lagging behind.

"No, thanks. We're okay, but you girls should be careful. Stick together," Dustin said.

Emily drew her legs up, wrapped her arms around her knees, and tried to still the trembling of her limbs. Her breath came in short bursts. She couldn't seem to fill her lungs.

"You're in shock." Dustin rubbed her back. "It's okay. Take your time."

"It was horrible. I thought I was going to die," she said, her voice cracking.

"I know."

"Who was he? Where did he go? Did you see anyone? I'm pretty sure he ran in your direction." She looked at him with tear-filled eyes.

"I didn't see anyone. Did you get a good look at him?" he said, his eyes narrowed.

"No, nothing at all. I couldn't."

He wiped dirt from her face. "You may have a bit of bruising."

"I don't care. I'm lucky to be alive. Besides, you won't look so good, either," she said, eyeing the cut on his face. Her gaze met his. "It was him, wasn't it?"

"I would think so. Who else would be after you?"

"No one." Emily rubbed her arms. "I'm scared, Dustin."

"I know. We have to find out who's behind this. C'mon, let's get out of here." He grabbed her elbow and helped her to her feet.

There was no question of continuing to the top. They descended the trail to the truck, the beautiful views ignored. Emily's mind raced, wondering who had attacked her, what she was going to do, and who she could turn to for help.

• • •

"I tell you; it was deliberate. Someone took this very seriously, much more seriously than you are."

"Ms. Burton, I can assure you we consider this an important case. We're in contact with Ted Bowen every day. We're working hard on this investigation," Inspector Wallace said.

"How can you be working on it when you're not even here? You're sitting in an office in Vancouver."

Emily stood in her living room with the phone pressed to her ear. She imagined the tall, thin man as he admired his view of the Vancouver skyline from his air-conditioned office, his suit rumpled and his tie askew.

"We've shared files back and forth between Clear Point and Vancouver. Don't worry. We're on it."

Emily huffed out a breath and braced herself for her next question. "Did you talk to Alan?"

"We did."

"And?" She wanted him to say Alan had a perfect alibi and would never consider harming his ex-wife.

"He hasn't been ruled out yet."

"He hasn't? He didn't have an alibi?"

"We're still checking it out."

Emily didn't like something about his tone. "I hope you're being honest with me. I need to know what's going on."

"Look, I know you're frustrated, and you're scared. You're doing the right thing by never being alone, keeping your doors locked, and being vigilant. However, after this latest attack, I'd suggest you leave town. Go stay at your sister's house or with your father. It'll give us time to move further along with the case."

"But I've also moved along with the case. I told you everything I found out about my grandmother."

"Yes, and it's fascinating, but I don't see the correlation between the two cases, not with a sixty-year interval. Humble agrees with me."

"But they're so much alike..."

"Granted, but criminals don't wait sixty years between crimes. It's impossible. The man we're searching for is young and in good shape. He's not in his eighties."

"I know that. I'm not stupid, but it can't be a coincidence either." Emily ran her hand through her hair.

"Yes, it can. I've seen coincidences before."

She closed her eyes and took a deep breath. "I guess we've hashed this over enough," she said. "We'll be in touch."

She hung up the phone and stared at Dustin. A sardonic smile played on his lips.

"Leave it to the Mounties," he said.

Emily stalked to the kitchen. He followed close behind.

"They won't even consider it," she said as she filled the kettle with water. "They treat me like a child. What am I going to do?"

"We keep doing what we're doing." Dustin leaned on the doorframe, his arms crossed over his chest. "We try to find the connection between your grandmother and you."

"What about this smuggling business?" Emily sat on a wooden chair and leaned forward with her hands clasped in front of her. "How likely do you think that is?"

"If you're asking me if I think it's still going on, the answer's yes. It could be more of a problem now than it was then. With time and technology, smugglers have gotten more inventive. It could be you got in the way of one of them, and he took you as a threat. And perhaps the same thing happened to Betty Wheaton."

"It's a bit of a stretch, isn't it?"

"A bit, but what else do we have?"

"Not much."

CHAPTER 31

Sleep is evasive. I'm told not to worry, that it was random, and there's no danger, but I can't help but worry. What if he's still here? What if he's watching me and waiting for another chance? I'm worried. My parents are worried. They watch me like hawks. I feel stifled.

Everything was a blank at first, but now little details are coming back to me. I have to speak to the authorities and bring them up to date. I don't know if I can help them, but I'm better to share what I know anyway, no matter how little it is.

I've lost my sense of security. I no longer go to the beach alone in the evenings, and it breaks my heart. It used to be one of the great pleasures of my day, listening to the waves and feeling the breeze toss my hair, the smell of salt heavy in the air. I curse the man who did this to me. All I can do is hope he will be brought to justice soon.

I even have trouble writing this diary, my thoughts scattered everywhere, floating like feathers disturbed by a breeze a second before they can settle to the ground. Is this going to be the portrait of the rest of my life? Will I have to leave this home I love so much?

"I could have written this. She's describing my feelings and emotions the same as I would have."

They were in Emily's living room, and she had narrated the passage from her grandmother's journal in a muted and mystified voice.

"It's eerie," Dustin said.

"There doesn't seem to be anything in here that gives us any clues. Yes, it's similar, but I don't know what we can do with it." Emily rubbed her hands over her face. Her sleep had been disturbed the previous night as she relived the attack on the trail. But she had woken up with fresh determination to get to the bottom of the cases.

"We have to figure out who the other people were, everyone who was involved. Then maybe we'll be able to find the connection. We need to delve into it more," Dustin said, his voice filled with intensity.

"How? We already googled it, and it didn't give us anything more than what we found in the police reports and in the journal."

"We have to talk to people who were around at that time. They'll be able to tell us things the police may not have known, or they didn't put into their report. And we have to finish reading this journal." His gaze followed her as she paced the living room.

"I have no problem reading the journal, but sixty years is a long time. A lot of people have moved on since then or died. We already spoke to Rob's grandfather. Who else could there be?"

"You're the one who knows everyone in Clear Point," he said. "You tell me."

"There aren't many left who were around then. I'll talk to Trevor. His family has been here for ages. He may know."

"Okay, you get on that. I'll do more web research," he said, as he left the room, presumably to find his laptop.

Under normal circumstances, Emily would have walked to Trevor's place but, with recent events, she decided to take the truck. She headed to the store and found him there.

He was partially hidden by a red and white surfboard he was showing to a customer, so she browsed the racks for a few minutes. A shiver ran through her at the sight of the wet suits lined up along one wall. She detoured around them.

"Hey, Em, nice to see you," Trevor said from behind her.

She turned with a smile and welcomed his hug.

"You want a coffee? Or, I have some kombucha in the fridge."

"That'd be great. I need something cold."

Trevor made a sign to one of his staff as he led Emily to the back room. She sank into a comfortable chair as her friend pulled two bottles of the brew out of a bar-sized fridge. The messy but homey-looking room was almost an extension of his living area, which was on the second floor of the building.

"Trev, your family has been a part of Clear Point for a long time. Do you remember anyone mentioning a murder sixty years ago?"

His brows drew together. "Sixty years ago? I thought this one was the first one ever?"

"Apparently not. Rob set me on the track. I spoke to his grandfather. There was one almost exactly like the one I witnessed. A woman was stabbed on the beach in the evening."

"You've got to be kidding me," he said, his eyes wide. "That's the first I ever heard of it."

Emily's shoulders drooped.

"I had hoped your grandfather would've told you about it. He didn't happen to keep a journal, did he?"

"Not that I know of. I could ask my dad. He may know something about it."

"How's he doing?" she said, referring to the man she remembered so well from her childhood, who now lived in an assisted-living residence.

"Okay, I guess. He has good days and bad days. The bad days are starting to take over a bit. I'll give him a call tonight, and see if he remembers anything, but I can't make any promises."

Emily knew Trevor's father was ill with emphysema, which slowly drained his life away. She wouldn't expect too much from Trevor's phone call to him, but anything, no matter how small, could help lead them to something else.

"I'd appreciate that. I'll check with Will too. His grandfather may have mentioned it to him."

Emily thanked him for the drink and gave him a hug and a promise to join the group of friends the following night at the pub.

Will was as easy to find as Trevor had been. He worked at the dock, elbow-deep in another motor that evidently needed repairs.

"Ah, you've come to save me from the tedium of the downside of fishing."

"Every job has a downside, Will." She laughed at his dramatic expression. She was thrilled to see the old Will had returned, apparently having gotten over his displeasure with her.

"Lately, this one has seen a lot of money going into repairs. That's why I'm trying to fix it myself."

"Are you going to win the battle?"

"I doubt it. Mechanical work was never my strong point. My grandfather, on the other hand, could take a motor apart, fix it, and put it back together with his eyes closed."

"Speaking of your grandfather, would he ever have mentioned anything about a murder that took place sixty years ago?" she said.

"A murder? No. What are you talking about?" He set down his wrench and focused his attention on her.

She glazed over the details of the crime that had uncannily similar circumstances to the present day killing, without mentioning her grandmother. Will's face was just as puzzled as Trevor's had been.

"Did he keep a diary?" she said.

"My grandad? Not that I know of, but I've got a box of things that belonged to my grandparents, so I'll check it out."

"That'd be great, Will," she said. The mention of a box reminded her of her grandmother's belongings, and her spirits lifted. "I appreciate it. I'll let you get back to work."

"Hey, I have an idea," Will said. "Maybe you and I could make a day trip to Victoria by boat. We could walk around downtown, have a nice dinner somewhere."

"That sounds like fun. But give me a bit of time to put this whole murder thing behind me. I'll be able to enjoy myself so much more."

"It's a deal," Will said with a wink.

He wrapped his arms around her and gave her a strong hug. A strange sensation swept through Emily, and she forced herself to return the hug. It was something that had never demanded any effort before.

She had always liked and trusted Will. She enjoyed his company, and when he had been angry with her, it had cut her to the bone. But now, for a reason she could not define, something had changed.

She tried to analyze their conversation and the things that weren't mentioned aloud. Nothing Will did or said made her suspicious, but for some reason, she couldn't bring herself to confide in him. She hadn't discussed the case with him, asked his opinion, or used him as a sounding board. Why was that? In the past, she wouldn't have hesitated.

Had this case made her distrustful of one of her best friends? Would she turn her back on all of them, one by one? Emily didn't know what was worse, living in fear for her life, or losing her best friends and living the rest of her life without them.

CHAPTER 32

Emily felt stifled, isolated, and restless. She didn't enjoy being forced to stay at home with the door locked and a personal bodyguard to protect her. Dustin had gone to his house to get some work done, something mysterious that required concentration and no distractions from Emily.

She, in the meantime, had a lot of painting to do. She fired up the kiln for a new batch of pottery and set to the task with little enthusiasm. She would have preferred to be outdoors. She wanted to hike in the mountains or run on the beach, but both of those activities had proven to be too dangerous of late. She was frustrated that her life was affected to the point she could no longer indulge in her favorite activities and she was a prisoner in her house. She had worked so hard to have an independent life.

Emily abandoned her pottery, knowing her level of creativity had dipped to a low point. Instead, she busied herself with the animals. Both the chicken coop and the goat pen needed to be cleaned. The goats were excited to see her and insisted on playing. She gave in to their demands if only for the distraction.

In the chicken coop, all the birds appeared healthy, except for one, who was a little more lethargic than usual. Emily took note to keep a closer eye on her.

Next, the vegetable garden required weeding. Her plants were coming along. She knew she would have plenty to both give away and preserve this year, something that made her content. Emily placed importance on sustainability.

And on self-preservation.

That was why she didn't give in to the temptation to go for a run on her own. The devil on her shoulder told her to do it, while the guardian angel buzzing around her head told her to stay put. She went with the angel this time. She didn't always do so.

At loose ends, Emily returned to the workshop. After an hour spent painting a difficult piece, she realized she had glanced at her watch at least ten times, willing it to move faster. She knew she wanted Dustin to come back, even if it was just to have a bit of company. Maybe she could convince him to go for a run with her, even though it wasn't his preferred form of exercise. But if she asked nicely enough, she thought, he might give in.

She wondered if she wanted his company for any other reason. Her first impression of him had been of a standoffish, almost rude person. He was undeniably reserved. He had wanted to keep his distance from her and perhaps from others also. His apparent about-face surprised her. *Why did he suddenly want to help her at every turn?* She didn't think he had developed an attraction for her. That wasn't a vibe she got from him, despite his occasional teasing. Yet there was...something. There was an elusive, evasive something. And maybe that something was what made her enjoy his company.

There was a lot about Dustin she didn't know, yet she had put her life in his hands. She trusted him, and she knew she needed to trust him. There were a lot of other people she had known longer and better, but for some reason, her neighbor inspired her to rely on him.

The sound of steps on the porch shook her out of her thoughts and made her pretend she worked hard on her latest creation.

"That's interesting," Dustin said.

"Oh, you're here. I didn't hear you come in. Do you like it?" She stepped back from her work.

"I guess, but what I find fascinating is how you're able to paint with the wrong end of the brush."

Emily glared at the errant brush and grimaced.

"It's a habit of mine," she said, her cheeks warm. "I twirl it around as I'm thinking."

She demonstrated by changing the position of the brush a few times until she fumbled and dropped it on the table.

"Hmm, the bizarre habits of creative people," he said.

"You must have some. You're an artist."

"Yeah. You wouldn't want to know what my habits are."

"Try me."

He shot her a smile and left the room without giving her an answer.

"Is drinking one of your creative habits?" she asked as she followed him to the kitchen.

His eyes narrowed as he glanced over his shoulder at her. "I've been good lately. You shouldn't get on my case."

"I'm not on your case. I just wondered. You seem to like to tie one on."

She leaned back in her chair and crossed her arms.

"I'm a big boy. I'm allowed."

"I didn't say you weren't. I wanted to know the reason for it."

"There doesn't always have to be a reason, you know. It could be just for the fun of it." He looked in the fridge, apparently trying to decide what snack he should choose.

"I never found it to be all that much fun," she said.

"We're different people. I don't get much of a kick out of running on a beach, but I don't bug you about it."

He twisted the cap off a large bottle of orange juice and poured himself a glass. He held the bottle up to Emily and offered her some.

She shook her head. "You're right. I won't mention it again...today."

They had taken to eating meals together, even though Dustin liked to grumble about her choices. She allowed him to bring some meat to cook for himself, but there were strict rules about not touching her food with the same spatula, pan, or plate that had touched the meat. She introduced him to quinoa, hemp hearts, and bean sprouts. She even sneaked a bit of tofu into his diet when he didn't pay attention.

"Dessert?" he said. "Wow, this is a special occasion."

"I had some time on my hands this afternoon and decided to make something light."

"Light? What do you mean by light?" He glared at her.

"There's no refined sugar or gluten."

"Oh." His expression reflected his disappointment. He gazed at the cookies like they were clumps of dirt. "They looked good for a minute."

"They are good. Try them. They're full of dates and seeds."

"Dates and seeds. Yeah, sounds great."

He opened his mouth to take a bite as Will stuck his head in the kitchen. The newcomer's smile slipped when he spotted Dustin.

"Oh sorry. I didn't mean to interrupt your dinner."

"Don't worry about it," Emily said, as she stood and offered him a chair. "We were just having a cookie. Would you like one?"

"No, thanks. I just wanted to make sure you were okay." He slid a glance toward Dustin, whose face remained poker-steady. Will turned his back to him and focused on Emily. "I haven't seen you for a couple of days. What have you been up to?"

"Working. I've been getting a lot done." She tried to keep her tone light. "That's one advantage of having to hide out; it gives me time to catch up."

Will faced Dustin, his shoulders braced.

"Are you living here now?"

"Most of the time, yeah. I go back and forth between here and my place, but it's a lot more fun here." He directed a leer at Emily.

Will's expression hardened, but he made a visible effort to cover it up with a brittle smile.

"I guess I'll be going then."

"There's no rush." Emily laid a hand on Will's arm. "How about a coffee?"

"No thanks. I got a few things to do tonight."

When the door slammed behind him, Emily glared at Dustin, her hands on her hips. "Did you have to do that?"

"Do what?"

"Make him uncomfortable like that?"

"We have to make people believe we're a couple."

"No, we don't. I can just tell them the truth. They're my friends."

"What if your friends are involved in the murder?"

Emily's eyes widened. "Are you crazy? None of my friends would murder anyone. That's absurd."

"Maybe they're not wittingly and directly involved. But what if they let something slip to the wrong person, a person who is involved?" He reached for another cookie.

"You're stretching now."

"You can't be too careful."

"I'm not happy with all this."

"That's obvious, and it's understandable, but ultimately we'll find out what's going on."

"What seems to be going on is someone is trying to eliminate me. For what reason, I don't know."

Silence fell between the two of them until Dustin broke it.

"If you want my opinion, the first attack against you could have been either random or targeted, depending on what we learn about your grandmother. I think the subsequent attempts were to eliminate a potential witness in the murder of Mr. Hart."

"Yes," Emily said, her voice low. "You're probably right."

• • •

Emily stood back to admire a bowl she had just created. As she wiped the clay off her hands, she heard the crunching of tires on the gravel in her driveway. The thud of a car door followed. Max responded with a loud bark and tore down the hallway with Emily following close behind. Dustin stood at the door when she reached it.

"Glad to see you're keeping it locked." He brushed past her.

"It's become a habit, unfortunately. I was going to make myself a cup of tea. Would you like one?"

As two mugs of chai tea steeped on the counter, the phone rang. Emily glanced at the call display.

"It's Lisa," she said. "I imagine she's looking for an update."

"Do you want me to leave you alone?"

"No, I have nothing to say that you can't hear." She leaned back in her chair and put the phone to her ear.

Emily told her sister about the attack on the hiking trail but dialed down the intensity to preserve her sister's sanity. She added a summary of their conversation with Rob's grandfather.

"So, you think this is all tied to our grandmother?" Lisa said, distress apparent in her voice.

"I don't know. It's far-fetched, but don't you think it's a hell of a coincidence?"

"It is, but what would be the connection? Whoever was involved in the first murder sixty years ago would have to be at the very least in their eighties by now. Do you think an eighty-year-old threw Dustin down a hill and wrestled you to the ground?"

"No, I don't. It can't be the same murderer, but somehow, someway, there's a connection. I want to find it."

"You think it's in the diary?"

"If it is, I haven't found it yet," Emily said.

"Maybe there are others."

"It's possible. I have no idea where to look. I don't have anything from Gran other than what Dad gave me, and I think if he had other boxes, he would've given them to me."

"You're right, but you can't give up. Why don't you follow up with Will's grandfather, and see if you can identify some of the other people in the pictures?"

"Don't worry, I will."

"So, tell me what's going on with Dustin."

"Going on? Nothing's going on," Emily said with a quick glance over her shoulder.

"A total stranger decides to take it upon himself to be your knight in shining armor, pretends to be your boyfriend, tries to help you solve the case, and nothing is going on?" Lisa didn't hide her incredulity.

"Put that way, I agree it sounds a little strange, but it's true."

"Why is he doing it then?"

Emily hesitated. *How many times had she asked herself the same question?*

She stood and strolled out of Dustin's earshot. "I don't know. I think he's just bored and looking for something to do."

"Yeah, right. I'm sure that's the answer. When do I get to meet him?"

"Whenever you make it out to see me, I guess."

"Why don't you come to visit me? You can stay a while. You'll be safe here."

"I'll be safe, but I'll be no closer to finding the person responsible. I have to stay here to do that."

"Here's an idea. Why don't you leave it up to the RCMP?"

"You don't have to be sarcastic. They're doing their thing, and I'm doing mine."

Emily knew the next time someone told her to hide out and leave the investigation to the RCMP she would scream.

"But they're the professionals," Lisa said. "They're trained for this kind of thing."

"I know," Emily countered as she gathered her patience. "I won't do anything dangerous. I'm just trying to collect information. Once I find something useful, I'll hand it over to them, and they can run with it."

"Promise me you'll stay safe."

"I promise. You don't have to worry about me."

"Okay. Now, let me talk to Dustin."

"What? Why?"

"I just want to introduce myself."

Emily hesitated. God knew what her sister would say to him. It could be embarrassing, but she also knew Lisa well enough to know she wouldn't give up. If she wanted to talk to Dustin, she would find a way to do it, whether Emily was around or not. Being here for damage control was a better option.

Dustin's brows furrowed when Emily handed the phone to him.

"My sister would like to talk to you."

He put the phone to his ear and greeted Lisa. He remained expressionless and silent for several moments before he grunted a goodbye and cut the connection.

"What did she say?" Emily asked.

"She instructed me to keep you safe."

"That's all?"

"And to not break your heart."

"Oh my God," Emily said with an eye-roll. "I'm sorry about that. Lisa tends to get a little dramatic."

"I hope it was a case of simple drama because I don't want to have my private parts cut off and fed to the goats."

Chapter 33

Emily did not need to feel the wind to know rough weather would soon be coming their way. The trees gave it away. The leaves had turned over as if trying to protect themselves from harm. And if that wasn't enough, she sensed the growing tension in Max, a master herald of storms.

She sat outside on the double swing with the black lab perched beside her. Normally, the dog would doze with his head in her lap, but he remained seated, his gaze fixed on the trees that separated them from the ocean, his entire body twitching. The sound of the waves crashing on the beach reached their ears, and Emily imagined the froth and foam as they rushed over the sand and the logs.

Emily enjoyed the coastal storms. She loved to hear and watch the waves beat with anger on the shoreline. She loved to tuck herself into her cozy, warm home, and listen to the wind and rain declare war on nature. It was part of her attraction to this area of the world. It could go from nature's paradise to nature's battlefield in a matter of minutes.

But Max was nervous of the storms, likely worried they would be blown away or swept out to sea. They would soon have to move indoors to make it through the evening without too much anxiety on his part, Emily thought. Before she could make that move, a strong tunnel of wind blew through the trees and bent most of the smaller ones almost sideways. She glanced at Max and saw his eyes widen with fear.

"C'mon, Max, let's get you inside so I can move the animals into the shelter."

The dog didn't need any further encouragement, following his mistress indoors with an unusual energy. Emily zipped up her jacket, pulled the hood over her head, and went back out to the goat enclosure. The animals were skittish and needed some corralling to get them into the small lean-to shed she had for their protection, but eventually it was done. The chickens had already moved to huddle inside their coops, but Emily secured the doors and removed all loose objects that could become dangerous projectiles in windy conditions. When she was sure everything possible was done, she made her way back to the house.

Emily stifled a laugh at the sight of Max huddled on the couch in the living room. The high winds, lightning flashes, and deep rumbles of thunder left him trembling. Emily had seen so many Clear Point storms they no longer bothered her.

Her thoughts turned to Lisa, who had inherited her fear of storms from their mother. As children, their parent would gather the family in the middle of the house, far away from any windows, and pray under her breath, clutching the girls close to her. Emily would always wriggle away to join her father at his spot on the porch. They would share the loveseat and enjoy the spectacle.

Emily joined her dog on the couch and hoped to take his mind off Mother Nature's stage play. When the lights flickered once, she didn't react. When they flickered again a moment later, she knew they were in for a blackout. She went in search of candles, matches, and a flashlight. They weren't far. It was a common occurrence to lose power in this area. The winds that came off the ocean were often strong, and the trees were abundant. Put the two together, and the power lines were often the victims.

She had no idea how long it would be off, but experience told her it could be anywhere from two hours to two days.

As the thought entered her mind a crack of thunder and lightning shook the house and doused it in darkness. She used her flashlight to find and light candles and set them in various corners of the room.

"Isn't that pretty? There's nothing nicer than candlelight."

Max gave his opinion with a drawn-out whine.

Tension filled the next half-hour. Emily tried to keep her pet calm, but the unrelenting howl of the wind and the continual flashes of lightning made her task almost impossible. Both of their heads swiveled to the left when they heard a loud crash come from outside. Her heart jumped. She recognized the source of the noise. She rushed to the door, grabbed her rain poncho, and slid her feet into tall waterproof boots.

Her left foot slipped as she took the first step off the porch, almost landing in the mud, but she caught the railing and righted herself. She didn't slow her pace. Instead, she fought against the wind for speed. It pushed her backward as the rain pelted her face and blinded her. Her route was memory-driven.

As she turned the corner of the house, her fears were confirmed. The goat shelter lay flat on the ground, the fence gaped open, and the goats were nowhere in sight. Emily moved her flashlight beam through the bushes and hoped to find animals seeking shelter under the branches.

Emily thought she spotted movement and pushed ahead, keeping her destination in sight. She raised her arms to protect herself from wildly swaying branches, but she still received a few stinging swats on her cheeks. There was no clear plan in her head about what she would do with the goats once they were found, but she had no intention of leaving them to fend for themselves in the storm.

Emily crept toward what she hoped was an animal when she was struck from behind. The blow glanced off the side of her head and hit her shoulder. Twisting to the right to see what had hit her, she lost her footing on the slippery ground. As she fell backward onto the rain-soaked earth, a flash lit the sky, and she witnessed the outline of a shape that loomed over her with a large branch in its hand.

Emily screamed and struggled to gain purchase with her heels to push herself out of harm's way. She didn't know when he would strike again. The darkness was complete. Her flashlight had fallen out of her reach, its beam pointed toward the trees.

She rolled to the right a split-second before she heard the branch hit the ground where her head had been. Scrambling onto her knees, she grasped for the flashlight. Emily was within a couple of inches of the grip when a foot descended on her wrist. She screamed again, this time in pain. Crazed barking came from the direction of the house. The sound was thrown in different directions by the equally crazy wind.

A body pushed Emily down into the dirt and straddled her back. A strong hand grabbed her ponytail and pulled her head back until she thought her neck would snap. Another hand wrapped around her throat. She was immobilized and at someone else's mercy.

Hooves pressed into her back at the same time as the attacker grunted in surprise. Words were unintelligible in the cacophony of the thunder and the pounding rain. She knew the goats bunted the person with their heads, and she hoped their little horns hit their mark. A struggle ensued between her attacker and the protective goats, freeing Emily's head.

Seconds later, the weight left her body, and she braced herself for another blow from behind. It never happened. Instead, two strong hands grabbed her arm.

"Emily! Are you all right?"

"Dustin?"

"What happened?" he shouted as he turned her over and shoved the goats out of the way.

"Where is he? Did you see him?"

Emily sat up and looked around her, but the force of the rain and wind blocked everything from view.

"Who?" Dustin said. "I didn't see anyone. I heard the goats and came over here to check on them. What happened to the shelter? Who did this?"

"It was probably him that did it."

"What? Let's get inside. I can barely hear you."

"I have to do something with the goats." Emily grabbed hold of his arm. She hated the thought of spending time outside while the attacker could be anywhere nearby but worry for her animals kept her from running into the house.

"I'll take care of them. You get inside, put on some dry clothes, and stay close to Max. I'll be there in a few minutes."

Emily didn't hesitate. She followed his instructions to the letter.

Wrapped in a warm sweater, she stood by the window and caught glimpses of Dustin as he persuaded the goats to follow him to the house. Once the animals were congregated on the porch, he put a ladder across the top of the stairs to keep them in.

"That's the best I can do for now. Hopefully, they'll stay there," he said as he entered the house and dripped water on the floor. He shrugged off his coat and hung it on a hook near the door, never taking his gaze off Emily.

She moved to the couch and wrapped her arms around a still-trembling Max. With the trauma of the attack in the forefront of her mind, the déjà vu of the heavy body on top of hers sent shivers down her spine. *How many times would she go through the same type of attack? Which time would be her last?*

"Where are you hurt?"

The light from the candles reflected in the raindrops that clung to his face as Dustin knelt in front of her.

"I'm okay. I don't have any serious injuries."

"Tell me what happened."

"You should get into dry clothes," she said, dazed.

"I'm fine. Tell me what happened." His tone didn't encourage light banter. Emily told him the details, her voice low and steady. She fought to keep her emotions under control and balanced on a thin rope that was strung between composure and hysteria.

Dustin stared at her with an unwavering intensity.

"I know what you're thinking," she said. "It was him. And you also think I should call the police, but that won't do any good. The cops won't come out here tonight. They're tied up with calls about the power lines, flooding, and God knows what else."

"I didn't know you were a mind-reader, along with everything else," Dustin said. "You're very calm."

"I'm far from calm. I'm terrified. But right now, I don't think it's productive to panic. Nothing else will happen tonight. You're here, and we'll be safe."

His lips twitched. "You've got a lot of confidence in me."

"Shouldn't I?"

His shoulders lifted in a shrug.

"I'm going to make some tea," she said. "Would you like some?"

"I'd prefer coffee. I'll come with you and give you a hand."

"That's not necessary. I can handle making coffee."

"I'll come with you."

Emily grabbed a candle to light the way to the kitchen and pulled a small camping stove out of a cupboard. While she filled a kettle with water, Dustin leaned on the counter next to her. "I'm only going to be able to make instant coffee with this," she said.

"That'll be fine."

"I don't know if you'll..."

"It'll be fine. Did you get a look at him?"

"No, it was too dark." Her hands trembled as she used a match to light the stove.

"How about his voice? Did you recognize it?"

"No, I don't think he said anything. What with the goats and the wind..."

"What's wrong with your arm? You're not using it."

"It hurts a little."

Dustin took hold of her forearm and pushed up the sleeve. Her wrist throbbed, red and swollen. "That's nasty. What did he do?"

"He stepped on it."

"It needs ice."

He prepared an ice pack while Emily waited for the water to boil. She sighed and leaned her forehead against the cupboard door.

"When will this be over?" she said with a sigh. "It's just one thing after another."

She straightened and turned toward Dustin. "Perhaps the RCMP are working on it, but if they are, they're secretive about it. Am I the only person who's interested in finding this guy? I can't give up. I can't go on like this anymore."

"Do you think you can catch a murderer? You're a potter, not a cop. You don't have the skills for that," Dustin said. "But, lucky for you, you have me."

Emily glared at him with a frown. "You're not a cop either. You write books on obscure topics. What do you have to bring to the table?"

"I have a few investigative talents from my days as a journalist."

"Ah yes, you were a crime reporter. But that didn't mean you solved crimes. You just wrote about them."

"I worked with the authorities on a lot of cases. I developed friendships with cops. Along the way, I picked up some knowledge of how they work."

"And you left all that behind to write about botany?"

"You have to admit it's different."

"This from the guy who has trouble eating a salad."

"It's not the same thing."

The wind howled around the house, not ready to settle down. Emily shivered, set the ice pack on the table, and wrapped her arms around herself.

"If I'm going to put my life in your hands, I'd appreciate complete honesty," she said to Dustin.

"You have it. I used to be a journalist in Calgary, and now I'm writing full-time. That's the truth."

"Writing full-time on what subject? We've already established it's not about holobionts. What are you keeping from me?"

"It's nothing for you to worry about. You're very suspicious, you know."

Emily snorted. Up until now, she had been an over-trusting person without a suspicious bone in her body. But too many terrible life experiences had piled up on her, throwing her nature into a state of flux.

Chapter 34

"Why don't you sit down? You'll drive me nuts with your pacing," Dustin said from his position on the couch. He soothed a nervous Max who was not getting the comfort he needed from his mistress.

"I can't. It's impossible to relax. Maybe Lisa's right. Maybe I should leave until it blows over."

The candles flickered as Emily stalked back and forth. The force of the wind had lessened, and the storm rumbled in the distance, but the electrical power had yet to return. It had been hours since the attack, and she had too much time on her hands. The never-ending series of attacks against her occupied her thoughts.

"How will it blow over?" Dustin said. "It'll end when the guy is caught. And I'm sorry, but I don't have a hell of a lot of confidence in Ted at this point."

"I know, but he's all we have."

"No, I already told you, you have me."

"Dustin, I appreciate all you've done to help, but at least Ted has some sort of training, and I know his heart is in it. If he needs help, he'll ask for it from the RCMP."

"Trust me."

"I do, strangely enough. But I think we've hit a dead-end. The diary hasn't told us anything to help us solve the mystery, and whoever is after me seems to be escalating. I'm a nervous wreck."

"The diary hasn't told us anything so far. It still may. And yes, he seems to be escalating. That's why we'll take extra precautions."

"Like what?"

"Like sharing the same bedroom, not just the same house."

"No way. I won't sleep with you."

"I promise to behave. You need round-the-clock protection, and I'll give it to you."

Emily put her hands on her hips and glared at him. She wasn't certain if he tried to ease the tension with levity or not, but she intended to rid him of the crazy idea outright. "You will not now, or ever, share my bedroom. Either you're satisfied with the guest room, or you can go back to your own house. Those are my conditions. Besides, I could ask Will or Trevor to help me," she said, lifting her chin.

"No."

"Why not?" She clenched her fists. "They're my friends. I've known them much longer than I have you."

"I don't care. They're not qualified."

"And you are?"

"Do they have a gun?"

"Of course not. They're not like that."

Dustin laughed. "And I'm 'like that'?"

"You're the one with a gun. None of my friends would even consider having one."

"Not even for hunting?"

"Definitely not for hunting. We don't understand the need to slaughter innocent, defenseless animals for no reason."

"It's a sport handed down by our forefathers."

"It'd only be considered a sport if the animals were also armed with weapons. Besides, our forefathers relied on hunting to feed themselves and their families. They didn't know any differently. You do, or at least you're supposed to."

"Spoken like a true vegetarian."

"Laugh if you like. You won't laugh when the planet is destroyed."

"I don't think eating a steak every once in a while, or the odd chicken, will destroy the planet."

"A lot you know," she said.

"Why don't we get back to the topic at hand, namely your protection?"

"How will you protect me around the clock? You have your work to do, and so do I."

"My work is portable. I'll continue to work from here. I should never have left you alone tonight. It won't happen again."

"We'll drive each other crazy."

"Finally, something we can agree on."

●　　　　　　●

The next day was literally the calm after the storm. The leaves on the trees remained still, and the sun thirstily dried up the puddles. Dustin and Emily worked together to repair the goat shelter. They also rebuilt the food trough, which had been broken in two. It took them most of the day to put everything to rights. Emily wondered why anyone would do something so destructive.

The next challenge was to herd the goats into the newly-repaired pen. They had enjoyed their stint on the porch and seemed to feel they had moved up in the world. But Max got the message across; they were not welcome in what he considered to be his territory, and the goats made it back to where they belonged.

Emily gathered fresh eggs for a lunchtime omelet, and they continued their reading of the diary. She had gone through most of the journal and had told Dustin about the more interesting sections.

"Apart from the fact it mirrors what happened to me almost exactly, there's not a lot in here that's helpful."

"I disagree."

"I'm so surprised. But, please, tell me what you disagree about."

He ignored her sarcasm. "Twice that I know of, she's mentioned someone who seems to show an interest in her."

"I didn't notice that," Emily said, sitting up straight.

"Go back a few pages."

Emily flipped through the pages, her brow furrowed.

"Give it to me." Dustin held out his hand. She handed him the book and watched him zero in on the passage. "Here it is."

I went to the grocery store today. They had just received some fresh tomatoes, celery, and carrots. I picked up some meat, having a real hunger for stew. I would make it as a surprise for my parents. He spoiled my excitement.

"I don't understand what you see there," Emily said.

"He spoiled her excitement."

"Yes, she probably meant her father. Maybe he was a grouch."

"You made an assumption there," he said, holding up his index finger. "That's not a good idea."

"You assumed it wasn't her father. It's the same thing."

"No. I've kept an open mind. Yes, it could be her father, or it could be another man who's bothered her. Besides..." He flipped through several more pages. "Listen to this."

I went out on the boat with my father today. I love to help with the catch. I don't do it often enough. The smell of the ocean and the salt and the fish, I think it's all a part of me too. It would be perfect except for him.

"I assumed…"

"You assumed it was her father," Dustin said.

"Right. So, if it isn't, then who could it be?"

"That's what we have to find out."

"How? It was so long ago."

"That's the challenging part. First, we have to read the diary with the assumption it isn't her father who disturbed her."

"I'm on it." She sat forward in her chair, and Dustin laid the book in her outstretched hand.

Emily started from the beginning and read her grandmother's diary again, searching for any references to an irritating person. She kept a pad of paper beside her elbow and noted any mention, no matter how small or insignificant it seemed. In the earlier part of her diary, it was clear her grandmother had fallen in love. She didn't name anyone specific but, from her account, the affection was reciprocated.

Emily thought the lucky man could be her grandfather but found it strange he hadn't been mentioned by name in the diary. *Was Betty afraid it would be discovered by her parents? Did she think they wouldn't approve of him?* It was likely. Emily had heard stories of people who eloped because their parents wouldn't allow them to marry.

On the other hand, maybe it was someone else, her first love perhaps. Near the end of the journal, her grandmother's feelings toward the unknown man seemed to change. And, after the attack, any and all references to men vanished, apart from the few where she seemed to be bothered by someone. Vanilla - the one term Emily could think of to describe her grandmother's writings after her attack. Plain old vanilla. That and 'constrained' would be another word. Perhaps it was the emotional distress that caused her musings to change from vibrant and emotional to contrived and bland. Or maybe it was fear.

It made Emily think deeper about her grandmother's feelings, and she wondered if her predecessor had known the man who had attacked her.

Chapter 35

Dustin worked on his computer in one room while Emily worked at her wheel in another. She couldn't see him, but she knew he was just a shout away.

Despite her troubles, or maybe because of them, creativity flowed from her hands and mind. She tried some new designs and experimented a little with more delicate items. She wouldn't know if she succeeded until the pieces were fired, but a desire to take a risk poked at her.

Hours passed. When her stomach rumbled, she glanced at her watch. It was well past time to think of preparing something for dinner. Her back cracked as she stretched and twisted, working out some of the kinks. She had been bent over too long.

Dustin was also hunched over his computer at the desk in her living room. He didn't seem to notice her arrival but continued to do whatever it was he did. Not wanting to disturb him, Emily slipped into the kitchen and pulled ingredients out of the fridge.

"What's up?"

She jumped and stifled a screech at the unexpected intrusion.

"Nervous, are we?" Dustin said.

"You don't have to sneak up on me."

"I didn't realize I was sneaking. I thought I was walking."

"Next time, please walk louder. And to answer your question, I'm making something to eat."

"I don't suppose you have any steak on hand, do you?" he said, his expression hopeful.

"No, I don't. I promise I'll pick some up tomorrow, but you'll have to cook it yourself. I won't be involved in that part."

"Sounds good. Tonight, we'll have rabbit food."

Emily made a face at him. She chopped vegetables and made no comment when he grabbed a knife to help her.

"What is that?" He pointed at a bowl of small, oval-shaped, green objects.

"Edamame."

"Never heard of it, but I'll give it a try."

A tinge of triumph boosted Emily's smile. "I'll convert you if it's the last thing I do."

"Don't count on it."

Despite his carnivorous nature, Dustin dug into his meal with gusto. Emily didn't dare comment on his enthusiasm, not wanting to spoil the moment.

"I'll check on the animals before it gets dark," Emily said as she set the dishes on the counter.

"Hang on. I'll take a quick look at your computer. Then I'll go with you."

Dustin had gotten into the habit of checking her e-mails every few hours.

"There's no need," she said, as he grabbed her laptop. "I'll be right outside the door."

'I'm going with you," he said in a voice that discouraged any argument. "Your memory is pretty short. He came here a couple of times, you know."

"Okay, I'll wait." Her shoulders slumped.

"Damn."

"What is it?"

"Another e-mail."

Emily's heartrate quickened as she peered over his shoulder and read the new message in her inbox.

You don't learn, do you? You keep prying. It's not going to get you anywhere, especially not with your new friend helping you. Get rid of him. You'll be safer in the long run.

"What does that mean?" Emily said.

"It doesn't make a lot of sense. How can you be safer without me around? You'd be alone and at his mercy."

"Just how he wants me to be." She ran her hands through her hair. "IHIT didn't have any luck with the other e-mail. This guy seems to know what he's doing."

"A techie surfer. Do you know any of those?"

She threw herself into an armchair, laid her head back, and closed her eyes. "Too many. Everybody under forty knows his or her way around a computer."

"Good. We've eliminated all non-surfers and people over forty."

She opened one eye to scrutinize him. "Are you being sarcastic?"

"Just a tad."

She shoved herself out of the chair, startling Max from his nap.

"I hate this." She wrung her hands. "I don't like being played with. I want to know who this guy is, and I want my life to return to normal."

"I'd like to tell you to be patient, but I know how you feel. Unfortunately, we have to work with what we have, and that's not very much."

CHAPTER 36

"I need to go into town to get some groceries."

Emily leaned against the doorframe of the kitchen. Dustin had claimed the room and one end of the table as his office and desk.

"All right. We can do that," he said.

"I also have to see Ted at the same time. I have to show him the e-mail I got last night."

"Yep, maybe by some miracle, he'll read it and know who the guy is."

"Has anyone ever told you you're snarky?"

"That's a new one. No, I haven't been told that."

"Consider it done."

Dustin stood and put his hands on his hips. He surveyed the crates stacked by the door. "I guess we'll stop by the shop too."

"No need to waste a trip."

"Absolutely not. And no need to waste an extra set of arms either."

"I thought of that," Emily said with a smile.

"Obviously."

The avid surfers and the early influx of tourists were not hindered by the overcast sky. People crowded the downtown area and filled the sidewalks and stores. Mary's shop was no exception. The owner waved Emily and Dustin toward the back room while she tended to customers. Within minutes, the two of them were outside, their first task completed.

They decided to leave the truck parked by the store, and they walked to the police station. Ted had just hung up his jacket when they knocked on his office door.

"Come on in. Have a seat," he said. "Dustin, it's good to see you're keeping an eye on Emily for us."

"Is this a good time, Ted?" Emily ignored his speculative stare.

"As good a time as any. I just got back from eating a big burger at The Joint. I should've walked back." He rubbed the stomach that protruded over his belt buckle.

"I wanted to let you know I've received another e-mail." Emily laid the printed copy in front of him. Ted reached for his eyeglasses and pulled the paper closer. "Hmm. Strange."

Emily and Dustin exchanged a glance. Dustin's look seemed to say, "I told you so."

"Any ideas, Chief?" Dustin turned his attention to the cop.

Ted stared over his glasses at the younger man. Their gazes held for several serious seconds. "There's not a lot there to jump out at me," Ted said. "Do you have any brilliant thoughts to share?"

"Nothing other than the obvious."

Ted sat back, crossed his arms, and looked at Dustin with lowered brows. "Which would be?"

"He's still here. He's still got some sort of obsession with Emily. And he's not going to let up."

"I agree all those things are possible. The hard part is figuring out who he is. We're doing everything we can."

"I know that," Emily said. "We just wanted to give you a copy of the e-mail to see if it would help in any way."

Ted looked at her and smiled. "Thank you for doing that, and if anything else comes in, or you have any other thoughts, don't hesitate to let me know."

"I'll do that." She stood and waited for Dustin to do the same. The two men glared and nodded at each other before they parted ways.

"I expected one of you to declare a shootout at high noon," Emily said, as soon as they stepped outside.

"Just wanted to let him know how I feel about their lack of progress."

"Oh, I think he knows how you feel."

"Emily, wait up."

They stopped and turned to see Doug jogging toward them.

"Hey, stranger," she said to her smiling friend.

"You're the stranger. We never see you anymore." He turned to Dustin. "I guess we can lay the blame for that at your door." Doug's smile didn't reach his eyes.

Dustin flung his arm around Emily's shoulders and grinned.

"Yeah, we've stayed in a lot."

Emily stiffened and shrugged off his hand.

"Doug, nothing is going on between Dustin and me." She knew she had opened a can of worms and could expect a frantic phone call or visit from Francie later that day. "He's just acting as my bodyguard."

This information earned glares in her direction from both men, but Doug responded first. "What about me? Or Will or Trevor? Why didn't you ask any of us? We're your friends. This guy's a stranger."

"It's because…"

"And why the big act? Why couldn't you have been upfront with me? With us?"

His expression was incredulous, and everything he said made sense. At a loss as to how to explain, it broke Emily's heart to see the hurt in her friend's eyes.

Dustin intervened. "It's my fault. I'm the one who wanted to keep it a secret and make it look like we're a couple." He held up his hand as Doug opened his mouth to comment. "And, the reason why she chose me is because I can work from anywhere, whereas you guys have businesses that require you to be somewhere else." He gestured toward the open water.

"We could take turns," Doug said.

Emily hid a smile. She knew her friend well enough to know he was coming around. The sulkiness in his voice reminded her of a little boy who had been mollified, and she felt a surge of relief.

"You're right," Dustin said. "Why don't you two work that out while I do a few things?"

He slapped Doug on the back, threw a smile in Emily's direction, and spun on his heel to head down the street. Emily watched him walk away and wondered what he was up to, but Doug distracted her.

"I mean it, Em. We could take turns staying with you," he said. "I don't know why you didn't say something in the first place. We all offered."

"You did, and I appreciate it, but at first I wanted to take care of myself. As time went on, and things became worse, I couldn't take a chance anymore. And Dustin insisted. It's worked out better than I expected. He does his work, I do mine, and we don't get in each other's way. I think that's best for now, rather than disturbing everyone and having the changing of the guard every few hours."

Doug's eyebrows furrowed.

"But I swear," she continued. "If I ever need anything or anyone, you'll be the first one I'll call."

"You know we care, don't you?"

"I know you're a great friend and I can always depend on you, on all of you. And yes, I know you care, just as I care about you."

She wrapped her arms around him and gave him a hug.

Chapter 37

"Doug, have you ever heard about seaplanes being used for smuggling operations in Clear Point?" Emily asked as she placed some tomatoes in her cart.

"Smuggling?" He picked up a butternut squash and tossed it between his hands. "What're you talking about?"

Doug had accompanied Emily to the grocery store and insisted on taking charge of the cart for her.

"Apparently, Clear Point is the ideal place for smuggling, and they use seaplanes these days," she said. "I thought, since you're a pilot, you would've heard about it."

"I don't know who's filled your head with crap like that, but they're dead wrong. If something like that was going on, I'd be the first one to hear about it." He put the squash, not too gently, back in the bin.

Emily had seemingly touched upon a sore spot, and she thought she might be better to bring it up with Francie instead. Wondering if there was more to the story than she had first suspected, she let it drop and changed the subject.

Fifteen minutes later, outside the store, their arms loaded with bags, they both turned at the sound of tires on gravel beside them.

"I've unlatched the back hatch. Just dump them in there," Dustin said through his lowered window. "Do you need a lift somewhere, Doug?"

The pilot declined Dustin's offer and set off toward the dock. Emily's gaze followed him. She felt as if, one by one, she had put roadblocks between herself and her friends. Her hope was that she would be able to tear them down, with a minimum of damage to their relationships.

•　•　•

It was late afternoon by the time they pulled into Emily's driveway. She craved a nice cup of green tea. It would give her a much-needed boost before getting back to work. She also needed to have a conversation with Dustin about the problems he had created with her friends. Her foot was on the first step of the porch stairs when her shirt was grabbed from behind.

"Wait a second," Dustin said when she yelped in protest. "Something doesn't look right."

That got her attention. Her gaze swung to her house.

"What do you mean?" she said, her voice breathless.

Dustin pointed at her front door. "I don't think it's fully closed."

Emily squinted. It was hard to tell from this distance, but she thought he could be right. He motioned for her to go back to the truck. She didn't argue with him. Within seconds, she sat in the driver's seat with the doors locked.

From her vantage point, she had an excellent view of the front door, but when Dustin opened it and disappeared from sight, she began to worry. *What if there was someone dangerous inside? What if Dustin was attacked and harmed? Should she call 9-1-1 right away to get help?* She wrapped her hand around her cellphone and decided to give it another minute. On the other hand, she thought, it would take Ted or one of his cohorts at least ten minutes to get here. By then, there could be all kinds of chaos.

Every second seemed like minutes as she waited until she couldn't wait any longer. She flipped the latch for the trunk and climbed out. In the back, she found a crowbar, slung it over her shoulder, and headed for the house. At the front door, she stopped and listened for a sound from inside. Silence reigned.

As she laid her hand on the doorknob, a loud crash sounded from inside the house. She gripped the crowbar with both hands and ran inside, not knowing what to expect, except it likely was not good.

The living area was clear, as was her view into the kitchen. When she heard a man's voice come from her workshop, she made her way in that direction, being sure to make as little noise as possible. She rounded the corner, and her heart crawled into her throat.

Dustin stood in the middle of her workroom with her fire poker in his hand. At his feet lay a pile of rubble. It contained the remains of her pottery wheel, topped with the crumbled pieces of her most recent work.

Emily was stunned. She couldn't speak, unable to wrap her head around what lay before her. Her precious wheel, a necessity for her livelihood, was destroyed, nothing more than scrap. Her bins of clay had been dumped all over the floor. The room resembled a war zone.

"It can be replaced," Dustin said quietly.

She lifted her gaze to his, her eyes filled with tears.

"What...why...I can't believe it."

"I know. It's awful, but you can get a new wheel. At least you weren't at home, and you weren't hurt. You have to look at it that way."

"Did you see anyone? I heard a crash."

"No, there was no one here. I caused the crash. That shelf hung by a thread, and when I opened the door, it fell down."

Emily glared at the offending shelf that now resided on the floor. It used to hold her bottles of paint, paintbrushes, and cleaning supplies, most of it now irrecoverable.

Emily had a sudden thought and pivoted to face the other side of the room. A breath of relief escaped her lungs. Her kiln remained intact. It hadn't been vandalized.

"I'll call Ted," Dustin said from behind her. She nodded, still having a difficult time comprehending what had happened. Someone had broken into her house while she was gone and wreaked havoc on her workshop. He hadn't been able to hurt her, so he went after something that was important to her, something that put food on the table.

The first flush of anger came upon her. *How dare he. How dare he invade her home and destroy her belongings.* She wanted nothing more than to get her hands on him and beat him senseless.

She heard Dustin outside the room. He told Ted about the latest development, but Emily knew it would achieve little. She doubted any evidence would be found amongst the mess of her broken pottery and tools.

She thought of how long it would take her to find another wheel. They weren't cheap. She would have to find a good second-hand one and hope for the best. She would also have to salvage as many of her tools as she could. The clay was a total loss. She would call her insurance company to see what they could do to help.

In her mind, the days loomed in front of her, filled with time wasted with insurance adjusters and salespeople, days in which she wouldn't be able to work. She straightened her shoulders. She had been through worse times. This too would pass, but it would be inconvenient.

Ted and his deputy pulled into her driveway ten minutes later. Their expressions were grim as they stood with their hands on their hips on the threshold of her workshop. Emily heard them grumble to each other before Ted turned to her.

"I'll contact IHIT. They'll get a team in here, and we'll do it up right," he said, shaking his head. "It's a real mess. I have to tell you again..."

"I know. Be careful. I'm doing everything I can. I'm never alone."

"You should get out of town," Ted added.

"And what if he follows me? Am I going to put Lisa or my father in danger? No, I'll stay here and help with the investigation the best I can."

"Now…"

"You don't have to say it." Emily held up a hand. "I won't do anything dangerous, and I'll leave the real investigating to the professionals. I know."

Those professionals arrived two hours later by helicopter. By the time they were finished their work, Emily's entire workshop, once again, had been turned upside down and covered in fingerprint powder, as was a good portion of the rest of her house, just in case.

Once everyone cleared out, Emily and Dustin began the long, slow process of cleaning up. A few minutes into it, their gazes met when they heard voices at the front door. Within seconds, four faces appeared in the doorway.

Francie, Doug, Trevor, and Will, each in turn, stepped up to give her a comforting hug. It brought tears to her eyes to have them show up, unasked, to help her. Especially with the way she had treated them of late, keeping secrets from them and putting her trust in a stranger. She had even suspected her best friend was the attacker, and a wave of guilt flooded her as Francie's arms wrapped her in an embrace.

They pitched in and made a noticeable effort to keep the atmosphere light. For the most part, their efforts were successful, until Emily would come across the remains of a piece of work she had been pleased with, or a tool that had been given to her by her mentor and was now in pieces. Sadness and grief would descend upon her again. She tried her best to hide her mood from her friends, but they weren't accustomed to seeing Emily as anything other than upbeat and optimistic.

It was mid-evening when someone mentioned food. Pizzas, both meat-lovers and vegetarian, were ordered, delivered, and consumed. Conveniently, someone had wine and beer in their car, and it became an accompaniment.

By midnight, everyone had left, and Emily and Dustin were alone.

"I'm exhausted," she said. "And I can't look at it anymore. Tomorrow's another day. I'm off to bed."

"Good plan. And Emily," he said, making her turn back to look at him. "We'll find this guy. I swear."

Chapter 38

Emily woke before six the next morning. Mental images of her ravaged workshop prevented her from going back to sleep. Before she ventured near the devastation, she sat at the kitchen table with a large mug of coffee and two pieces of toast and made a list of supplies that would need to be replaced.

She searched online for a new wheel and grimaced when she saw the cost of buying one and having it shipped across the island to Clear Point. She considered shipping it to her father's condo to be picked up there. She would have to come up with a plausible explanation for buying a new wheel, or her father would ask questions.

"Did you find the worm?"

Emily glanced up to see Dustin standing in the doorway.

"What?" she said, her mind elsewhere.

"The worm? You know, the thing the early bird finds?"

"Oh, no. There aren't any worms around this morning. I'm shopping for a wheel, but they cost more than I'd expected. I think I'll send it to Dad's place. I'll save a chunk of change on shipping."

"We can kill a few birds with one stone while we're in the city," Dustin said as he poured himself a coffee.

"What do you mean?"

"You can have a little visit with your father, and I'll drop in to see an old friend of mine."

"What are you up to?" she said, her eyes narrowed.

"Yesterday, when I left you with Doug, I went to visit the newspaper office. It's a small weekly, but they have records from sixty years ago. Their coverage of the murder back then was extensive, as you'd expect, but nothing that wasn't already covered in the police reports. What I found interesting was it had also been covered by an investigative journalist from Vancouver, and it just so happens I have a friend who works for the Vancouver Sun. I'll give him a call today and see when we can get together. We'll try to coincide it with the delivery of your wheel."

"Why do you think the Vancouver Sun would have more than anyone else?"

"I don't, but any journalist worth his salt would've taken a lot of notes. Maybe there's something in those notes that'll help us out, if they still exist. It's worth a try."

Emily shrugged and stood. "I'll get started in the workroom. There's an entire section I haven't touched yet."

"I'll drink my coffee and join you."

In the light of a new day, everything looked worse, despite the clean-up that had already been done. The dust had settled and turned everything a dull grey. Her friends had worked with care the previous day, sorting through the broken bits, and hoping there would be something salvageable, but Emily realized little of what was left in the room would be of use to her.

She stepped through the dust and shards of broken pottery to make her way to the opposite corner. A storage cabinet had been overturned and broken, and the contents had spilled onto the floor. Francie had cleaned up most of the debris, but the cabinet needed to be righted and perhaps repaired. It seemed to suffer from a broken leg.

"Let me help you with that."

Dustin took the brunt of the weight, and they propped the cabinet up with a box to replace the missing leg.

"Oh no. It's smashed," Emily said, pointing toward the corner.

The chest, which had survived at least sixty years, lay on the floor. The lid, crushed and split, revealed the carefully-preserved contents.

"Damn it," Emily said, kneeling beside it.

"Maybe I can fix it." Dustin lifted the box by the side handles.

"Wait." She put a restraining hand on his arm. "It's breaking apart."

The bottom of the chest fell onto the floor, along with two large brown envelopes. Emily stared at them, puzzled. She glanced up and saw Dustin peering in through the broken lid of the box with an equally puzzled expression.

"The chest is still full. That was a false bottom," he said.

Emily gathered the envelopes and hurried to the kitchen, upending one of them onto the table. Black-and-white photos slid out, and they were clearly old. The edges were yellowed, and on the back of some of them was faded writing. It was almost illegible, not only because of the fading but because the handwriting was difficult to read.

"This isn't my grandmother's handwriting," Emily said.

"No, it isn't. If I were to hedge a guess, I'd say it's a man's writing."

"Can you make out what it says?" She handed it to Dustin.

"It seems to be the name of someone, but it's hard to say." He squinted at it. "It could be the name of a place. Do you recognize anyone in the photo?"

"No. It's two men, that's all I can see."

They sifted through the rest of the pictures, not able to make out many words, but they recognized it as the same person's handwriting.

"What does this mean?" she said. "Why were they hidden in the bottom of the box?"

"I don't know. What's in the other one?"

Emily opened and emptied the other envelope.

"Letters."

At least a dozen of them littered the table.

"It's the same handwriting." Dustin unfolded one of the letters "Damn, how did anyone read this? The guy must've been a doctor."

"They won't be of much use to us if we can't read them."

"We'll find a way, don't worry."

"They must be important if she hid them like that," Emily said.

"Maybe. Or they could've belonged to whoever owned the chest before her. Maybe they have nothing to do with her."

"You're right. I shouldn't get my hopes up."

"Let's continue in the workroom for a while, and then we'll decide what to do with this stuff."

Over the next two hours, they worked side by side, but Emily's mind remained on the mysterious envelopes and their contents.

The workroom returned to an almost livable state, except the new state did not include her wheel, some of her tools, all of her finished products, and most of her clay. It was depressingly empty to Emily's eyes.

Over a lunch of quinoa salad, they discussed the next step.

"First, I have to order a wheel," Emily said.

"How long do you think it'll take to get it?"

"Online, it said they have them in stock. It'll be shipped from Toronto, so at least a few days before it arrives in Vancouver."

"Fine. You can let your dad know we'll be there, and it'll give me time to get in touch with my friend at the Sun. He may need a couple of days to find the information we need."

"What precisely are we looking for?" Emily set down her fork and focused on him.

"I'm leaning toward the smuggling theory. That's what was tossed around in 1959, although it was never proven."

"Are you suggesting my grandmother was involved in a smuggling operation and she was a criminal?" Emily said.

"I didn't suggest anything. She may have been in the wrong place at the wrong time, as you were. All I'm saying is they thought the person responsible for the attack at that time was a smuggler, and I think we should look into it."

"And you hope your friend will be able to find this other journalist's notes. What about the journalist himself? Is he around?"

"No. He passed away five years ago."

"I find it far-fetched," she said, shaking her head.

"It is far-fetched. I'll grant you that, but it's all we have. Either that or we sit here on our hands and wait for the RCMP to come up with something, or for the guy to try again to attack you."

"No, I don't want any hand-sitting." Emily thought of the destruction in her workroom. "Whoever it was did a number on my equipment. Is it just me or does he seem to be getting angrier?"

"He may be. Thank God you weren't around yesterday."

"He probably knew I wasn't home. That's why he did it."

"Or he thought you were home, and it made him furious to find you gone."

Emily hadn't thought of that.

"This isn't good," she said, her brow furrowed.

"I'll get on my computer and track down my contact at the Sun."

"I'll order my supplies."

CHAPTER 39

Three days later, they once again crossed the island to take the ferry to the mainland. Rain made the roads slick, and the fog hampered visibility. On the winding mountain roads, Dustin drove at a crawl in some sections, not able to see more than a few feet in front of him, whether it was another car, or wildlife choosing a bad time to cross the road.

They arrived as the ten o'clock ferry pulled away from the dock, leaving them to drink coffee in the terminal as they waited for the next departure an hour later. The bad weather and the delays made Emily antsy. She had more and more trouble finding her good humor these days. It hid away somewhere with her good luck.

On the ferry, she huddled on the top interior deck and listened to the rain pound on the windows. The coast was invisible under its shroud of fog. Emily found herself mesmerized by the sloshing of her coffee caused by the rockier-than-usual crossing.

She thought about her phone conversation with her father. She had explained her wheel needed repairs that were too costly for such an old piece of equipment, and she had decided to invest in a new one. He accepted her explanation, but she hoped he didn't ask her too many questions in person. She had a difficult time lying face-to-face.

"Who are you texting?" she said to Dustin, more to make conversation than out of curiosity.

"Jason, my friend in Vancouver. I want to let him know we're running late."

"Did he tell you what he'd found?" she said, her interest piqued.

"No, not specifically. He said he found the notes, but he didn't know if they'd help me or not."

"That doesn't sound promising."

"I'll decide when I see them. Jason doesn't know the whole story." He didn't take his eyes off his phone.

"Neither do we. Are you sure you don't want me to go with you?"

"There's no need. Stay with your dad and take advantage of the time you have to visit with him. Jason and I will do some catching up."

"You're enjoying this, aren't you?"

He glanced at her.

"Am I enjoying the fact there's a killer on the loose and you're the target? No. Do I enjoy getting into investigative mode? Yes, I guess I do."

"If you miss journalism, why don't you get back into it?"

"I may, at some point. I've got my project to finish first, and then I'll decide."

A tinny voice came over the intercom system to tell them they would soon dock in Horseshoe Bay, and all passengers should make their way to their vehicles. In short order, Emily and Dustin were on the highway, headed toward Vancouver.

The mainland was also encased in fog, and traffic crawled like a line of tortoises. The weather cleared as they drove into the southern region of the city, and by the time they reached Abbotsford, they donned their sunglasses to protect themselves from the glare of the sun.

As usual, her father was elated to see Emily, but he complained about Lisa never coming to visit. And as usual, Emily explained Lisa lived so much farther away, and she had children to raise.

"They delivered that thing," Harry said. "I had them put it in the storage room. It's big and heavy. How will you get it into your truck? I won't be able to help you."

"Dustin's with me. Between the two of us, we'll get it in."

"Oh, he's still in the picture, is he?" Her father's eyes lit up.

"There's no picture, Dad. He's just a friend. He had to see someone in Vancouver, so he came with me. That's all."

"I had a good feeling about him right from the start," he said with a knowing smile.

"There's no...oh, never mind. Tell me what's new with you."

Her father launched into a litany of the latest gossip in the residence, followed by comments on the general state of the world, the crime rate, and the quantity of illegal drugs on the streets of Vancouver.

Emily puttered around the kitchen and made herself an herbal tea from a stash she kept in her father's pantry. The coffeemaker brewed a cup for her father, and cookies sat on a plate for a snack. She had the perfect opening.

"Dad, did you ever hear anything about smuggling off the coast of the island?"

"Smuggling? Smuggling what?"

"Weapons or drugs."

"Well, I can't say I've heard anything lately, but that doesn't mean it doesn't exist."

"What about years ago? Like when Gran lived on the island?"

"Hmm. Well, of course, I wasn't very old at that point, but I do remember someone talked about it. Apparently, Clear Point had been a drop-off point for smugglers, until they were caught and had to find another place."

"How were they caught?"

"I seem to remember they had a snitch. Someone spied for the Mounties. I'm not sure if it was at the same time as your grandmother lived there."

Emily kept her back turned to her father. Her hand was suspended above her cup of tea. *Had her grandmother been the snitch? Was that why she was threatened? It was possible, but if that was the case, what did it have to do with herself sixty years later?*

"How's my coffee coming along?"

"It's ready."

"Why are you asking all these questions about smugglers?"

"I talked to Will's granddad the other day, and he brought up the subject. I was just curious." Emily's eyes were lowered, looking over the assortment of cookies. "So, did you hear about Lisa's kids and the chickenpox?"

An hour later, the doorbell rang, and Emily buzzed in Dustin. As he came through the doorway, they exchanged looks. She tried to read his expression to see if his visit had paid off, but his poker face was firmly in place.

Harry greeted Dustin like an old friend, and Emily knew her father wished this could be his future son-in-law. She hoped Dustin didn't pick up the same vibe.

Now that they were together, Emily was impatient for them to be on their way, but her father insisted they stay longer. She didn't have the heart to say no. He spent a lot of time alone and enjoyed her company so much a couple more hours wouldn't make a difference.

Emily wondered whose company her father enjoyed more, hers or Dustin's. Most of the time, she was ignored while Dustin discussed everything from sports to politics with her parent. It gave her time to mull over the fact her grandmother may have worked as an informant for the RCMP while she lived in Clear Point. Perhaps she had been discovered, and one of the smugglers tried to kill her but had failed and killed someone else instead. And maybe that's why she left the island. Her secret life had been discovered, and she was in danger. It all seemed plausible until you tried to find a connection to the present-day events.

"We should hit the road if we want to catch the six o'clock ferry."

Emily glanced at the clock and realized Dustin had a point. They didn't want to leave too late. It would be dark and foggy to cross the island, and those were never the best conditions.

Harry accompanied them to the storage unit and watched them load the wooden crate that held the pottery wheel into the back of the SUV. Emily gave her father a tight hug and promised another visit soon. Dustin received a firm handshake and a good-natured slap on the shoulder and was told to be sure to come with Emily the next time she came to Vancouver.

"You sure won him over," she said, once they were on the road.

"I'm a natural." Dustin flashed her with a wide grin.

"You weren't a natural with me when we first met."

"Are you implying I've now won you over too?"

"You wish. Just because my dad thinks you're God's gift, it doesn't mean everyone does. He's just an easy target."

"Don't get carried away with the compliments. I wouldn't want them to go to my head."

"Enough of this. I've been dying to know how it went with your contact."

"He gave me a pile of material to go through." He motioned with his head toward the back seat. Emily half-turned and saw a beat-up cardboard box.

"Is that full?"

"Yep. The guy was a big note-taker."

"Had your friend gone through it?"

"Quickly, but he didn't have time to do an extensive study. He said the journalist leaned toward the theory it all had to do with the smuggling operation, but we already knew it wasn't proven."

"I asked Dad about it."

Dustin glanced at her. "What did he say?"

"He remembered talk about Clear Point as a drop-off for smugglers. But there was an informant. They were caught and had to start up somewhere else."

"An informant? That's interesting."

"The more I think about it, the more it makes sense in a way. I mean, it makes sense for it to have been my grandmother at that time. But it doesn't make sense for it to be tied to me now."

"At least we can study it from a different angle. I think we have to take a closer look at those pictures and letters that were hidden in the chest."

They spoke little for the rest of the trip. Emily thought about the fact her grandmother could have been an informant and lived the rest of her life in fear of reprisals. *Why would she have agreed to it in the first place? Did she seek adventure? Was it a case of being bored in a quiet island town? Or had she been involved with the smugglers, or maybe one particular smuggler, and the police had approached her to work with them or face being prosecuted?*

Emily had read her grandmother's journal, and apart from the fact Betty had been deeply shaken by the attack, there had been nothing to indicate she had been involved in any other way. Surely, she would have mentioned it. It was her diary, after all. She used it to record all of her deepest thoughts and secrets. *Or had she worried about the journal being found and used to further incriminate her?*

There were too many possibilities, but Emily thought Dustin could be right. The photos and letters had to hold more information. They would have to dedicate more time to studying them.

The ferry ride was smooth, but the drive through the curving, mountainous pass was arduous. On the unlit road, hampered by the fog, hardly a word was spoken. When they reached the main road on the other side, the tension eased.

"Thank you, Dustin, for everything you did today," Emily said. "That was a lot to ask of you."

"You didn't ask. I volunteered, so don't mention it."

"I have to, especially when there's nothing in it for you."

"I already explained it to you. First, it interests me. Second and most importantly, I won't sit around while a woman is threatened. Enough said."

He returned his concentration to the road. They may have been out of the worst part, but the fog near the ocean, combined with the complete darkness, made driving difficult.

"I hope everything's okay at home," Emily said.

"If you think there may have been another break-in, look at it this way. He's already done enough damage. He knows that. I don't think he'll be back."

"I know, and the main thing is no one was hurt."

"Do you want to pick up Max tonight?" The dog had been left with Will for the day.

"It's late. I'll get him in the morning."

When they pulled into her driveway, Emily studied the outside of the house for a sign something wasn't right.

"Stay here," Dustin said. "I'll go have a look."

"Be careful."

"Don't worry," he said. He twisted around and removed a baseball bat from behind the seat.

Dustin circled the house and checked the doors and windows. He disappeared inside for a few minutes before he reappeared in the doorway. He waved at her, the bat hanging loosely by his side.

Emily climbed out of the truck and lifted the back hatch.

"You want to bring that in tonight?"

"I'd feel better if we got it safely inside," she said.

They decided it would be easier to dismantle the crate before taking the wheel inside. Dustin removed a crowbar from the hatch. Within a few minutes, pieces of wood were scattered on the ground, and Emily had her first view of her new wheel. Despite the darkness, she smiled in appreciation. She had loved her old equipment, but there was nothing like a shiny new apparatus.

With several grunts, a few swear words, and a stubbed toe, the two of them carried it up the steps onto the porch and maneuvered it through the doorway and into the workroom. Emily ran her hands over it, knowing it wouldn't stay shiny and clean for long. By tomorrow, it would be put to good use, and from then on, it would be splattered with clay.

She heard Dustin's footsteps behind her and turned to see him deposit the bucket of clay and the bag containing her new tools on the floor.

"A new beginning," he said.

"Yes, it is, at least as far as my pottery goes."

"It could be a new beginning for other things too, you know."

Emily looked at him. A wistfulness flickered deep inside her, and she sensed it showed in her eyes.

"I can't, Dustin. I just can't."

"You know it doesn't matter to me, don't you?"

"I can't," she said with more emphasis.

"I'm not him."

"I know you're not, but I'm still me, and I can't change the feelings I have. You have no idea how badly I was hurt."

"I think I do."

Chapter 40

"Do you like that one?"

"It's a bit girly for me. If I have to drink tea, why can't it be normal black tea?" Dustin's voice was sulky.

"Because I don't have any normal black tea. I'll make you a coffee. I just thought this would help you relax."

"I'm relaxed. I don't need this stuff."

Betty Wheaton's photo albums littered the kitchen table, along with the old black-and-white images and the letters that had been hidden in the bottom of the wooden chest. Note pads and magnifying glasses completed the ensemble.

The tea dispute out of the way, they got to work. Emily compared the photos from the chest with those in her grandmother's album. She also tried to decipher the words on the back of the photos. Dustin had the job of reading the letters and trying to make out as many words as possible.

"I'm not getting very far with these. I can decipher about three words per page," he said. "But I do have good news."

"What is it?" Emily set down the photo album and turned a wide-eyed gaze in his direction.

"The person who wrote the letters signed his or her name with their initials; LDJ."

"LDJ," Emily repeated. "So, the last name begins with J."

"Jones, James, Johnson...you know anybody?"

"I know a few, but they're not eighty years old. We're going to need more than that."

"You keep going through the pictures, and we'll keep it in mind."

Emily pored over the photos and tried to find a match between those that were found in the chest and those that had belonged to her grandmother. The grainy images weren't made any clearer by the magnifying glass, but she noted two of Betty's photos included a man who had a sharp resemblance to one of the men in the others.

"I think I've found someone," she said.

"Who?" Dustin leaned over her to look at the pictures spread on the table.

"That's the part that doesn't work out so well."

Even though her grandmother had written the names of the people on the back of her photos, there were a few other men in each one, and they would have to work through a process of elimination to do a proper match.

"It`s too bad we don't have someone who'd recognize these people."

"There's Rob's grandfather in Nanaimo," she said.

"That's a little far. There must be someone here."

"Will's grandfather is alive, but his memory is almost completely gone."

"It's worth a try to ask him." Dustin handed her the phone handset.

Emily heard the roar of the waves in the background when Will answered. She knew he would have a difficult time hearing her, so she kept it brief. He said he would set up a meeting for them with his grandfather, but he wasn't optimistic the old man would be able to help them.

The next morning, Emily and Dustin met Will in front of the small nursing home just outside of town.

"He has good days and bad, but even on a good day, he's at about fifty percent," he said.

"I understand," Emily said. "I know it's a long shot, but anything could help."

"Let me do the talking. Too many people and voices can confuse him even more."

Stuart McCade had been a tall, thin man in his youth, well over six feet tall. He stood before them now, stooped and unstable on his feet. Despite those problems, he seemed to like to walk. He walked around his room as if he would like to escape the strangers but was unsure how to do so.

Emily and Dustin sat in a corner and tried to fade into the woodwork, allowing Will to lead the conversation.

"Granddad." He took the older man's hand and guided him to a chair. "I have a couple of pictures to show you. I wondered if you could tell me who's in them."

The man's eyes lit up. "Oh, I'd like that."

His expression eager, he took the photos from Will. He held them close to his face and strained to make out the images.

"Well, will you look at that," he said.

"Do you know those people, Granddad?"

"Of course, I do. I'm not stupid, you know."

Emily smiled at Dustin, hope in her eyes.

"Who are they?" Will said with a sideways glance in their direction.

"There's Ricky, Toph, and Jack. And that's Loot!" His finger trembled as it ran across the old photograph.

"You're doing great. Can you tell me their family names?"

"Uh, now let's see. I'm not sure."

"Did they all live here in Clear Point?"

"Clear Point?"

The light was extinguished. The old man's face had been alive and animated a minute ago, but now he stared at the pictures like he had never seen them before.

"Do you have any cookies?" He turned his gaze toward Will.

"Yes, I do. Do you remember anything else about the people in the pictures?" Will's voice reflected his disappointment.

"Could I have my cookies now?"

"Yes, Granddad, you can have your cookies."

Will glanced toward Emily and shrugged an apology.

"It's okay," she said with a weak smile. "I'm happy. We have a few names. It's a big help."

"Betty?"

Emily turned her gaze to the older man. He looked back at her with a smile on his face.

"Do you remember me?" she said to him without hesitation. She moved closer and knelt on the floor beside him.

"Betty, it's so nice of you to drop by. I thought you'd left."

"I did, but I came back. Do you remember why I left?"

"He shouldn't have done that," the old man said, shaking his head. "He was wrong."

"What did he do that was wrong?" Emily said, afraid to hope they would have an answer. "His last name began with J. Do you remember?"

He looked at her and smiled. "Is it time for the sing-along?"

"What did he do that was wrong?" she tried again.

"Wrong? Did I do something wrong?" He turned at Will with tears in his eyes. It broke Emily's heart. She laid her hand on his arm.

"No, you're fine," she said. "You didn't do anything."

The older man grabbed his grandson's hand like a lifeline. "I'm tired now. I want to go to bed."

Dustin and Emily were silent as they waited on the sidewalk for Will to come out of the nursing home.

"I'm so sorry, Em. I told you it mightn't go well," Will said when he reached them.

"It went great." She wanted to reassure him. "We have names. That's more than I expected to get."

"I hope they're accurate. He might've been mistaken."

"We'll check it out, and I'll let you know. I'm just sorry I upset him," she said.

"He's already forgotten about it. Once he had his cookies, he was content," Will said, his mouth twisted wryly.

Emily wrapped her arms around him and gave him a strong hug.

"Thank you. You're the best," she said.

"Glad I could help."

Chapter 41

"Where do we start?"

"I think the best place would be the city registers," Dustin said. "At the very least, they'll have the names of the landowners at that time. If we're lucky, maybe they'll have a list of all citizens, but that's a longshot."

"It was a small town at the time, much smaller than it is now. Maybe they had a list. The real question is if they still have it," Emily said.

They were in the truck, driving down Main Street, having left Will at the docks. Dustin glanced at his watch.

"It's one o'clock. Why don't we stop in and see what they have?"

Millie greeted Emily with a wide toothy smile. A woman in her late fifties, she stood a few inches short of five feet with a round figure that stretched the limits of her vividly-flowered blouse.

"Well, Miss Emily, it isn't often we see you in here," she said. Her words were directed at Emily, but her avid gaze was glued to Dustin. Emily hastened to introduce him.

"Oh, of course," the city clerk said. "This is your new neighbor."

"You seem to know what's going on," Dustin said with a charming smile.

"It's a small town and, working here, I have to know who lives where," she said. Emily knew Millie loved to show off her self-importance in the realm of the city offices. As she said, it was a small town, and it was managed with less than twenty employees, Millie being one of the most senior.

"We have a bit of a strange request, and I hope you're able to help us, Millie," Dustin said, pouring on the charm. It worked. The older woman looked ready to sit up and beg. "We wondered if you had a list of residents from 1959."

"We do. We have the land registry since the beginning. But not everything is computerized. I'd have to search in the archives."

"We don't want to put you to a lot of trouble. If you showed us where to look, we could do it for you," he said.

"That's nice of you to offer, but I'm afraid it's not allowed. It won't take me long. I know where to look. I'll be able to get it for you by tomorrow."

"That would be wonderful," Emily said. "We appreciate it."

"May I ask why you need this information?" she said with a sly smile.

Emily opened her mouth to answer, but Dustin interrupted her.

"We're working together on a book about the area, and we need some historical background."

The perfect answer for a nosy civil servant, Emily thought.

"Oh, how interesting. But why that year in particular?"

"Our publisher won't let us divulge too much information at this point," Dustin said with a wink. "Let's just say we're looking at that year for now, and we'll be back for more."

"Well, I'll be more than happy to help you out with anything. You know I've dabbled at writing myself, mostly short stories."

"That doesn't surprise me at all. I could sense a kindred spirit as soon as I laid eyes on you."

Millie blushed with pleasure.

"You know how to lie, don't you?" Emily said when they were alone on the street.

"I didn't quite lie. I stretched the truth."

"What about 'We're writing an historical book together' is not a lie?"

"It may happen. Once this is over, we may decide to write about it."

Emily laughed out loud. "Once this is over, I don't even want to think about it anymore."

"Give yourself time. You'll see."

She stopped dead in her tracks and turned to stare hard at Dustin.

"Is that what you hope to get out of all this? A story?"

"Don't even think it. You're so sure I have a mercenary reason for helping you. Maybe I'm a nice guy. Did you ever consider that?"

She was silent, her brows furrowed.

"Emily?"

"Just a minute. Let's see. Dustin. Nice guy. Hmm, that's a tough one."

"Very funny."

The next day, as promised, Millie called Emily to tell her she had a list of property-owners in the town for the year 1959. As an extra bonus, she had discovered they had done a census at the time. She had the names, addresses, and birth dates of all the residents. She offered to e-mail the information, and, within a few minutes, Emily heard a ping as a message landed in her inbox.

She called Dustin from the other room, printed out two copies of the list, and they got to work. Since the total number of residents in that year was just a little over a thousand, it didn't take them long to go through the list. The problem was matching the names Stuart McCade had given them with the residents at the time.

"They're obviously nicknames," Emily said. "Ricky must be short for Richard, but there's no Richard that age on the list. Who would name their child Toph or Loot? What kind of nickname would that be?"

"Loot is the one we should be most interested in, but there's no 'Loot' on the list, and there's no one with a first name L and a last name J."

Emily sat back and ran her hands through her hair. "God, we'll never get anywhere with this."

"It may not have taken us anywhere at any rate. They were pictures in a chest. They probably had nothing to do with the murder. And maybe the guy wasn't a resident. Maybe he was a tourist or a summertime visitor."

"Yeah, I guess you're right." Emily sat up straight. "Wait a second. I just thought of something."

She hurried to her desk and retrieved her grandmother's journal from under a stack of notes. She perched in an armchair with the journal on her lap and flipped through the pages.

"Where is it? I saw it here somewhere. Ah, here. Listen to this."

I thought I trusted him. Actually, it was more than trust. It was everything. It was love, devotion, and trust, all rolled into one. I thought it would be forever. Why did this happen to me? Life isn't supposed to turn out this way. You're supposed to meet the man of your dreams, marry, and have a family. It's supposed to be happily-ever-after. But not for me.

"I read that as if it was a break-up," Emily said. "She had a man she loved, but something happened, and they broke up."

"Yeah, that's what it sounds like. So, what's your point?"

"Listen to the next part."

He knows that I know. I can feel it. Something has changed in the way he looks at me, in the way he talks to me. I have to decide what to do. I know what I should do, but just the thought of it is like a knife stab to my heart.

"You think she was the one to break it off?" Dustin said.

"Yes, but why would she? She was in love with him. What did he do that was so terrible? What changed?"

"She may have found out he was a smuggler."

"Maybe. It's possible. Or he could have been anything – a thief, a cheater, a child molester. There was something about him she couldn't accept anymore."

"And she confronted him, and he tried to kill her?" Dustin said, deep in thought.

"It's a theory."

"And a damn good one."

"Are you laughing at me?"

"Not at all. I like how your mind works."

Emily paced back and forth in front of him and tried to piece it all together. "I'm going for a run. I need to get rid of this restlessness."

"I'll come with you," he said, standing.

"You don't have to."

"Yes, I do, and you know it. You can't go alone, and I shouldn't spend all my days sitting on my ass. Let's go."

Chapter 42

The following afternoon, murder stories and nickname mysteries took a rest while Emily and Dustin went to their separate corners and worked on their own projects. He had set himself up in the kitchen with his laptop and the box of notes from his journalist friend. He sorted through the files and created distinct piles of documents.

Emily retreated to her workshop to paint some pottery, feeling the need to distance herself from the case for a while. She was frowning over a difficult piece when the discordant ring of the phone interrupted her. It was Lisa, calling for her twice-weekly check-in.

A few days ago, Emily had told her about the break-in, the destruction of her equipment, and the subsequent purchase of a new wheel. As expected, Lisa had been distressed about this latest development. Today, Emily tried to keep it light.

"You should see the stuff I'm getting done with this new wheel. It must have magic powers."

"You shouldn't have to go through that."

Emily imagined her sister's sulky expression. "It's okay. I've moved past it."

"You've spent too much time moving past things. Why is this happening to you?"

"I don't know, but I won't let it beat me."

"Em, you've got to do something."

"I'm doing everything I can. The authorities are on it, and so are Dustin and I. We're going through journals, photos, letters, and notes. We're trying to figure out what's going on."

"I've been wondering about Dustin."

Emily didn't like her sister's ominous tone of voice. "What do you mean?"

"Can you trust this guy?"

"Why wouldn't I? He's been helping me."

"Exactly."

"You're talking in riddles. Get to the point," Emily said. Her sister's negativity annoyed her at times.

"He's always been there, sis. Every time something has happened to you, you always tell me Dustin showed up right away, coming to the rescue. Don't you find it strange he's always a couple of steps away whenever anything goes wrong? Why is he there so fast? Have you ever thought of that?"

"No, I haven't, and I don't think you have all your facts straight either."

"You don't think so? Why don't you think back about all that's happened? Because I think I'm right. It's gone too far, and it's gone on too long. I don't trust him, and I don't think you should either."

"I'll deal with Dustin. Don't worry, I'll get to the bottom of this."

For the rest of the conversation, Emily was distracted. Her thoughts returned to all the attacks and incidents.

Using the excuse she had work to do, she said goodbye to her sister. When she disconnected the call, she sat like a statue and listened to her heart, which beat faster and faster. A wave of heat flooded through her.

When she had been attacked while hiking, Dustin had been nearby, but that was to be expected. They had gone together. When her truck had been run off the road, she had gone to his house, and he had been at home and awake. His truck had been splashed with mud and dirt, but she had never thought of it being him who had followed her.

She crossed to the window, and stared out, not seeing the ocean peeking through the trees. Her mind's eye was filled with Dustin when he showed up to help her after the goat shelter was destroyed during the storm. He had arrived seconds after the attack. It was obvious he had been close by. *But what about the day her house had been ravaged? He had been with her in town.*

Emily's eyes widened. Dustin had left her with Doug while he went to take care of something. *He had told her he went to the newspaper office. But had he?* He'd had plenty of time to return to her house and trash it before going back to town to pick her up.

Was it possible she had been so close to the killer all along? No, she couldn't believe Dustin was capable of something like that. He had been nothing but kind to her. He had saved her from gas poisoning. My God, she had even considered having a real relationship with him. It wasn't possible. It couldn't be.

Emily wanted to brush off Lisa's worries, but she couldn't help but wonder if there was a kernel of something in there she should be concerned about.

She returned to sit in the chair and bent over to put her head in her hands. *What about the event that had started it all, the attempt on her life? Dustin didn't come to her rescue for that one. But he may have been living just down the beach from her at the time.* She considered each other mishap and close call she'd had, and with dismay, she realized Lisa was right. Dustin had always been just around the corner.

But it didn't make sense. He was living in the house with her. If he wanted to harm her in any way, he'd had every opportunity to do so. On the other hand, everyone knew he lived here, so he would have to make it look like an accident.

The destruction of her workshop had not been aimed at her physically. Instead, it had been something to threaten her livelihood, or at the very least, something designed to inconvenience her. *What was going on? If it was Dustin behind all this, what was his goal? Had she misjudged him, and he was a sociopath that got his kicks out of tormenting people? Did he intend to kill her once he was done toying with her?*

Emily couldn't believe the path her thoughts took, but the seed was sown, and the more she thought about it, the more merit the idea had. Yes, her sister was the pessimistic type while Emily tended to be the opposite, but it was hard to ignore all the signs now that they had been pointed out to her.

What should she do? Confront him? That might not be wise. He was bigger and stronger than her. She could always arm herself before a confrontation, but she would rather find proof before she made any moves or flung accusations at him.

He was busy now, Emily thought. Normally, he would work for hours without a break.

Being careful not to make a sound, she slid open the window and said a silent prayer of thanks that she lived in a bungalow. Dropping down an extra story to the ground would not have been either pleasant or safe.

Her feet firmly on the ground, she didn't waste any time. She headed to the path through the trees and was on the beach within a minute. Her feet flew across the sand until she reached the familiar house she had visited so often.

Dustin had made renovations, but she knew he hadn't changed all the windows. Several times, Mr. Felch had complained about the window in the back of the house and how it never latched properly. He said it didn't matter because he had nothing worth stealing. Besides, he would say, people around here wouldn't break into a house.

Emily discovered, under the right circumstances, she would.

It took a lot of strength to slide open the broken-latched, rarely-used, heavy window, but Emily's muscles were well-honed from years of molding clay and working a pottery wheel. She opened it wide enough to slide her body through and drop to the floor into the spare bedroom. It was the room in which she had slept the night she had run from the man in the woods. *Had she made the mistake of running back to the person who had been chasing her?*

When she stepped into the hallway, she took a moment to orient herself to her surroundings. There were two more bedrooms. One would be where he slept, and the other would be an office or storage room. She chose the room that would most likely be the office and opened the door. A desk, chair, and filing cabinet made up the furnishings. The computer, of course, was missing. At the moment, it was at work on her kitchen table.

Emily tugged on the top drawer of the filing cabinet to find it unlocked. It seemed to contain invoices, bills, and other personal business documents. She didn't waste time with it. The second drawer contained at least a half-dozen file folders wrapped in elastic bands and bursting with papers.

Emily removed the first one from the cabinet and perused the documents inside. They were police reports from five years earlier concerning the murder of a woman by the name of Melissa Holmes. The details of the homicide could be buried among the papers, but she set aside the file and removed another, laying it open on the desk in front of her.

Inside were legal documents, the top one addressed to Dustin Holmes. It referred to the death of Melissa Holmes, his spouse. Papers rattled as she flipped through them. The woman had been murdered by strangulation, and her husband had been the prime suspect. *But were Dustin Holmes and Dustin Reeves one and the same?*

Emily threw aside the file and pulled out another. This one contained newspaper articles about the murder and the subsequent questioning of the husband. A younger version of Dustin was displayed on the front page, with longer hair and a haggard look. Another man in a suit, presumably a lawyer, stood by his side.

Emily's heart thumped against her ribs as she skimmed the article. It told the story of a young woman murdered while she ran through a park in her hometown of Calgary. The most obvious suspect was her husband, a journalist and a person who stood to inherit a hefty estate from the only child of a late successful businessman.

The article had been printed the day after Dustin was questioned. Emily didn't know if he had been arrested and tried for the murder. Apparently, he hadn't been convicted, but he had changed his name and moved to Clear Point. *Was he a fugitive? Or hiding from the press that used to employ him?*

Emily lowered herself into the chair and held her head in her hands. His wife had been a murder victim, and he had been accused of her murder. If it was true and he had killed his wife, she had been rubbing shoulders with a killer. If it wasn't true, and he had been falsely accused, along with losing his wife in the worst possible way, he may be unhinged.

Emily's stomach turned. *Maybe that was the problem. Maybe he hadn't come through it unscathed. Maybe the experience had made him want to hunt down and hurt people or try to kill them.*

Her heart raced. She needed to get out of here. *What if he realized she was missing from the house, and he came looking for her?* She wrapped the files in the elastic bands as quickly as possible and put them back in the drawer, not caring if they were in the same order. She closed the door of the office and took a quick peek in his bedroom. Nothing seemed to be out of the ordinary. She no longer knew what she should look for, but she hoped if anything seemed off, she would realize it.

The kitchen and living room were both clean and tidy. No weapons lay out in the open, and no list of intended victims was taped to the fridge door. She opened the hallway closet, and what she found made her heart crawl up her throat until she could barely breathe. A black neoprene wetsuit.

Dustin had never mentioned surfing to her. He seemed to have no hobbies or interests besides working. Apart from keeping an eye on her.

CHAPTER 43

Emily left the house the same way she had come in, through the bedroom window, but she didn't struggle to close it this time. She sprinted for the bushes and got out of sight in case Dustin was prowling the area.

She drew her cell phone from the back pocket of her jeans and hit Will's number. It rang too many times. She hung up and called Trevor. He picked up on the second ring.

"Hey Em, what's up?"

"I need your help."

He must have heard the urgency in her voice. "Where are you?" he said, his own voice serious.

"I'm hiding in the trees near Dustin's place. It's him. He's the one who's been trying to kill me."

"Go out to the point. I'll pick you up there."

Emily understood where he meant. Just south of Dustin's house, a rocky outlet protruded into the ocean. The water was deep enough beside the point for diving. She had watched her friends do it often enough. Trevor could pull his boat alongside the rocks to pick her up.

She knew she would be visible for a couple of minutes while on the beach but hoped Dustin hadn't noticed her absence yet. Even if he did, he might not assume she was here. Emily dashed out of the trees and across the beach. She reached the outlet, scampered up onto the rocks, and jumped from one to the other, hoping not to slip. Near the edge, she crouched behind a larger rock and kept out of sight of anyone on the beach.

The sound of an approaching boat reached her, and she knew Trevor was close. Seconds later, the boat pulled up to the rocks, her friend at the wheel and a concerned expression on his face. She scurried down and accepted a hand to help her into the rocking boat. His arms closed around her once her feet hit the deck.

"Are you okay? You're not hurt?"

"No, I'm fine. He doesn't know I know about him. I need to get to Ted."

"You didn't call Ted yet?"

"No. I know I should have, but my first thought was to get as far away from there as possible. Thank God I got hold of you."

"I'm glad you thought to call me first," he said, accelerating the boat.

Emily didn't mention she had called Will first. The two men were equal in her eyes. She scrolled through her phone contacts to find Ted's number and was about to hit the call button when the boat swerved sharply to the left. She fought to keep her balance. The phone slipped from her hand, landed on the floor of the boat, and continued its journey toward the front.

Emily chased it, but the boat hit the waves at such an angle she couldn't remain upright.

"Trevor! My phone. It's right behind you. Be careful."

He turned to glance in her direction, obviously having trouble hearing her over the noise of the engine. As he did so, he glanced down, swayed on his feet, and his heel went down on her phone, crushing it beneath his boot. He grimaced and mouthed the word 'Sorry' before he turned around again.

"Damn it. I need to call Ted." Emily got on her hands and knees and crawled toward her phone. She hoped it was simply a cracked screen she would have to deal with. She didn't understand why the water was so rough, not now when she most needed to contact the police. Dustin had to be arrested before he realized she had discovered his story.

Her phone was demolished. Emily pulled herself up beside Trevor and hung onto a seat to steady herself.

"Give me your phone," she yelled.

"I don't have it."

"What?" she said, incredulous.

"I left it at the dock. I was in such a hurry to get to you, I set it down and forgot it."

"Oh my God," Emily said. She couldn't believe this comedy of errors. She looked out at the water and realized they made progress, unhampered by waves and the weaving of the boat. But something was not right.

"Trevor, you're going in the wrong direction. We have to head back to town," she said.

"I know. I wanted to check something out first. Your friend Dustin may have left some evidence in the cove."

"What do you mean? What could he have left there? And why the cove?"

She tugged on his arm, wanting an answer, but his face was set, his lips clenched in a tight line.

The cove was a small lagoon a little farther south, which had remained undiscovered by the tourists. The locals sometimes gathered in the spot for swimming or campfires on the beach on weekend evenings. Emily and her friends knew it well, but as far as she was aware, Dustin had never been there. She couldn't imagine what he could have hidden there and why Trevor would consider such a thing.

"Do you know something I don't?" She fixed her gaze on his face.

"I can't say I know something. Let's just say it's a suspicion. I haven't trusted that guy from the beginning."

"You and my sister both. I don't know why I didn't see it sooner. I thought I was a good judge of character."

"You're way too trusting. You prefer to think the best of everyone."

"I guess you're right, but at least I know my real friends," she said, relieved to be in safe hands. Her burst of adrenaline had faded, and she knew this whole nightmare would soon be over. They would look for whatever Trevor suspected, and they would go see Ted.

The cove came into sight, and Emily thought how beautiful and serene it appeared. She used to come here alone at times, just to soak in the peacefulness. It was hard to imagine anything sinister rested here.

Trevor pulled the boat up alongside the dock.

"Get a little closer, and I'll hop out to tie us up," Emily said.

"That won't be necessary. We're not going on land."

She turned and looked at him. "Why not?"

"I just needed to get out of sight."

Emily frowned. Trevor never talked in riddles. "What are you going on about?" she said.

He dug into the storage box at the back of the boat. When he turned around, he held a rope in one hand, and another object in his other. Emily gestured toward the thick rope attached to the side of the boat. "What do you need that for? We have a rope."

"It won't be painful if you cooperate, Em."

"Trevor?" she said, her body frozen in place.

Emily had never seen him like this. Her kind, soft-spoken friend had changed before her eyes. With a hard and determined expression, his hands were clenched around the objects in them, and his eyes were glazed. Sweat beaded on his forehead, despite the cool breeze that ruffled his hair. She worried he was in the middle of a breakdown.

"Trevor, why don't you sit down and rest a bit. I don't think you feel well."

"I'm fine. I need to do this."

"Do what?"

"Don't be so dense, Emily. You know what's happening. It was supposed to be your grandmother, but she left. It's up to me now."

"What are you talking about? What do you know about my grandmother?"

"He was devastated. She turned on him, accused him of terrible things. He was just trying to get enough money so they could have a good life together. She didn't understand. She didn't want to understand."

Trevor took a step toward her, and Emily took a step back. The boat rocked, she lost her balance, and landed on the seat behind her. She scrambled to her feet.

"Explain it to me. I want to understand more. I want to help you." She saw by the crazed look in his eyes he was beyond help, but Emily needed to buy time.

"You're just like her. You even look like her. You're fickle, pretending to be nice, pretending to be interested in me. But you fall for Will's charm, and then that other guy comes along. You'll turn on us and leave. Just like her."

Nothing he said made sense to her, but instinct told Emily to get off the boat as fast as possible. She swiveled and prepared to leap onto the dock, at least four feet away. She knew there was a good chance she would land in the water, but it was a better alternative for her than being on the boat with Trevor.

She didn't make it. A strong hand grasped her from behind and pulled her back against him.

"Stop this! What the hell are you doing?" Her voice was high-pitched and panicked. "You're my friend."

She was shoved facedown onto the floor of the boat. The smell of fish and motor oil filled her nostrils as Trevor straddled her back. Her hands were yanked behind her and securely wrapped with duct tape until she thought her arms would leave their sockets.

"Yeah. I know I'm your friend," he said, his voice filled with sarcasm.

"Stop it. I love you!"

A hand grabbed her ponytail and yanked her head back. His voice growled in her ear.

"No, you don't. You love that bastard. You're a traitor," he said, as he let go of her hair and dragged her up by her arms. The pain made her suck in her breath.

"I don't understand. Stop. Talk to me." Her mind raced. She didn't know how to appeal to this Trevor, a stranger she had known since childhood.

He picked up a fishing net and wrapped it around her, mummy-like. She couldn't move her limbs. His arms wrapped around her, as they had so many times, and he threw her overboard.

Chapter 44

The cold engulfed her. The water soaked into the heavy netting and dragged her toward the sandy bottom several feet below the boat. Emily gulped in air before she hit the water, but she was rendered helpless with her hands taped and the netting all but paralyzing her. The water was murky with dirt, stirred up by all the action, but she spotted the wooden legs of the dock a few feet away and knew they were her only hope.

Emily kicked her legs like a mermaid and propelled herself across those crucial few feet until she bumped against one of the dock legs. The netting had loosened, either from the weight of the water or from her movements. She positioned a knee on each side of the wooden post and shimmied upward. Her lungs burned. She swallowed water a split-second before her head broke the surface.

Her reprieve was brief. The tide was high, and the air space under the dock was small. Each gulp of air brought a swallow of water along with it.

Emily tried to remain quiet. She wanted to scream for help, or at least in pain and frustration, but Trevor was there, and he was dangerous. She took a mouthful of air and lowered herself until just her eyes were above water. Trevor stood in the boat, alternating between tidying up any sign of the scuffle and peering into the water for a glimpse of her body.

The impassive expression on his face drove a stake into her heart. He didn't care that he attempted to murder someone who considered him a beloved friend. What all of this had to do with her grandmother was beyond Emily's understanding. For the moment, she needed to concentrate on keeping this whole experience from escalating from attempted murder to murder.

Her thighs screamed in pain. She didn't know how much longer she would be able to use them to keep herself tethered to the dock. Somehow, she needed to free her hands. She bent her head back and took several deep breaths of air before she let herself sink below the waterline. The water had cleared and gave her a better look at her surroundings. The shore lay at least thirty feet away. *Even if she succeeded in doing the mermaid for that distance, could she escape him?*

She rose to the surface once more, both for air and to keep an eye on Trevor. What she witnessed made her realize she didn't have the luxury of time.

Trevor was halfway into his wet suit, his air tank at his feet. He set his mobile phone on the seat of the boat, the phone he had supposedly left behind in his haste to help her. He would dive down to make sure she would never come up again. It wouldn't take him long to find her clinging to the dock, and he would finish off his job.

Emily took another breath and sank again, this time pushing herself farther down. She knew what she searched for, but she didn't know how long it would take to find it. She moved from one dock leg to the other until she had to push herself up again for air.

She was tired. She had never been a strong swimmer, and to navigate through the water without the use of her arms was a major feat. The sight of Trevor adjusting his air pack made her take another deep breath and close her mouth.

This time, she was successful. She spotted a rusty piece of metal attached to one of the legs. It was difficult to position herself to cut the tape, but she had no choice except to try. To her right, a dark shape lowered itself into the water. She moved behind a leg and hoped she wouldn't be found. She had a few seconds before she would have to surface for air again.

As Trevor lowered himself into the depths, she took the opportunity to inch upward for air. After a few quick gulps, she descended again and returned to the ragged piece of metal.

Emily struggled to get her hands in position and felt the resistance of the metal pulling on the tape. Desperate, she sawed her hands back and forth. Fatigue threatened to overcome her. She had no idea if she made any leeway but prayed her hands would soon break free, and she would be able to rid herself of her binding.

Having no choice except to lift herself for air, she gasped in shock and sucked in dirty ocean water. The mask-clad face of Trevor hovered in front of her. A strange mixture of amusement and anger danced in his eyes as his hands closed around her throat and shoved her below the surface.

Emily could do nothing to stop him. Her hands were taped, and her lower legs were tangled in netting. She pleaded with him with her eyes and hoped he would see reason and get over whatever madness had overtaken him. Either he couldn't read her expression, or he didn't care. She continued to sink along with him as her lungs burned, and he breathed with ease through his apparatus.

Emily realized these were her last moments on this earth. Her lungs would soon fill with water, and that would be the end. She didn't want Trevor to think she would accept it.

She threw herself against him, attempting to hit him with her head, but the force of the water, her flagging strength, and his protective gear all worked against her. All she succeeded in doing was to breathe in more water. She didn't give up. She struggled and hoped to break his grasp. He tightened his arms around her, and Emily heard laughter beside her ear.

Until she didn't hear it anymore. Instead, Trevor's breath grew raspy and forced. As her vision darkened, the last thing she saw were his alarm-filled eyes and the terrifying sound of someone gasping for his life.

Chapter 45

Emily coughed until water spewed out of her lungs and onto the sand. Someone yelled at her, but she couldn't make out the words. All she was aware of was a roaring in her head as she puked up water and sucked in life-saving air.

"You did it. Good girl," a man's voice said in her ear. Then he yelled. "Do you have him?"

An indistinguishable shout answered in the distance.

Hands lifted her into a sitting position, and she looked up to see Dustin staring at her, his face twisted with worry. She remembered what had happened and how she had been certain her life was over. She didn't know how her circumstances had been reversed, but she was alive and grateful for the fact.

Until a thought occurred to her.

"Trevor." She grabbed Dustin's forearm. "We have to get away from Trevor. I'll explain later." The urgency of her words was heightened by the scratchiness of her voice.

Emily struggled to get to her feet, but Dustin eased her back onto the sand.

"You don't have to worry about Trevor. We have him."

"You do?"

For the first time, she realized Dustin was dripping wet. She glanced around to see Will at the edge of the water. He stood over the prone form of Trevor, still in his wetsuit with his air tank on his back.

"Oh my God! Is he...?"

"No, he's alive. If we had our choice, he'd be in worse shape, but we thought we should let the cops do their part."

Emily stood on wobbly legs. Dustin wrapped an arm around her waist to steady her. She couldn't pull her gaze from the man she had always considered to be a friend, who had tried and failed to kill her, several times.

"Why? I don't understand why."

"We all have a lot of questions, but we'll be able to get the answers soon enough."

Emily turned her head to meet Dustin's gaze. "How did you find me? You and Will? How did that happen?"

"I got a text notification. I have security cameras set up around my house. I watched you go into the house and come back out a little later. I saw you hide in the bushes and call someone. I knew it was either the cops, Trevor, or Will you'd call."

Emily was stunned. She had thought she was so clever, but the man she had run from had watched her on his phone from the comfort of her own home. So much for stealthiness.

"But how did you find me here?"

"I knew you were headed to the point. That meant you had called someone with a boat. I went to town to find someone else with another boat to find you. Will said he'd seen Trevor leave in a hurry. He was concerned."

"He was? Why?" Nothing made any sense to her.

"Because I'd gotten strange vibes from Trevor," another voice said.

Emily turned to Will. "Like what?"

"It was just weird things he'd say every once in a while. It got a little creepy. Out of the blue, he'd say something like 'She deserves it.' I'd ask him who he was talking about and he'd change the subject. Or he'd say, 'I have to do it.' I asked him what he had to do. He said it was nothing, but he had a strange look on his face."

Emily was aware of the strange face Trevor could make. Today was the first time she had witnessed it, but she didn't think she would ever forget.

"Dustin called me," Will said. "All the weird behavior fell into place, especially when he told me about the initials. I was able to make the connection between LDJ and Trevor."

"So, we took Will's boat and tried to follow Trevor," Dustin continued, as Emily's gaze swiveled from one to the other. "Luckily, Will knew of this place. We saw the boat, but nothing else. We were heading to shore when we spotted the oxygen tube. I jumped in the water and followed it, while Will had the great idea to pinch the tube to slow Trevor down. When I got to you, you had blacked out and were sinking to the bottom."

"There was a bit of a struggle when we pulled Trevor from the water, but we were able to immobilize him," Will said, flexing his right hand. Emily saw signs of swelling on his knuckles.

Emily wavered on her feet as she thought about how close she had come to losing her life. Dustin's arm came around her waist again and pulled her close to his side. All three of them gazed at Trevor's inert form, each of them filled with their own thoughts of dismay, horror, and sadness.

Their heads lifted as a sound reached their ears. The police boat rounded the corner and headed their way.

"Here they come," Dustin said. "We'll have more answers soon."

•   •   •

It did not seem possible. Her grandmother had been victimized sixty years earlier by a man who had claimed to be in love with her, a man with whom she had wanted to spend the rest of her life. They had grown up together in the same small town, Clear Point, and fallen in love while in their early twenties. Her parents hadn't approved of him. They couldn't give her a reason for the way they felt. It was something they couldn't put their finger on.

The couple had a spot where they always met, away from prying eyes. A cluster of trees stood beside a certain spot on the beach, near the big rock. Within those trees, they had a secluded section where they would lay a blanket. Betty would go for a walk at the same time every evening, and he would be there to greet her.

As time went on, her lover pressed her to convince her parents to accept him. She had tried on several occasions to speak to them about him, but they were adamant they didn't want to see 'his type' around their daughter. So, their love affair continued in secret.

One night, unable to sleep, Betty returned to the beach and spotted a strange incident. From a distance, she saw an exchange between some men; several had arrived by boat, and one was on the beach to meet them. She was too far away to recognize any of them, but crates were transferred from the boat into a truck. Given the lateness of the hour and the stealthiness of their behavior, she suspected their work was illegal.

Betty discussed the incident with her lover the next evening, and he convinced her she had witnessed a late return from a fishing expedition. However, curiosity got the best of her, and she returned to investigate the site again a few evenings later. She was attacked by an unknown person and almost killed. Another woman came upon them and lost her life.

Over time, Betty began to realize what the something was that bothered her parents about her boyfriend. She suspected he worked as the eyes and ears of the smugglers in Clear Point. It was his job to let them know when it was safe to drop off their merchandise.

The realization devastated Betty. Her conscience told her it was her civic duty to turn him in as a criminal. But she loved him and couldn't imagine being responsible for him spending years in jail. She decided she would attempt to make him stop.

The night she confronted him was the night their love affair ended. She recognized him for what he was, an immoral madman. The man she had given her heart to was the person who had tried to kill her. To make matters worse, he threatened to implicate her and her family in the smuggling operations if she revealed his secret.

I will never forget the horror I felt and still feel. Those hands that caressed me and loved me were used to try to kill me. I survived, but only physically. My spirit is crushed and dead. I don't know how I will go on living. The future appears bleak. I will no longer have a life with the man I loved. I have nowhere to turn. I can't go to the police. I can't confide in my family or friends, and it adds to my despair. I have aligned myself with a criminal, and that makes me guilty as well.

It gives me shivers when I see him around town. How had I not seen his true self? Was I so blinded by love? Does he truly have contrived evidence to incriminate me and my family? I can't take that chance.

I can no longer look at the beach and not think of him. I can no longer look at the ocean and not think of the smuggling boats. I will carry this to my grave, and part of my penance will be having to leave this place in paradise I love so much.

Emily lifted her head and stared out the window, mesmerized by the trees that swayed back and forth in the wind. It was too much to absorb; Trevor, her grandmother's story, and the events that connected Emily to it all.

Trevor was questioned by the police, and his home was searched. He didn't hold back any information. His grandfather, Luther 'Loot' Dalton Junior, had been the man who tried to kill Emily's grandmother sixty years earlier. He had passed away several months ago and left his belongings to Trevor, who in turn, found letters and other evidence pointing to his grandfather's activities two generations earlier. Instead of being repelled by the revelations, Trevor was fascinated. That fascination turned into an unhealthy feeling of kinship. He had sympathized with the plight of his ancestor and believed his grandfather had been wronged by Elizabeth Wheaton, emboldened by the older man's journal that portrayed the woman as unfaithful and dishonest. Trevor then projected those feelings on Emily, someone who thought of him as one of her best friends.

He had wanted to reproduce the attempted strangling, with the idea he would complete his grandfather's work. When it backfired, he waffled between trying again and covering his tracks. He decided to play with Emily, to instill fear and doubt, even going so far as to stuff a rag in the ventilation outlet for her kiln. He removed it while she was being loaded into an ambulance. But each of his attempts failed, thwarted by circumstances. His anger increased, along with his madness.

He trashed her workroom in a fit of frustration. There was another journal hidden by her grandmother at the bottom of the chest. Trevor found it on the floor and took it with him.

That, along with letters left by his grandfather, was how the rest of the decades-old story was uncovered. Now the members of this generation had to deal with the fall-out.

Emily had lost a dear friend. Trevor would be tried and possibly convicted of murder, along with a string of other crimes, including attempted murder, assault, breaking and entering, and destruction of property. Emily didn't know if he would ever see the outside of a prison. A young man who had always been wonderful in her eyes had cracked under some mysterious force carried through the years. *What had caused it? Or had it been something that had always been there and simply needed an impetus to reawaken it? They would probably never know.*

Chapter 46

"I thought it was you," she said, her voice soft.

"Yeah, I figured that out. It was the sneaking in and out of windows that gave it away."

They sat in deck chairs on the end of Dustin's dock and watched the sunset. The previous day had been spent with the authorities, repeating their story, time and time again. They had slept in their respective homes the night before, or in Emily's case, she had lain awake in her own home.

"I shouldn't have doubted you," she said, her eyes downcast.

"Why did you? What did I do to make you think I'd do something that terrible?"

"It's just you were always there."

He snorted a laugh. "Well, excuse me for always being there for you."

"No, I mean, you were always so close when something bad happened to me. It was Lisa that pointed it out to me."

"Ah, Lisa. She doesn't like me too much, does she?"

"She doesn't know you."

"You know me, and you still thought I was capable of trying to kill you, among other things."

"I'm sorry. But there were just so many secrets and, like I said, you were always there. I was stupid. What else can I say?" She held her hands out to her sides.

Dustin looked at her, his gaze piercing.

"I didn't kill her."

Emily remained silent. She knew he referred to his wife, and the hurt in his eyes made it clear to her he told the truth. She didn't want to hear the rest of his story, but she knew he had to tell it.

"I loved her with all my heart." His gaze returned to the undulating waves. "She was everything to me. Most of the time, I ran with her, not because I love it, but because I loved her, and I wanted her to be safe. That night was one of the few times I didn't go along. I had a deadline to meet the next day, and I didn't have time to leave the house."

He shook his head.

"A deadline," he said. "She lost her life because of a deadline. It's ironic, isn't it?"

"You can't blame yourself."

"Oh yes, I can, and I did. I would've let them prosecute me and send me to jail if it hadn't been for a friend of mine, who was also my lawyer. He wouldn't let it happen. They couldn't find any evidence to prove it was me, and they had to let it go. But there were always people who never stopped believing I'd done it, her family in particular."

"So, you changed your name."

"Yep. I needed a certain amount of anonymity. I wanted to start over somewhere else, and I didn't want someone to remember my name and have the same suspicions start all over again. I had it legally changed, and I bought this property."

"Are you really writing a book, or are you trying to cover up something else?"

He smiled wryly. "I'm writing a book. It's fiction, but it resembles my life story."

"Telling people about your experience."

"You got it."

"Have you decided how it'll end?"

He met her gaze. "I think you're the person who'll decide how it ends."

"You'd be taking on a lot of baggage. Then again, there's some baggage missing," she said, glancing at her chest.

"Do you think you're the only one who's got baggage? I think I have my fair share of it."

Emily looked at him speculatively. "I suppose you're right. You know, this would be a big step for me, a step I never intended to take again."

He sat forward and took her hand in his.

"I didn't either," he said. "But I can promise you this. You'll never run alone again."

Note from the Author

Word-of-mouth is crucial for any author to succeed. If you enjoyed the book, please leave a review online—anywhere you are able. Even if it's just a sentence or two. It would make all the difference and would be very much appreciated.

Thanks!
Anita

ABOUT THE AUTHOR

A.J. McCarthy grew up with books by Agatha Christie, Sidney Sheldon, and many other masters of mystery and suspense. She has three published suspense thrillers to her credit and plans to have many more to come. She's a member of *International Thriller Writers* and *Sisters in Crime*. For more information about A.J. and her work, please go to www.ajackmccarthy.com.

Thank you so much for reading one of our A.J. McCarthy's novels.
If you enjoyed the experience, please check out our
recommended title for your next great read!

Sins of the Fathers by A.J. McCarthy

"McCarthy has certainly established herself
as a writing force to be reckoned with."
—Authors Reading

View other Black Rose Writing titles at
www.blackrosewriting.com/books and use promo code
PRINT to receive a **20% discount** when purchasing.